An Un

Love by a Twist of

Fate

STAND-ALONE NOVEL

A Western Historical Romance Novel

by

Lydia Olson

Table of Contents

Let's connect!

Impact my upcoming stories!

My passionate readers influenced the core soul of the book you are holding in your hands! The title, the cover, the essence of the book as a whole was affected by them!

Their support on my publishing journey is paramount! I devote this book to them!

If you are not a member yet, join now! As a FREE BONUS, you will receive my Novella "A Race to Save His Childhood Love":

FREE EXCLUSIVE GIFT
(available only to my subscribers)

Go to this link:
https://avawinters.com/novella-amazon

Letter from Lydia Olson

"There is no better place to heal a broken heart than on the back of a horse"

This is my moto; this is how I grew up.

My name is Lydia and when I am not baking cookies with my daughter or riding the bike with my son, I am a Western Historical Romance writer. It is my passion, my hobby and my career.

After I received my BA in Psychology I realized that this would help me create believable characters. Characters that are based on real people. I want my readers to feel as if they have lived themselves in the West.

Growing up myself in a ranch I have a lot of tales to share. Stories that will help you not escape reality, but rather navigate you through reality. You will feel what it would feel to go through situations that make your heart pound and your palms sweat. You will access the depths of someone else's mind; you will open yourselves to new experiences and different point of views.

What do you say? Do you want to take a vacation with me?

Lots of hugs,

Lydia Olson

Prologue

May 3rd, 1867, Goldsprings, Nevada

In the predawn light, shadows stretched the length of the spacious kitchen as flames danced in the hearth. David, lost in thought over an incident with his brother, snatched his hand away from the scorching cast iron griddle sitting over the fire in the stone fireplace.

"My word," he cried, shaking his hand.

He'd been making sourdough pancakes for himself and his brother, Gabe, and he'd been so preoccupied, he'd burned himself. His hand struck the metal coffee pot resting in the embers. It overturned, sending boiling water hissing all over the floor.

Unaccustomed to such clumsiness, a garbled exclamation left David's mouth. *Keep your mind on your task, David Brown. No sense stewing on the look of satisfaction on Gabe's face when he wooed away Leslie.*

David had been courting Leslie for only a short time. It wasn't much of anything, but Gabe had swooped in like a vulture to steal her right out from under David's nose. Even though it had happened a couple of months ago, it still left a long splinter of bitterness festering in David's insides.

Gabe sauntered into the room, his hair still wet from his morning ablutions.

Dressed in woolen trousers and a long-sleeved cotton work shirt, his feet clad in leather boots, Gabe hustled toward the hearth, grabbing a sturdy cotton cloth from the wooden counter. As he dabbed at the water, he said, "There goes breakfast, I take it?"

David said nothing.

"You could have used the range," Gabe pointed out, gesturing to the massive cast iron stove next to the hearth. "Mother bought the best range money could buy."

"Since I can't cook over the flames, what makes you think I can cook on that cockamamie thing?"

Gabe kept up with his teasing. "Trying to let Cousin Ada know she's not needed?" A cheeky grin appeared on his face as he spoke.

Unlike David, Gabe could find humor in just about any incident.

"Oh, she's needed, all right. But right now, her sister needs her more." David's cheeks flamed with heat. He had yet to master the art of breakfast since Mother died five years ago.

After that tragedy, he and Gabe had joined the fight for freedom in the Civil War, leaving thoughts of learning how to cook far behind. Left limping from a war incident, David had returned home with his uninjured brother to find their father—a wealthy man, thanks to the gold rush—had died of a heart attack.

So, he and Gabe were on their own at their farm outside of Goldsprings, Nevada, with plenty of money to their names.

But money did nothing to staunch the lonely hardship of daily life, living in the Nevada high desert and trying to turn the farm into a viable ranch. They had calves to brand, livestock to tend to, horses to train, buildings to build—they even thought to construct another house once they each had wives.

That's if Gabe can let me build a relationship without snatching the girl I'm interested in out from under my nose.

"No, I'll get it done," David said with a determined grimace. "Fetch me some more water, will you?"

While Gabe hurried outside to fill the coffee pot with water, David pitched the burned flapjacks out the window for his dog, Blue. Then, he hooked the iron griddle above the flames once more and scooped more pancake batter onto it with an iron ladle. *It sure would be good to have a woman besides Ada around... someone to keep me warm on a cold winter night.*

He scoffed at the folly of his thoughts. Even if he found a woman, Gabe would unfailingly woo her away with his charm and good looks. *Unless, of course, this tomfool mail-order bride business turns out in his favor.*

A few minutes later, he heaped his and Gabe's plates with the fragrant hotcakes, limped toward the heavy wooden table in the middle of the kitchen, and set the plates down with a clatter.

Once Gabe returned and the coffee pot sat nestled in the embers once again, the brothers settled down to eat their breakfast.

David said, "So how's your correspondence going with... what's her name again? Amanda?" His insides rankled as he spoke.

After Gabe had stolen Leslie, he'd promptly dropped her like a hot potato and started up a correspondence with Amanda Kennett, a young woman from way up yonder in Virginia City.

Gabe's face brightened, just like the dawn sun peeking through the window. "It's going well. It's been weeks of writing—I'm sure looking forward to meeting her."

David wanted to be excited about his brother's upcoming nuptials to a relative stranger. But, as the oldest brother, he shouldered all responsibilities for Gabe and himself like a fortified mule. There was no cause to get excited about nonsense. Especially since Gabe went through potential brides like a dying man at a water hole.

There could never be enough women in the world to quench his brother's thirst.

"She'll arrive here in a few weeks," Gabe said, forking a mouthful of pancake.

David shook his head as he chewed his food. "How can you settle for marriage without love? Unless you foolishly think that what you have with her *is* love."

Gabe glanced at the water boiling in the pot. He rose, crossed to the hearth, and picked up the tin of coffee David had ground earlier, adding some "finings" or burnt sugar to the mixture to give the coffee a rich, brown color. "Oh, it's not what I'd call love by a long shot. But she seems kind and nice, so why not? Someone's got to cook us breakfast around here when Cousin Ada's away." He winked at David.

David rolled his eyes, and he shook his head. "You're crazy, you know, for even going through with this whole plan. Mail-order brides," he muttered, adding a grunt. "I wouldn't be caught dead marrying someone I've never seen. What if she's hideous? What if she looks like that crazy, old wolf who's been skulking around the property? That thing's a bag of bones that needs to be put down. In fact, I might do the honors next time I see it." He lifted an imaginary rifle and pretended to shoot it. "Blam! We'll have to put your fiancée down two seconds after you meet her."

Gabe laughed. "She won't look like an emaciated wolf; I can feel it in my bones. What if she's the most beautiful girl you've ever met?" He tossed a scoop of ground coffee into the pot to let it boil. Every rancher knew that boiling the coffee killed any contaminants that might be lurking in the water.

David snorted. "Fat chance of that." He rose from his seat and walked the now-empty plate over to the metal counter with the recessed basin filled with water. After resting the plate in the metal basin, he retrieved a couple of tin cups and a piece of burlap and crossed back to the hearth. Using the burlap to keep from burning his hands, he poured two cups of coffee for him and Gabe.

"Here you go," he said, stepping closer to the table to put Gabe's coffee in front of his plate. He parked his behind once more on his wooden chair to wait for the coffee to cool. "What are you up to today? I've got some errands to do. I'll be heading into town to pick up a few supplies."

Gabe's sunny disposition clouded over like a sudden storm had appeared on the horizon. "Nothing much," he said, glancing out the window. His fawn-brown eyes had taken on the look of a broody sky at midnight. He ran a hand through his shoulder-length hair, which was the same color as the coffee. "Except for the usual—taking care of chores around here."

David's eyes narrowed as he studied his brother. *Something's bugging him, I know it.* "Come on, now. It looks like there's more to the story."

Gabe's lips parted as if to speak as he met David's eyes.

An indecipherable mystery lurked behind his brother's gaze, but David couldn't tell what it was—nervousness over his impending nuptials?

Gabe's mouth snapped shut, and he pasted a sunny smile on his face—a smile that didn't reach his eyes. "It's nothing. I just got to write a letter."

11

"To Amanda?" David said.

"Maybe…" Lines appeared around his brother's eyes.

"Why are you being so secretive? Gabe… if you can't talk to me, who can you talk to?" David picked up his cup and blew on the coffee, taking a tentative sip.

"I know. But it's nothing, really. I've got everything handled, under my belt. Including your delicious pancakes." Gabe patted his flat abdomen. Then, a frown flickered across his face. "If and when it comes to something, I'll let you know."

An unsettling sensation rocked David's insides. *What is he not telling me? What's going on in that head of his?* Figuring he'd learn about this mysterious "whatever it was" soon enough, David decided to let it go. Anyway, he didn't care enough to pursue it. His brother was always going on about something. Still, he couldn't shake the feeling that something was terribly amiss—something that might change things between him and his brother forever.

Chapter One

May 21st, 1867, Virginia City, Nevada

An odd wind kicked up outside the home where Amanda resided, blowing dust devils down the road. Seeing them today sent a shiver up her spine, and she made the sign of the cross over her bosom. Her gaze followed the whirlwinds until she stared down the street at the low mountains in the distance, wondering what her life would become once she left this home.

In less than a week, she would be leaving Virginia City to meet her husband-to-be, a man named Gabe.

Gabe lived south, a five-day trip by horse-drawn wagon in Goldsprings, Nevada.

Julia's dad, Mr. Williams, would be taking her, saying he needed to meet with a horse trader in Goldsprings and might bring home a horse or two. Apparently, Goldsprings was known for a particular breed of horse.

Nervously, she nibbled on her lower lip.

Getting married hadn't been on her mind, but what else could she do? No prospect courted her, and she was nearly twenty-three—practically an old maid. So, when her closest friend, Julia Williams, had insisted she try offering herself as a mail-order bride, Amanda had reluctantly grasped the opportunity.

I wonder what this Gabe fellow will be like? Tall and handsome or short and stumpy? Will he be mean to me? Will he be kind?

The whole idea of marriage curdled the contents of her stomach. She'd been engaged once already—to John, Julia's brother.

And look how that turned out? He died in a fire, along with Jacob. And there went all the joy in my life...

Before nervous jitters seized her stomach, she headed outside to retrieve the clothes that had been baking in the noon-day sun. She'd washed everything at dawn, wanting to start her new life with freshly cleaned laundry.

Standing in the yard, with the late-morning sun beating down on her back and the top of her head, she began unpinning the clothes from the line with trembling fingers. *I don't know the first thing about being a wife. What will he expect from me?*

Her hands shook so hard one of her favorite pieces—a robin's-egg blue and white pinstriped blouse, fell to the ground.

She tsked, picked it up, and dusted it off as best she could.

Once she'd removed every garment from the line, she clutched the crisp, warm clothes to her bosom and hustled inside the back of the house. Scooting through the kitchen, she nodded at Clara, the Williams' housekeeper.

Clare stooped and removed a fresh apple pie from the cast-iron oven.

"Morning, Miss Clara," Amanda said. She often marveled at the extravagance of having a housekeeper. Her parents could never have afforded such a luxury, especially after her brother Jacob crossed to the afterlife. *After that tragedy, Ma gave up on life. And Pa spent his meager earnings from the silver mines at the saloon, where he drowned his sorrows.*

"Morning, Miss Amanda. Looking forward to your journey, are you?" Her graying hair held high with a red-checked, flour-spattered scarf, Clara rested the pie on the windowsill. The cheerful apron tied around her waist did nothing to hide her generously sized belly.

"No," Amanda said in a small, weak voice, pausing in the doorway.

"Now, child, getting married is a natural occurrence in a woman's life. You should be excited. My husband was the rock in my world until he died, and the Williams family took me in." Clara turned to stand at the massive oak table in the center of the white-washed room. She picked up a sharp knife and began whacking at a freshly killed chicken. Once the bird lay in pieces, Clara turned and fetched a ceramic bowl from a cupboard along the walls. "You'll be fine," she said.

"If you say so," Amanda said, unconvinced, pushing away from the door frame to continue upstairs.

"You'll see," Clara said, placing chicken parts in the bowl.

A warm breeze blew through the window, playing with Amanda's long hair and teasing her with the scent of cinnamon-infused apple pie.

The aroma made Amanda's stomach growl. She'd been too nervous this morning to eat much.

Ignoring her hunger, she scrambled up the stairs to the second landing.

Amanda's toe caught the doorjamb as she scurried into the bedroom she shared with Julia. "Ouch," she cried, hopping about on her non-injured, black leather-booted foot. As she jumped, she dropped the slightly stiff clothes. "Oh, no!"

Hurrying to pick them up, she shook out each one, hoping they'd still be clean and not covered with dust bunnies. After inspecting them and finding them suitable, she continued into the bedchamber, where she dropped the clothing on the pink and white quilt-covered bed. Then, she lifted them one by one, trying to determine which would make it into the nut-brown leather suitcase resting on the ground by her feet.

As Amanda considered her options, Julia sashayed into the room.

Julia always appeared elegant and composed—a distinctive contrast to Amanda. Today she wore a blue and white-checked gingham day-dress, complete with blue-velvet trim on the collars and sleeves that set off her iridescent eyes.

The dress had been fashioned by Amanda's own hand.

With her glossy, raven-colored hair held back in a stylish up-do, Julia strode in the room like a fine-show horse.

Amanda had always felt like a colt who never found her footing, all gangly legs and awkward movements. A tomboy at heart, she loved to climb trees and go fishing in the water hole at the edge of town, catching the fat catfish that patrolled the bottom of those waters. Or she loved to run through the desert, chasing the wild hares. When she was younger, she'd climb on top of old Red, their pony, and set off into the hills to explore with John and her brother Jacob.

But, as much as she loved to be outdoors, God hadn't done her any favors in the grace department—she was as bumbling as a bow-legged toddler.

Dressed in an off-white work shirt and an mud-colored ankle-length walking skirt—the same outfit she'd wear for the journey ahead—she nibbled her lip as she studied Julia's poise. *I'll never carry myself with that much grace. It's a wonder I can even roll out of bed each day and not fall to the floor.*

"What are you thinking about?" Julia asked, her sky-blue eyes twinkling. "The man you'll soon be wedded to?"

"No," Amanda said. "I'm considering sending you to meet him instead. He'll never know the difference."

Julia glided closer to Amanda and took her hands. "Oh, honey. Besides the fact that Marshall and I are courting, why would I do that? Do you think you're not pretty enough?"

Amanda blushed, casting her gaze at the black wrought-iron bed frame. "Maybe..."

"You're beautiful, Amanda. Don't you see?" Julia seized Amanda's shoulders and pivoted her to face the full-length mirror propped in the corner. "Look at this gorgeous young woman."

Amanda shook her head, unable to look at her freckled cheeks or unruly hair.

Determinedly, Julia seized Amanda's chin and forced her to face the looking glass. "*Look.* You've got a fetching figure, flaxen hair the color of winter wheat, eyes the color of a summer lake, and sweet, heart-shaped lips. When Gabe meets you for the first time, he'll be tongue-tied."

"More like worried he caught the wrong fish. He'll toss me back into the stream for certain," Amanda quipped.

"Silly girl." Julia giggled, wrapping her arms around Amanda. "Oh, how I will miss you."

"I know," Amanda said, returning the heartfelt embrace. "I'll miss you, too. Besides, I'm indebted to you. You and your family saved my life." She sniffled, thinking again of the tragedies that had brought her to live with Julia five years ago.

It started when her fiancé and Julia's brother, John Williams, and her brother Jacob died, completely derailing Amanda's family and Julia's, too.

John and Jacob had both been downtown at the general store, purchasing supplies for their respective families, when a fire had broken out in the store. They'd tried to save the owner, old man Bentley. But the ceiling had collapsed in a pile of burning lumber in front of the entrance, blocking egress.

According to Julia's neighbor, Jim Taylor, the boys' efforts had been heroic.

"They tried to save old man Bentley, they did. I spied them through the window as I was rushing to get help. They was helping him around the counter, what with his bum leg and all. No way they could have known the ceiling would have collapsed," Mr. Taylor had said, tears moistening his red, rheumy eyes when he'd come to the house to bring the news of the tragedy. "Everyone inside the store was caught unawares. By the time people started trying to put the fire out, the flames had already consumed most of the building." He'd bore down on the hat he held in his hands, crushing the worn gray felt.

And Amanda, standing behind her Pa, had burst into sobs, the same way she did right now.

"Oh, honey, what's this?" Julia drew away from the embrace, shaking Amanda out of the past. Grabbing her shoulders, she said, "Why the sorrow? Shouldn't you be happy?"

Amanda wiped at her eyes. "I am happy. I was just thinking about John and Jacob and how they died. Such a tragedy!"

Guilt stabbed at her insides as her next thought arose.

I would have had a loveless alliance with John, not true love. She shook her head, trying to rid herself of these gloomy thoughts, but they wouldn't stop. It was as if she'd opened a dam inside her soul, and she was helpless to cease it.

Amanda gazed out the window, framed with lacy white curtains, at two cowboys who rode past on their Palomino steeds. For one brief second, she wanted to climb on the back of one of the horses and disappear into the high desert. She sniffled, returning her gaze to Julia's.

Her friend retrieved a linen handkerchief from her sleeve and dabbed at Amanda's eyes. "There, there..."

"Maybe I could stay here forever," Amanda suggested, hope filling her heart. "I could set up a little seamstress shop in town and earn my keep."

"You're so good at it, Amanda. You made this dress, didn't you?" Julia twirled in a circle, making her voluminous skirts soar like a hot air balloon, a wonder Amanda had only seen once at an exhibit in Virginia City.

The balloon had been shaped out of blue, green, gold, and red striped fabric, and, floating in the desert sky, it had looked magical—just like her life had once been.

"Thank you," Amanda said through her sobs. "After Jacob died, I did manage to make enough money to put food on the table."

"Yes, you did. You're a strong and capable young woman." Julia clutched Amanda's hands again and looked at her earnestly, no doubt trying to lift her spirits.

Amanda gamely tried to put a smile back on her face, but the tragedies that brought her to live with Julia kept her caught in a whirlpool of sorrow. Starting with Jacob's and John's deaths, all the sunlight and soaring joy in her life had ceased. And then, a year later, both her parents died. With no more marriage prospects on the horizon, and no place to go, Amanda had been orphaned, swamped with grief, and unable to take proper care of herself.

Same as when Clara lost her husband, the Williamses had insisted on taking her in.

Julia trained a stern gaze on Amanda's face. "Where are all these bad memories coming from? Are you certain you're excited about the journey ahead to meet Gabe?"

Amanda gave a quick toss of her head. "I'm nervous. I'm certain something's going to go wrong because that's what happens to me. Luck is never on my side—luck left me in the general store when my brother died. He was only twenty-two! So much life left... I loved him so much." Her weeping started once more.

Julia guided them both to the bed and sat, drawing Amanda to sit next to her. She wrapped her arms around Amanda and comforted her as she sobbed.

"You're the best friend in the whole wide world," Amanda finally said, as her crying began to cease.

"No, you're the best friend in the whole wide world." Julia pulled away and grinned, lifting her handkerchief to Amanda's face once more. She wiped at Amanda's tear-stained cheeks. "We both lost our brothers, and you lost your husband-to-be. But now you're going to head south and get married. Isn't that exciting?"

Amanda frowned, wondering what life with John would have been like. Since they'd known one another since birth, their families had arranged for their betrothal when they were young. But she didn't love John any more than she loved the man she would soon marry—Gabe. To her, it felt like a transaction, like buying one of Mr. Taylor's donkeys. "Maybe becoming a seamstress could be exciting."

"This again? And just be a lonely spinster? Honestly..." Julia tsked. "I won't be here forever. I'm to be married to Marshall in the spring, you know that." She tweaked Amanda's nose. "You're acting like a silly, nervous girl when the truth is you're going to go meet a handsome man who will cherish you and adore you forever. You'll see. Trust me."

Somehow, she doubted that very much. But since she had no other options, she figured she might as well go. Resignedly, Amanda picked at the quilt with her short fingernails.

"Think of this as an adventure," Julia said with shining eyes. "Maybe it will even be *fun!*"

"Will you come and visit me?" Amanda said, suddenly feeling like a child.

"Of course, I will!" Julia enthused. "As soon as Marshall and I are married and settled, I'll ask him to take me to visit you. But you'll be too busy to miss me, just you wait and see."

"Okay," Amanda said, with a wan smile. But as hard as she tried, she couldn't catch onto Julia's enthusiasm. Apprehension rooted itself in her heart, clinging to her like an invasive vine. Something was going to go wrong; she just knew it. With her life and her string of bad luck, it could be no other way.

Chapter Two

May 24th, 1867, Goldsprings, Nevada

David sat in the kitchen, his head propped in his hands, unable to make a single decision about what to do next. A cup of lukewarm coffee sat next to him, as well as cold bacon and eggs.

Gabe was dead. He'd been found out in the field a couple of weeks ago, with a bullet hole shot clean through his skull. The image of finding his dead brother staring up at heaven with a bloody hole through his head still haunted David's nights and rode on his shoulder all day long.

I'll have to live with that nightmare image for the rest of my days.

Sheriff Slinger had come out to the ranch to see to the body. The man always seemed to have an oily appearance, like a weasel, with narrowed eyes, gaunt cheeks, and bushy eyebrows that dominated his face.

Slinger hadn't been sheriff long around here—only a couple of years. But he'd arrived in town with a chip on his shoulder the size of the building he occupied, and David had never cared for him.

So what if Slinger had grown up poor, as he liked to whimper about at Dirty Dave's Saloon? David and Gabe hadn't been lucky when they were little—but Father had taught them about the value of hard work and "making something of your life with your own hands."

And Slinger always went on about "making a name for himself" and being "determined to turn every obstacle in his way into his own fortune."

His demeanor never sat well with David, and it sure didn't sit well with him the day the sheriff came out to inquire about Gabe's death.

Slinger and David didn't say much that day—what was there to say? Gabe was dead. But before the sheriff left with Gabe's cold, dead body laid out in the back of the wagon, he had said, "This is a crying shame. Gabe was a fine man. Don't you worry, now. We'll get to the bottom of this."

His words had blown past David like the wind. "Getting to the bottom" of Gabe's death wouldn't bring his brother back.

Since then, David had barely had time to grieve, let alone mull over this mail-order bride business his brother had set in motion. He still had to keep up with all the chores he and Gabe had shared, like milking the dairy cows, roping the calves to brand them, tilling the garden, feeding the chickens, and...

But this morning, his legs just wouldn't move. A persistent thought kept buzzing around his head like a blow fly. *I was too busy to inquire further about what was bugging him that day. I knew he was troubled about something, but I didn't press the issue. The truth was, I was still right peeved at him for taking Leslie out from under my nose before he started all that tomfoolery with the mail-order bride.*

He'd dated Leslie for a time. David had never liked her all that much, but when Gabe had wooed her away, he'd been mad.

And instead of helping out my blood kin when he carried a load of trouble, I sucked on a grudge that day.

As he sat there, moping, Ada hurried into the room, fresh brown eggs cradled in her crisp, white apron. Her graying hair was held back from her face in a severe bun that smoothed all the lines of her wrinkled face.

"David!" she exclaimed. "What's this? You haven't touched a bite of the breakfast I prepared for you." She opened the wooden, zinc-lined icebox in the corner and deposited the eggs into a bucket with her free hand. Then, she wiped her hands on her apron. "Wasn't it to your liking?"

David politely picked up a piece of cold bacon and took a bite, tasting nothing. "No, it's fine, Ada. I'm just moving slowly this morning. Can't figure out why my get up and go has got up and gone."

Ada flashed him a sympathetic gaze but said nothing.

A distant cousin of Mother's, she'd cared for him and Gabe for as long as David could remember. After Mother died, she stayed on, telling them it was her duty and obligation.

David reached around and scratched the back of his head. "Gabe's death just doesn't make no sense. Everyone liked Gabe."

Whenever Gabe rolled into town, people offered to buy him a drink or smoke a fine cigar with him down at the saloon.

David couldn't recall anyone fawning over him the way folks did over his brother. And why should they? He kept to himself and kept his nose out of other people's business.

Ada tsked and set to washing dishes in the recessed basin. "You're as fine as any man in this here town. Don't you go saying things like that, or you might start believing them." A stiff smile formed on her face and, just as quickly, disappeared. "And you're right—there's no reason for Gabe to have been shot. He was the most joyous lad. Never gave no one no quarrel. I know you two got to bickering now and then, but that's just what brothers do."

David side-eyed her. *If you only knew the kinds of things we bickered about.* Gabe would sail through town, make a mess of things, and David would be the one to clean them up. *Like when Leslie dragged herself back to me like a lonesome dog and begged me to take her back...*

Ada sniffled and picked up the corner of her apron to dab at her eyes. "Now look what you've gone and done—you got me to cry. Crying won't do me a lick of good."

David's own eyes moistened. Despite David's grievances toward his brother, Gabe was his only remaining kin. And family should mean more than a grudge. So, he picked up his tin of coffee and took a long swig of the bitter stuff to distract himself. It worked as his whole body shuddered from the dregs he'd poured out of the pot.

"Do you think it had anything to do with his recent job assignment as a deputy sheriff? Gabe's death, I mean? He was always sticking his nose in some nonsense or another." His fingers rapped against the wooden table he and Gabe had made for Mother when they were barely teenagers.

"That's as good a reason as any," Ada agreed, setting a clean pot on the counter with a clang. "Some bandit he probably had thrown in jail sought his revenge." She picked up a cast iron skillet and set to scrubbing it fiercely. "He was such a good man," she said, a determined look on her face.

David took a bite of the now-awful eggs, considering the phrase "good man." In truth, he had shared a bitter rivalry with Gabe since Gabe always seemed to get what he wanted in life, and David had to work hard for everything.

His stomach cramped as he swallowed. He wished Ada would scurry on outside so he could dispose of the eggs without hurting her feelings.

But, no, Ada remained at the basin, scouring dishes with a fury.

She seemed to be lost in thought this morning as she buzzed about the kitchen.

David eyed her speculatively but didn't pry in her business. He had other things to think about, like, how he would manage the ranch without Gabe... and what he would do with a mail-order bride.

He'd thought about sending word to Virginia City about Gabe's death. The message might have gotten there in time. But there was this niggling, wormy thought in the back of his mind—what if Amanda was as pretty as Gabe claimed? And with no rival around, maybe he stood a chance with her?

David was lonely, with no prospects on the horizon. He'd given up on finding a woman after Gabe had stolen Leslie. It hadn't been that serious between them. In fact, Leslie came across as somewhat conniving—it never would have worked. But the stab to his heart when she'd gone to be with Gabe reinforced the bitterness he carried toward his brother.

Never mind that Gabe had dumped Leslie after stealing her. He'd probably snatched her right out from under David's nose just to prove he could. Besides, he'd gotten caught up in this mail-order bride business, and the prospect of a potentially prettier woman with a kinder disposition than Leslie's had seemed more appealing.

And when Leslie came crawling back to David? David had felt like he'd been served up Gabe's discarded leftovers, as always. So, when she left to visit her family for a few weeks, he hadn't minded one bit.

When it came to him and Gabe, David always seemed to be overlooked or passed by. He'd always been the quiet one who stayed in the shadow of his brother's sunny personality.

Wasn't it about time David got what *Gabe* wanted?

But that thought left the taste of soured mash in his mouth and sent him spinning into a world of guilt.

Hence, the last thing he wanted to do this week—or any week, for that matter—was pick up his dead brother's bride-to-be.

"Where'd Gabe stash his correspondence? I need to see to Miss Kennett's arrival."

Ada tapped her chin. "I think they're in his dresser drawer. I saw him tie a sheaf of letters with twine and place them in his top drawer as I was setting to change his sheets one day."

David nodded.

"Have you thought much about what you're going to do with her?" Ada asked.

"I thought maybe you could keep her busy." David picked up his coffee cup but then thought better about drinking the bitter liquid.

"I can keep her busy, but she came here to marry a man," Ada said firmly.

"What are you saying?"

Ada stayed silent.

David shook his head and got up from the table, ready to head upstairs to Gabe's room. He knew what Ada might be implying—he'd already considered it.

What would be the harm in marrying her? Especially if she's pretty? There's no way my brother can steal her away from his grave.

His stomach felt queasy when he stepped into the room. A stillness as dead as his brother's body clung to every piece of furniture, every rug, every window covering. It was as if the entire room mourned his absence. The queasiness turned into an all-out sea storm when he stood before the heavy oak dresser opposite Gabe's bed. *No way should I be looking at my brother's private correspondence.*

He pressed his fist against his mouth and considered this idea. But picturing that poor girl waiting downtown with no one to fetch her yanked at his sense of responsibility. *I'll pick her up, take her home, and feed her supper. But then I'll have to tell her the news—that her fiancé is dead. Maybe she'll just turn tail and run. Or maybe Ada can find her a place to live.*

Squaring his shoulders, he slid open the drawer.

Like Ada had said, there sat a sheaf of letters tied in light brown twine. Next to the bundle sat the ad Gabe had placed.

He swallowed hard as he picked up the ad and read.

I want to know some pretty girl of 17 to 22 years. I am 24, 5 feet 10 inches tall, hair the color of a fox. I can laugh for 12 minutes straight, and I want a pretty girl to laugh with me.

David's stomach tightened.

Gabe was the funniest person he knew. Everyone liked Gabe Brown.

David fought back his resentment and rifled through the letters, removing the contents and scanning them.

The pair had exchanged light-hearted correspondence, and David understood right away why Gabe wanted to meet this gal. Love or no love, she was a smart young woman. He paused at her confession about losing both her brother and fiancé in a tragic fire. After that, both her parents died sometime later, within days of one another. He ran his hand through his hair. *Oh, no one so young should experience such a thing. But then I lost my parents, too… and now my own brother is dead.*

Finally, he found what he was looking for—the date of her arrival—Monday, May 27th. It was in three days. No way could he reach her in time now to tell her of Gabe's demise.

Hastily, he shoved the letters back in the drawer, slammed it shut, and turned to lean against the solid wood, his heart racing. Shame noosed his insides at having glimpsed their exchanges. More than that, apprehension made his mind go blank. *What in the blazes am I going to do with a mail-order bride? How can I be so disrespectful of my dead brother as to marry her myself?*

And why am I even considering it?

***

Over the next few days, he stayed as busy as a man could get, dreading the coming Monday. He'd tilled the field, moved the cattle to new grazing land, and the barn was as clean as a whistle.

But try as he might, he couldn't fathom what he would do when Miss Kennett arrived. Whenever the topic had come up between him and Gabe, he'd hammered on at the notion of ordering up a bride.

"What in the tarnation has gotten into you?" he'd said on their last argument. "Why'd you steal Leslie only to turn around and order up a bride by mail?"

"Because I wanted to," Gabe had replied. "You know Leslie had a mean streak. I was doing you a favor, brother."

After that, he'd laughed like it was the funniest thing in the world.

But all the hilarity in the world couldn't erase David's shame and heartbreak at having had yet another thing stolen by Gabe.

At night, however, laying in his lonely bed, his thoughts softened. Maybe Gabe had been right... perhaps a mail-order bride might be a welcome change.

At dinner the night before Gabe's bride was due to arrive, his nerves got the best of him, and he dropped the porcelain plate Ada had insisted on using for supper—and broke it.

"Goodness gracious, David, what's gotten into you?" Ada chided, scurrying to pick up the broken porcelain.

"Miss Kennett, that's what. What am I going to do with her?"

Ada dropped the shards in a waste bucket. "Why don't you marry her? She's coming here to get married. Don't disappoint her."

Even though he'd thought that very thing, David reacted strongly to this suggestion and not in a positive manner. He'd be doing it out of revenge toward his brother, not because he actually wanted her.

Sweat beaded on his forehead, and he felt like he might faint.

"Come now, honey, you look like I've signed papers for your execution. It might be nice for you to have someone to care for you."

David hustled from the room with some lame excuse to check on his horse, Kickabilly. In truth, he thought he might fall to his hands and knees and throw up his supper. *This is not how I wanted things to go.*

When Monday came, he awoke at dawn, still unsure about marrying Miss Kennett. In the middle of the night, he'd gotten down on his knees and prayed on it. His brother looked down from heaven like a guilt-driving ghost.

After breakfast and chores, he cleaned up and dressed as nicely as he could, donning his best blue poplin shirt, a herringbone-patterned vest, and spit-shined cowboy boots. He dusted off his Stetson as best he could, hitched Kickabilly to the wagon, and set off for town.

Miss Kennett was said to arrive at noon, about forty-five minutes away. The sun bore down on his back as he rode through the high desert of scrub-covered plains surrounded by low hills. Clouds danced through the sky, like frolicking maidens with their hair stretched to the horizon.

Once he reached the bustling town, with a population of nearly six thousand transient and permanent residents, he slowed Kickabilly. The horse clomped through the dusty street, passing other horses and wagons. On the wooden sidewalk, women and their children hurried to fetch their supplies.

The wagon proceeded in a cloud of dust, adding to the already dusty street and sidewalk. In the winter, the roads would be muddy and foul, covered with snow at times, or deep troughs from wagon wheels in the rain at other times. But springtime baked the mud, and the horse hooves and carts would trample down the gutters.

David scanned the occupants of the wagons as he passed the red-painted façade of Dirty Dick's local saloon, where a few fur trappers and cowboys milled around the outside. He nodded to those he knew. Past the tavern, he rode by the drug store, dentist, and general store, heading for the stage stop.

The stage stop, consisting of a gazebo with a couple of benches for travelers to wait, stood near the town center. Here, exhausted horses could be replaced with fresh ones, and stagecoaches and wagons deposited weary travelers and picked up eager ones. Nearby, livery stables held well-rested horses to be bartered out for wagons and stagecoaches.

Spying an upheaval ahead, David pulled up on the reins.

Several yards before him, a small herd of mustangs, with sweat-soaked bodies and froth around their mouths, reared up and overturned a wagon empty of passengers. Dangling ropes hung from their necks.

David guessed that they'd been rounded up to sell in town.

One of the horses fell and landed beneath the wagon. The rope wound around its neck caught on the metal frame of the wagon, and try as it might, the mustang couldn't free himself.

Around the bustling station, people gawked at the equines but did nothing to help.

"By jingo, those horses need some assistance. You stay here a mite, Kickabilly. I've got to go talk to those animals." He climbed off the wagon and slowly walked toward the kerfuffle.

As he approached the fallen horse, someone yelled at David, "Stay away from that horse, you fool. You're going to get yourself kicked in the head."

David turned toward the helpful idiot. "Not if I stay away from his hooves, I won't."

Unable to free itself from the wagon, the horse writhed, and the whites of his fearful eyes shone as David came closer.

David pursed his lips. *That's precisely what I feel right about now at the notion of meeting Miss Kennett.*

He glanced at the horse's side. Bloody streaks covered the horse's flanks, as if the animal had been whipped. *No one should have to beat a horse as fine and wild as this to get it to do his bidding.* Crouching, he spoke to the horse in low, soothing tones. "Now, you're going to have to trust me to get you out of this mess you've gotten yourself into." He tried to ignore the bold stares and judgment of the crowd who watched him—he'd endured such ridicule all his life.

David had always been different when it came to animals.

The horse stilled, breathing hard.

"That's better. I'm going to cut this rope from your neck—can you stay still and let me do that?"

The horse, a bay with a tail the color of cream, directed one of his eyes, as richly brown as David's hair, at David.

"Good. I thought you'd agree with me." Slowly, David reached for the hunting knife strapped to his side.

The horse watched his every movement.

People huddled around David and murmured at one another.

He employed a couple of cowboys to manage the wagon, which trapped the horse as he freed it.

After some maneuvering, the equine quickly got his legs under him and scrambled away from the wagon. It stood several yards away from David and stared at him, its sides heaving.

The crowd cheered.

A cowboy raced down the street, waving his arms and yelling. "What did you do to my mustangs?"

"That man saved one of them," one of the cowboys who steadied the buggy said.

"Wanna buy it?" the man said when he stood a few feet away from David.

"How much?" David said, eying the dust-covered cowboy and glancing at the mustang.

"One-fifty," the cowboy stated.

"Given that this horse was running free a week ago, and now it's wounded, do you really think that's a fair price? Besides the fact that you're going to have to catch it again."

"Oh, never you mind, then." The cowboy waved his hand at David and turned away from him. "Where's the boy I paid to keep watch over my mustangs?" he bellowed.

David's eyes glanced at a cart rolling up the road, sending clouds of dust billowing into the air.

An older man sat on the seat, holding the reins of the steeds hitched to the wagon. And next to him sat the prettiest girl David had ever seen. A sight to behold with cornflower-blue eyes and pale hair fluttering around her face, she sat primly, clutching her hands together.

David's heart began to rattle around in his ribcage, considering escape, just like that mustang. His eyes darted right and left, landing on the distant hills.

Is that Miss Kennett? My, but she's a comely young woman. As he stood there, watching her, his nerves got the best of him. He considered mounting his horse and heading back home straight away. *I can't do it... this marrying business... I simply can't do it. I should turn around and leave. She ain't met me, so she wouldn't know the difference.* Thoughts of his brother swirled around his head like a ghost, churning a mountain of guilt. *No way can I claim what's rightfully yours, brother—not for revenge or responsibility. She's too darn pretty for the likes of me.*

His gaze skittered toward Dirty Dick's Saloon. *Maybe a stiff drink would do me right.* He'd never been much of a drinker, but right now, it seemed like a good idea.

He clutched his reins in a knotted grip, feeling his own tongue tangling in a twist in his mouth.

If that was Amanda Kennett, no way would he be able to speak, let alone ask her to be his bride.

Chapter Three

May 24th, 1867, Goldsprings, Nevada

Forty-five minutes earlier...

Amanda sat on the uncomfortable seat next to Julia's dad, Mr. Williams, tired of the bump and jostle of the long, arduous ride. They'd been traveling for days, and she hadn't gotten much sleep on the journey. Besides the lack of sleep, her once-clean outfit was now covered in dust and grime.

Goldsprings lay ahead in the distance, tiny structures shimmering in the heat. Nervous apprehension fluttered in her chest at the sight of the cluster of buildings nestled in the foothills. *Is Gabe waiting for me? What if he changed his mind?*

Suddenly, the notion of being someone's mail-order bride seemed the most foolish endeavor she'd ever done. *What was I thinking to have come all this way to meet and marry someone I don't even know?* She glanced over her shoulder at the distant mountains, wondering if she should jump off the wagon and disappear into the vista... or maybe ask Mr. Williams to take her home.

Mr. Williams had always been a man of few words, but, on this journey, he seemed to have lost what few words he possessed. Back in Virginia City, when he came home from the bank where he worked, he mostly spoke to his wife or his daughter, Julia. But during this trip, he'd been silent the entire way, save for the time some Indians—a group of Washoe—had appeared over the hills and stopped them.

Mr. Williams had managed to say, "Stay here," but he needn't have bothered.

Amanda was scared to death of Indians, growing up with tales of how the native warriors took what they wanted and slaughtered when it suited. As a result, she sat in the seat, clutching her hands together.

Mr. Williams climbed from his seat and approached the Indians, who sat like imposing statues on their noble horses.

The Washoe people were bare-chested, with deerskin leggings covering their legs. Their scandalous attire was downright shameful. Perched bareback on their steeds, they held leather reins in their hands and spoke to Mr. Williams in a language Amanda didn't understand.

Her fear built as she watched the exchange until she thought she might faint.

Finally, Mr. Williams returned.

The Indians remained, eying his progress until he'd climbed back into his seat, picked up the reins, and clucked at the two horses hitched to the wagon.

"Heyya, get up," he said to the horses, adding some clicking noises in the back of his throat. With a lurch, the wagon surged forward, and the bouncing, uncomfortable ride began anew.

The Indians turned their horses in the opposite direction and rode away.

"What did they want?" Amanda asked.

Mr. Williams side-eyed her as if surprised she'd said anything. "They wanted to know if I'd trade with them. The Washoe people make fine baskets."

Amanda marveled at the number of words emerging from his mouth, suddenly aware of how lonely this trek had been riding through the scary landscape for days with no one to talk to. They'd trekked through potholes, forged creeks, and slapped at buzzing insects with nary a word passing between them.

Continuing, Mr. Williams said, "They also asked if we needed any medical care. They have these healers called shamans who can supposedly bring a person back from the dead." He let out a snort. "That's what doctors are for."

"What was that language you were speaking?"

Mr. Williams glared at her as if her time for conversation was nearing its end. "The Washoe people speak a form of Hokan-type language. It's come in useful to learn it as best I can since my stable boy is half Washoe."

"Oh, my! A Hokan-type language," Amanda exclaimed, eager to keep the discussion rolling. In truth, she didn't know what a "Hokan-type" language meant.

But the set of Mr. Williams' mouth and the fixed gaze he directed ahead let her know that this rare burst of chatter had come to an end.

That had been nearly an hour ago, but the fear clutching her insides persisted. Meeting Gabe might be equally terrifying.

As the buildings grew closer, Amanda's anxiety grew with each turn of the wheels. A small town compared to Virginia City with its twenty-five thousand or so residents, she wondered what kind of ramshackle dwelling she'd be living in. From what she could tell, the town ahead held tiny homes at the edges and not much in the way of a town center. In fact, it looked like an odd assortment of mismatched structures.

I never thought to ask Gabe what kind of a home he owns or what he does to earn his keep. What if he's a silver miner like

Pa was? What if he lives in a tiny house like that one? She squinted at a small wooden dwelling with laundry hanging on a line between the house and the fence. Dirty little children, their feet bare, played outside in the yard.

She'd grown up clean and well-cared for in the foothills of California. But then, when Amanda turned fifteen, Pa had up and moved the family to Virginia City, Nevada, at the suggestion of Mr. Williams. He said silver mining was the means to a man's fortune.

Together, the two families made the long passage to Nevada. Only, Mr. Williams had gone into banking, instead.

Pa worked the silver mines, earning their family just enough to make ends meet.

Her heart was saddened at the thought of her deceased family. She suddenly wished her ma and her pa were alive, that her brother Jacob and Julia's brother John had lived. She and John would be settled in their own ranch in Virginia City.

Maybe I'd have two children by now. If I had a boy, I'd name him Paul. If it were a girl, I'd call her Charity. We'd have a housekeeper like Clara who would cook and clean for us. That way, me and my children could work in the garden or look for salamanders in the creek the way Jacob and I used to do when Ma and Pa were alive.

She waved her hand, shooing her silly fantasies from her mind.

Mr. Williams gave her another side-eyed glance but said nothing.

Amanda's thoughts took a pessimistic turn as she pondered the way her life had turned out instead.

After Jacob had died, Ma had grown too depressed to care for Amanda and Pa. She simply sat in her rocking chair on the front porch of their modest home and rocked, staring at nothing.

And Pa turned to the saloon for comfort, drinking his wages away.

So why do I think life's suddenly going to improve? God has it out for me now that Jacob and John are dead. God's probably punishing me for my foolhardy thoughts. 'Amanda, because you weren't looking forward to marrying John, I had to wrest both him and your brother away from you and make your life miserable from that point on.'

Those thoughts made her want to cry. But then she mused on the correspondence she'd had with Gabe. *Maybe this will be a fresh start so I can put the past behind me? He's not so bad.*

Gabe had been funny, telling her of the time he nursed a baby squirrel to life when his hound dog caught it. He'd said that baby squirrel had become his little pal until it decided to head for the hills and perhaps take a squirrel wife.

And he'd told her how the circus had come to Goldsprings, and a woman stood on the back of her horse and rode it in a wild circle, with a tiny monkey clinging to her back. He said it was the most marvelous thing to witness. He was sorry the squirrel had disappeared—riding a horse while standing with a squirrel on his back might have earned him some laughs.

Over the weeks of their correspondence, she'd grown quite fond of Gabe. But was it love? Not by a long shot, unless love consisted of lukewarm tea with half-baked biscuits—because that was the kind of enthusiasm she'd brought with her today.

One of the horses nickered and shook its head, pulling her back into the moment. She'd gone and lost herself in thoughts of Gabe. But soon, the man she'd shared weeks of correspondence with would be before her, in flesh and blood.

As the horses clomped along the dusty road, she began to feel anxious.

Ahead, some sort of skirmish had broken out involving a few horses. Amanda grabbed the metal railing next to her.

Mr. Williams leaned back on the reins and said, "Whoa."

The horses came to a stop.

Mr. Williams lifted his hand over his eyes, studying the scene ahead. "Let's hold up here a bit and wait for the dust to settle. Something's going on, and we don't want to get caught in the middle of it."

This time, Amanda was the one to grow mute.

Ahead, a man crouched in front of a horse underneath someone's cart, but she couldn't make out any details other than he wore a hat on his head.

Maybe that's his horse, and the horse fell or something. Amanda wrung her hands in her lap, scanning the street to see if there was anyone who looked like she imagined Gabe might look.

He'd given her a description in his ad, saying he had hair the color of a fox. *Well, what kind of fox?* Foxes came in many colors. She'd seen drawings in a book her mother had shown her once. *Why didn't I ask him for more details? What a ninny. I'm looking for a maybe red-haired, maybe brown-haired man, around 5-foot-10, who likes to laugh.*

Not a single man dealing with the horses up the way looked like he was laughing.

Oh, dear. I should have had Gabe carry a flower, or maybe a baby squirrel, so I'd know he was the right guy.

The mustang that had fallen to the ground scrambled out of the way of the wagon, and people cheered.

"Okay, let's go." Mr. Williams clucked at his horses, and their clopping hooves hauled the creaking, groaning wagon into action. "I sure hope those horses ain't the ones I'm coming to see. I don't need no wild mustang, that's for sure."

As they got closer, she nervously scanned every man in the crowd, shuddering at some and feeling hopeful at others.

But no one even glanced in her direction.

The man who'd crouched before the horse brushed off his pants with his palms. His head lifted, and he stared hard at her. He straightened his Stetson and strode toward the wagon.

Relief flooded her insides. *Gabe came to get me, he really came.*

Her stomach twisted as if Gabe's baby squirrel was playing in her belly. This man was as handsome as could be.

See? All your fretting has been for nothing. Gabe's a good-looking man. Maybe everything's going to turn around just fine—perhaps God has forgiven me and given me another chance. It will be my honor to marry the man approaching us.

A grin tugged at the corners of her mouth, but she held it back, not wanting to appear foolish.

The man continued to step in their direction.

Mr. Williams gently tugged the reins. "Whoa, whoa," he cooed.

The horses came to a stop, shifting back and forth, making their harnesses jangle.

"Easy, boys," Mr. Williams said.

Amanda's gaze stayed pinned to this Gabe fellow.

His gaze stayed pinned to hers, too. But there was a wildness in his eyes as if he might bolt at any second like that mustang.

Does he not find me to his liking? Am I not pretty enough?

When he stood before the wagon, he stayed mute, just like Mr. Williams. He removed his hat, nearly crushed it between his hands, and shifted side to side, same as Mr. Williams' horses.

Amanda glanced at Mr. Williams, but he stayed silent, too.

Finally, the handsome man cleared his throat, and his lips parted. He cleared his windpipe again... and again.

Amanda frowned. *Is he okay?*

"Are you Miss Kennett?" he finally said in a soft-sounding voice.

"Yes," she squeaked. "That's me."

"I'm here to take you home." The word "home" emerged with a nervous stutter. "My name is David. David Brown."

All her hopes and silly thoughts of a fresh new start flew down the street. Gabe didn't want her. He'd sent someone else to fetch her in his place.

Chapter Four

The knots his mouth had insisted on tying in his tongue persisted as David stuttered out his name and his intentions to take Miss Kennett home. Staring at her beguiling face with those blue eyes and hair the color of young wheat didn't help his cause. He simply had to tell her, right here, right now, that Gabe was dead. But remembering her story about losing her family and her fiancé gave him pause.

No way can I burden her soul by telling her that the man she came here to marry is dead, brutally killed by bandits. It would shatter her to tell her such a thing.

He lifted his hand to his head, removed his Stetson, and smoothed his hair before replacing the hat. He'd been instantly attracted to the girl, which confused him. Sure, he'd been attracted to other women in his life. Before he left to fight in the Civil War, he'd thought about asking Mary Anderson to get hitched to him.

Mary came from an upstanding family in Goldsprings. Her daddy was one of the best ranchers in these parts. David had even purchased stock from him when a cougar had culled his family's herd.

But when he returned from the war with a bad limp, he didn't think Mary would want him. Apparently, he'd been right because, while he was away, she'd gone and got engaged to old Rattlesnake Hank's son. Which was fine by him in the long run because he didn't fancy her as well as she deserved—he just thought he couldn't do any better. So, he'd begun courting Leslie, instead, until Gabe had swooped in and stolen her.

But if Mary was considered out of his league, the young woman before him was *way* beyond anything he might hope for. She was just too pretty for the likes of him—she was meant for a handsome man like Gabe.

He stiffened, realizing that Miss Kennett sat there looking at him with wide, fearful eyes.

"Are you going to remove her from the wagon, or what?" the man sitting next to her said. Annoyance was etched all over his sun-tanned face.

That frog that had been napping in his windpipe settled into position again, forcing him to clear his throat. *I'm clearing my throat so much Miss Kennett's going to think I've come down with yellow fever or typhoid, she is.* He extended his hand to her. "Miss," he managed to say.

She propped her dainty hand on his and stepped from the wagon.

He had to swallow his reaction to her smooth, smooth skin.

"What were you doing with that horse?" She nodded to the mustang that was now surrounded by men with ropes.

One of the men tossed a lasso at the horse's neck, attempting to catch him. The mustang reared, knocked one of the men on his behind, wheeled, and galloped away.

"That horse?" David pointed at the fleeing mustang. *What an idiotic thing to say. Of course, she meant that horse.*

"Yes, that horse. Is it yours?"

"No, miss, it's not mine. I just freed it. It got caught under a wagon." His face grew uncomfortably hot as he spoke to her. *Oh my word, the sun is warm today,* he excused himself in his mind.

"That was kind of you." As she descended from the wagon, her foot came down hard on his boot.

He winced and flattened his lips in a thin grimace, making her blush.

"I'm sorry," she said, casting her gaze at the ground.

He ignored the apology, scanning the back of the wagon. "Is this your luggage?"

"Yep, it's hers," the cart's driver said. "That, and that bag of potatoes. The missus thought you might need some seedling potatoes, so she sent them along with me."

David touched the brim of his hat before seizing the luggage and the burlap bag. "That was mighty fine of her. I don't believe I caught your name."

"It's Williams. Nick Williams." The man nodded.

"Mr. Williams, I'm pleased to make your acquaintance," David said as the manners his mother had pounded into him surfaced.

Mr. Williams grunted. "Make sure her fellow takes real good care of her. She's my daughter's favorite friend."

"Will do," David said. *Too bad her fellow is six feet under.*

"Know a good place to put up for the night? I've got to see to some horses and won't be starting back today." Mr. Williams retrieved a handkerchief from his pocket and dabbed it at his brow.

"Try Miss Mae's hotel at the end of the street." David lifted his hand and pointed. "It's right next to Dirty Dick's Saloon. You can't miss it."

"Much obliged," Mr. Williams said. He directed his attention at Miss Kennett. "You take care now, you hear?"

"I will. Give Julia my love when you return." Miss Kennett stood stiffly with her hands clutching one another like she might lose one of them if she loosened her grip.

Mr. Williams clucked at his horses and they lunged into a forward walk, leaving David and Miss Kennett without another word.

As David guided Miss Kennett toward his wagon, where Kickabilly rested with his head down in a deep drowse, he couldn't think of a single thing to say.

"Is Gabe held up somewhere?" she said in a small, weak voice that broke his heart.

"Gabe's unavailable at the moment," David said bitterly. *When he should be the one to be marrying the beauty by my side. All my thoughts of revenge were foolishness. I'll never be good enough for Amanda Kennett.*

The "beauty by his side" seemed a bit bumbling as she stumbled when she got close to the wagon. When she put her hands out to brace her fall, they collided with Kickabilly's belly.

The horse side-stepped out of her way.

"Oh! I'm so sorry. What a clumsy one I can be," she blurted.

David glanced at her as he hefted the potatoes and leather case into the back of the wagon.

Miss Kennett's eyes glistened.

Poor thing's scared out of her wits. "That's okay. Kickabilly is a gentle beast. He forgives you." He patted his horse's neck, affection warming his heart.

Miss Kennett put her hand next to his and caressed Kickabilly's neck, too.

Her touch practically sparked his hand, so David quickly snatched his arm away. "Here. Let me help you into the buggy, and we'll be on our way."

"Thank you," she said.

He put his hands around her waist and hefted her into the seat. She let out a little gasp. Once again, he yanked his hands away, well aware of how soft and sweet she felt. He quickly brushed those thoughts away, picturing his brother glaring at him.

But wormy notions of revenge slithered their way into his mind, making him feel like a sinner. *Come on, David. You just want her to get back at Gabe. And she don't deserve to be treated that way... she looks kind and innocent.*

Once he climbed into his seat, Miss Kennett sat with her back rigid, eyes staring straight ahead.

"If you're going to sit like that the whole way home, you're going to bruise your backside," he said, a slight smile curving the corners of his lips. "Kickabilly's going to do his best to give you a smooth ride home, but even he can't account for all the potholes and the rough terrain we'll encounter."

Miss Kennett let out a breath and gripped the leather seat on either side of her. Still, her eyes stayed glued to the horizon. "What made you name your horse Kickabilly?"

He smiled. "Gabe used to rescue animals all the time, so he brought home this billy goat one day. That dumb old animal used to rear up on its hind legs and head-butt anything in its path. I'd just gotten my horse and hadn't figured out what to call it. So when the billy goat tried to head-butt my horse,

Kickabilly kicked... he missed the goat because they were facing each other, but his name was born."

No need to tell Amanda about the momentary satisfaction I experienced over my horse trying to kick anything belonging to Gabe. Gabe always took the best for himself, even horses.

After Dad had gotten rich, he'd given David and Gabe some money to buy horses. Gabe had chosen his pick of the herd, leaving Kickabilly and a few scrawny mares for David. David had poured his heart and soul into making Kickabilly a sound, saddle-worthy animal, even when Gabe showed up on his fine stallion. David figured Kickabilly shared his resentment toward Gabe and had shown his feelings by trying to kick that dumb goat.

After shaking those thoughts from his head, he glanced at Miss Kennett, pleased to see a smile crossing her too-pretty face.

The smile vanished. "Is Gabe waiting for me at home?" Her voice cracked when she spoke.

"He's somewhere around the ranch," David said.

That's not exactly a lie. He's buried beneath the Texas mountain laurel Mother planted in the backyard before she died. He pursed his lips.

Miss Kennett seemed to relax somewhat.

David grimaced. *How am I going to tell her Gabe's dead and convince her to marry me instead?* His brow furrowed as his thoughts soured. *I told him this cockamamie mail-order bride business was foolish. Only now, she's my foolishness to deal with—or worse, my stupid idea at revenge.*

As they rode home, he stayed silent, his mood grown as dark as midnight.

With the ranch looming in the distance, Kickabilly lifted his head, whinnied, and planted his feet in a wide stance.

"What's gotten into you, Kickabilly?" His gaze scanned the horizon, looking for signs of a cougar.

No predators could be seen. Instead, a bay-colored mustang galloped over the hills, heading straight for them. David let out a laugh, urging Kickabilly on with a few clucks and a tap of the reins.

"What's so funny?" Miss Kennett said, looking at the mustang.

"That's the horse I saved today. Guess it's come to express its thanks."

"Maybe the mustang likes you," she said shyly, looking up at him through her eyelashes.

David shook his head and rolled his eyes, taken aback by her beguiling innocence. *This is going to be more complicated than I thought—way harder.* "Not if he knows what's good for him," he said, not sure whether he was speaking about the mustang or himself.

Kickabilly began to beeline toward the pasture, knowing that food, water, and a good rest were soon within reach. The mustang watched from a safe distance away.

And Blue—David's black, white, and brown cattle dog and good buddy—launched around the barn corner and loped toward the wagon.

David tugged on the reins, and Kickabilly came to a halt, patiently waiting for his release. Blue leaped in the back of the buggy and wiggled toward David, licking and kissing his face with his pink, wet tongue.

"Hey, boy, where have you been? I didn't see you this morning, or I wouldn't have taken off without you. Did you keep Ada company?" David ruffled the dog's soft coat while Amanda stared at him, stirring a sense of discomfort.

The dog barked, then leaped to the ground, waiting expectantly for David to climb off. He did so and crossed to the other side, holding up his hand to Miss Kennett.

She took it and climbed down, this time thankfully not landing on his booted feet.

"Wait here a second, will you? I've got to get this harness off of my horse and turn him out into the pasture. I'll brush him down after I've got you settled."

The thought of "getting Miss Kennett settled" made his heart all warm and stupid. *Where's my good sense flown off to?* He scoffed at his nonsense.

The rescued mustang stood near the fenced pasture, boldly staring at them.

Kickabilly lifted his head again and whinnied.

The other horse whinnied back in a high-pitched squeal.

Kickabilly responded.

The mustang whinnied again.

"That's enough," David chided, softly chucking Kickabilly's nose. "You can have your little conversation on your own time. But right now, I need to get Miss Kennett into the house and get her some refreshments. You want yours, too, don't you?"

Next to him, Miss Kennett giggled. "Do you think he understands you?"

David thought a moment. "Sure, I do. Don't you?"

"I guess I never thought about it." Once again, she giggled.

The sound was as sweet as water gurgling down the creek.

As David removed the breeching strap, trace, breast collar, and other parts of the harness, panic replaced the gloom in his mind. *Can I really do this? Can I really ask her to marry me? I'm hardly what you call a catch.*

"I'll be right back."

He grabbed the bearing rein and led Kickabilly toward the pasture, with Blue trotting by his side. Next, he unlocked the gate and walked into the field. There, he removed the headpiece, browband, and bit from Kickabilly's mouth and sent him off into the grass with a pat on the rump. He paused for a minute, taking time to get himself in good order again as Kickabilly galloped away.

He turned to face the most challenging task of his life—asking Miss Kennett for her hand in marriage and informing her of his brother's death. He hoped she didn't take off with the mustang and head for the hills. He had no business asking for her to marry him—not for the horrible reasons he'd concocted to justify marrying her.

A woman as pretty as Amanda Kennett should never be married to exact revenge against anyone, but especially one's own brother.

Chapter Five

Standing near the fence, with a soft breeze tossing her hair about her face in the same way it ruffled the grass in the field, Amanda eyed David as he led his horse out to the pasture. *He's sure a good-looking man—but he seems a little on the shy, quiet side. I wonder if Gabe is the same way.*

Julia's brother John was the exact opposite. He'd cracked jokes, teased her incessantly, and was always going on about some such thing or another that she couldn't care less about. *What if Gabe's loud, like John? Will I really want to marry him if he is?* She didn't think so—she would have preferred someone more on the quiet side than a loudmouth like John.

Instantly, guilt tied a tidy lasso around her heart and tugged, transforming it into shame. *God's going to smite you if you keep on with thoughts like this, Amanda Kennett... the same way he smote you before.*

She inclined her head, studying David.

David stood in the field, his hands on his hips and his dog by his side. He stared at his horse while the mustang grazed outside of the pasture.

That wild horse acted as if he lived here—unlike Amanda, who felt pinned to the ground by a sense of not belonging. *Maybe David's disappointed in me and wants to warn his brother off... or send me packing.* She began to wring her hands the same way she'd done countless times today.

A faint, dizzy feeling overtook her, and she began to sway. Her face became cool and clammy even though the sun shone brightly on the land. She suddenly felt too hot, too small, too scared, too everything, and wondered if she might faint. As she reached her hand out to steady herself, David finally turned around.

His eyebrows shot high on his forehead and he hurried toward her with the dog trotting next to him. "Miss Kennett, are you all right?"

The dog sniffed her and sneezed.

"I'm just a bit peckish, is all." A wan smile formed then flitted away. "I don't recall eating much today."

"Goodness gracious, what kind of host am I? A poor one, that's what," he said, answering his own question. "Let's get you into the house." With one hand on her back, the other supporting her elbow, he ushered her from the barn and the field. The gesture evoked a sense of safety in her, and she wanted to melt into his touch.

Her eyes widened at the grand structure in her line of sight. *That's the most elegant home I've ever seen.*

David pushed open a small gate and guided her through a lovely yard, abundant with flowers and trees.

The gardens looked like something she'd seen in a children's storybook once, complete with butterflies flitting about and birds singing.

"Oh, my," she gasped as she stepped along the stone walkway. "What a pretty yard. I've never seen such a wonder."

"Thank you," David said. "It's all my mother's doing."

"How do you keep it so lush in this awful heat?"

"There's some sort of clay irrigation system buried in the yard. It's a German innovation. When Father became rich, Mother got her notions from the Queen herself. She read all those fancy publications—the kind that told her what to buy. The Queen of England supposedly endorsed the clay irrigation system." He snorted. "But Mother's no longer with us." A frown crossed his face, marring his handsome features.

"I'm so sorry," she said, still leaning into his steady touch.

He gave her a side-eye. "Nothing to be sorry about. You didn't do it. She caught a bad illness, is all—some fancy doctor called it a cancer. It took her real quick." His mouth formed a slit. "But her cousin Ada came to help out, and she kept us going. She's in the kitchen now."

"Is your father around?" Amanda asked in a fit of boldness.

"Nope. A heart attack took him." David's jaw tightened as he opened the front door and stood aside for her to enter.

The dog wandered off.

Embarrassed that she seemed to have evoked bad memories, Amanda kept her mouth shut as they entered the home. Her hand flew to her mouth as she took in the wonders of this fine house.

Rich mahogany furniture was artfully arranged over ornate red and gold rugs. A crystal vase sat on a sideboard, bursting with flowers from the garden, and heavy drapes hung at the windows.

Will this be my new home?

David placed his hand on her back and ushered her toward another room.

Ahead sat a massive kitchen, with the usual white-washed walls at the top and glazed brick covering the lower wall—a feature Amanda had never seen. A light-wood counter sat along the wall, with a cozy eating table perched in the center of the room. Tins marked with the words "coarse flour," "rye," "sugar," and more lined one of the shelves. A fireplace stood next to an ornate range, which an older woman opened to retrieve some sort of baked good that smelled heavenly.

"Ada, this is Miss Kennett," David said, presenting Amanda with his hands on her shoulders as if she were a prize he'd won at the fair.

Using her apron to keep her hands from burning, Ada swiftly deposited a tray of fragrant biscuits atop the range. Then, she picked up a spoon and stirred something in a cast iron pan, making Amanda's stomach rumble.

"I'll be with you in a moment, dear." She scooped some of the fragrant stew to her lips, blew on it, took a sip, and nodded. When she pivoted and smiled at Amanda, the corners of her eyes creased into laugh lines.

"Miss Kennett's a mite peckish," David said.

"Then, set her down, and I'll dish her up some venison gravy over sourdough biscuits. Does that sound good to you, dear?" Ada directed her almond-colored eyes at Amanda.

Ada seemed like a kindly woman, like Miss Clara, whom Amanda had come to adore. "Yes, ma'am, it sounds lovely. Can I help?"

"No, no. You're our guest. Please take a seat—you'll be helping out around here soon enough." Ada flashed a conspiratorial gaze at David.

Unless Amanda was mistaken, it looked like David shook his head slightly.

Whatever the gesture, he turned and exited the room as if his pants were on fire.

"Is he going to fetch Gabe?" Amanda asked, eager to get introductions over with.

Ada ignored her question and hurried after David, wiping her hands on her apron as she scurried from the room.

Furtive voices in hushed whispers floated from the front room, but Amanda couldn't make out a single word. *Oh, dear... they're not happy with me, are they?* She perched at the edge of one of the wooden chairs surrounding the table, ready to flee at any moment.

A few minutes later, Ada marched resolutely into the kitchen and beelined toward a shelf, where she retrieved two porcelain plates. As she rested one of the plates in front of Amanda, she scanned her with a critical eye. "You'd best relax, Miss Kennett. David's got some news to deliver."

This statement made Amanda's entire body stiffen as hard as the wood on which she sat. "What kind of news?" she squeaked.

"The kind best delivered by David, not me. David?" she called. "Get on in here and do what you intend to do." She turned back to the stove and grabbed the tray of biscuits.

Amanda's heart tried to exit through her throat. *This is where they send me away. I knew I shouldn't have come—I knew Gabe wouldn't want me.* She bit down on her lower lip to keep from crying.

Ada deposited a biscuit in the middle of her plate and called, "David! Get on in here!" She placed three biscuits in the middle of the other porcelain dish before she turned back to the stove with the tray and dropped it on the range with a noisy clatter. A few seconds later, she returned with the pan of gravy. She scooped out a hearty serving, which she slopped in the middle of Amanda's plate. "David!"

Boot steps thundered through the house, and a few seconds later, David appeared, his face as pale as the clouds gathering on the horizon, clutching something small in his hand. "I was fetching something, Ada. Quit yer hollering." He marched up to Amanda and blurted, "Gabe's dead. Might I have the honor of marrying you?"

Amanda's hand flew to her forehead. "What?" she squeaked.

"My brother Gabe was shot. Can you and I get hitched?" He thrust a ring in her direction.

The kitchen began to spin and the smell of venison stew, which had stimulated her hunger a few seconds ago, now curdled Amanda's stomach.

"I don't... I don't understand," Amanda stuttered.

"Take her into the drawing room and let her lie down on the sofa," Ada said. "She looks like she might faint. Hurry!"

David practically lifted her out of her seat. Without missing a beat, he hefted her in his arms as if she weighed no more than a sourdough biscuit.

Her consciousness wavered as he powered her into a smaller room and gently rested her on a loveseat, covered with a shiny blue and gold fabric. "There," he said, propping his hands on his hips. "Do you feel any better?"

"I feel... I feel... I don't know how I feel," Amanda said, her lower lip trembling.

"Oh, gosh," David said, his face still ghost-white. "I'm afraid I've gone and messed up this moment. But I don't know what else to say. My brother's gone, and you need a husband. What do you say to the idea of marrying me?"

Amanda's mind was blank—she couldn't think of a single word to utter. But what other option did she have?

Chapter Six

"Gabe's dead, Miss Kennett," David said again, longing to bolt for the door and see to his horses or something—anything, if it was outside, away from this situation.

The lovely young woman across from him looked as pale as snow on the mountains. She sat on the sofa, wringing her hands and endlessly blinking her eyes.

David didn't know what to do... where to sit, where to stand, how to hold his hands, nothing. So, he stood awkwardly in the front room with the sun streaming through the window that looked out over Mother's gardens.

It cast its light on Miss Kennett's flaxen hair, giving her an ethereal glow that brought a strange sensation to his chest. He threw his gaze back out the window, seeking distraction from her beauty.

I wonder if Miss Kennett's handy with plants and such. Maybe she can take over the yard.

He cleared his throat, a new habit of his that seemed to have sprung up since meeting the woman across from him. "Do you like to... um... do you like to fiddle around in the garden and such?"

Her blinking increased. "What?" she stammered.

"Oh, I'm sorry, Miss Kennett. I'm ill-equipped to deal with situations such as the one we got before ourselves. Gabe's no longer with us. That's a fact. A couple of weeks ago, I found him out in the back field with a bullet through his head. I've spoken to the sheriff, and he assured me he'd get to the bottom of the situation. It could have been bandits or cattle rustlers... we don't know. But whatever it was can't bring him back from the dead, no, sir, it can't." The words tumbled from his lips, buffeted by the winds of discomfort blowing through his body.

His head felt too hot, so he lifted his hat, smoothed his hair back, and replaced the Stetson. *How is it I'm standing here when this was all my brother's doing? And I'm making a mess of everything. Can't say anything in my life prepared me for this.* A well of anger at the injustice of Gabe's death warred with his barely contained resentment.

Miss Kennett didn't say a word to help him out. Instead, she stared out the window. The expression on her face was as blank as the last look he'd witnessed on his brother's.

David rolled his lips between his teeth and worked his jaw around.

Pots and pans clanged from the kitchen as Ada continued her chores and David's gaze slid toward the back of the house. *Maybe Ada can help me out—she's better at this than I am.* When that chicken-sized thought fled from his brain, he muttered, "I'll give you a moment to compose yourself. I'm going to head out and check on my livestock."

He turned to leave right as a lone tear slid down Miss Kennett's soft-looking cheek. Reluctantly, he pivoted around. His heart melted at her slumped shoulders and sorrowful disposition. She looked as small and vulnerable as a coon trapped in a tree by his dog, old Blue. *Fiddlesticks, I can't just leave.*

With a sigh, he shuffled across the room and sat stiffly by her side. Still unsure how to proceed, he patted her back with his work-worn hand.

She let out a small whimper, twisting a knife in his hard heart.

This whole situation plumb-near wore him out. He could rustle cattle from dawn to midnight, but dealing with a woman's emotions set his teeth on edge.

He kept up the whole pat, pat, pat movement until she shifted under his touch. Quickly, he withdrew his hand and placed it in his lap.

"I'm fine, David. It's just a shock, it is." Her voice came out soft as a whisper.

"I understand," he said, staring longingly at the front door. "You, uh... you think on it a bit—my proposal that is. You don't have to give me your answer until you're ready." *Which she'll never be... she expected my fun-loving, larger-than-life brother. Unless she likes a quiet man?*

At that thought, a wistful longing tugged at his chest. He huffed out a sigh. *Don't you be getting any foolish notions in your head, David Brown.* His jaw set in stone, he pondered what to do or say next. He lifted his hand to scratch the back of his neck, tanned to a crisp by the Nevada sun.

Finally, she lifted her head to face him. With her eyelashes all dewy moist and her face all puffy, she broke his heart all over again.

"I'm fine. You go on out and get to what needs getting to. I'm sure you have chores to tend to." She blinked, knocking a tear free from her eyelashes.

Without thinking, he wiped it away with his thumb. Her plump lips parted and she sucked in a breath.

Thinking he might have just made a bigger fool of himself than he already had, he bolted to his feet. "You're right, Miss Kennett. I've got a ranch to tend to. There's things that need to get done that won't be doing themselves."

A wan smile crossed her lips and, by golly, if it didn't light up her whole face.

His brother's face stared down at him from heaven, and an arrow tip of betrayal lanced through his heart. *I'm sorry, Gabe. I know, I know, I'd wanted to have my revenge on you. But truth be told, I don't mean to be liking your woman. She's just so pretty I can't help myself.*

Guilt wound its way around his chest and squeezed tight. He'd best get on outside while he still had a brain cell left. With a tip of the brim of his Stetson in her direction, he swiveled to depart. He raced outside, determined to talk himself out of any foolish notions he might be harboring about how nice it might be to be wedded.

The reason was easy to understand—the woman he'd just left was none other than *his brother's*—not his—mail-order bride. And, like the fool he was, he'd only wanted her out of revenge.

Chapter Seven

Silence settled itself around Amanda's shoulders like an unwelcome visitor at the door, bringing nothing but bad news. She felt a fool for crying in David's presence. It made her look weak, like the little lamb her ma had tried to raise once that didn't last the night; it was too frail. They'd bottle-fed that little thing after its mama got snatched by wolves, but it didn't matter. Weak things were meant to go back to their maker and start all over again.

When she'd arrived in Goldsprings, she'd mustered up the hope that she might get a fresh start. But bad luck followed her like a mongrel, begging for a bone. *I just can't escape my bad luck.*

The slow, measured cadence of a grandfather clock pulled her out of her cloud of gloomy thoughts. Since she'd been too stunned to even think when she'd been brought into this room, she took a moment to study her well-appointed surroundings.

David's home was one of the grandest places she'd ever seen. In fact, she'd never set foot in a house so elegant. Sure, Julia's parents did okay for themselves on Mr. Williams' banking business. But this place held treasures in every corner, like the gleaming candelabra on a polished hutch against the wall, or the china bowl painted with delicate violet flowers resting next to the silver piece. Even the sofa she sat on looked made from the softest fabric known to mankind.

I never dreamed I'd be living in a rich man's place. A frown tugged at the corners of her mouth. *Except I soon won't be living here... I can't possibly stay and accept David's proposal. He's just trying to do me a kindness.*

A sob stuck in her windpipe, making her chest flutter. *Where will I go? I can't possibly go back to Julia's... like she said, she's setting to marry Marshall. Maybe someone needs a maid in this little town.*

Her gloom-filled thoughts were interrupted by footsteps. She squared her shoulders and sat up straight and tall, not wanting to appear like that sad lamb her memory had conjured up a moment ago.

Ada strolled into the room bearing a silver tray, a teapot, two teacups, and a china plate full of treats. She rested the tray on the side table, settled next to Amanda, and took both hands in hers.

"I'm sorry for the upset in your life. You sure weren't expecting this situation, were you? And after having traveled for nearly a week... let's have a cup of tea and see if we can sort things out, shall we?"

The warmth emanating from Ada made Amanda feel safe and welcome. "Yes, ma'am. Thank you, ma'am. That would be sorely appreciated."

Ada withdrew her hands from Amanda and reached over to the lovely little teapot, painted with the same violet posies that appeared on the china bowl next to the candelabra. Securing the lid with her calloused fingertips, she poured some of the steaming amber liquid into each dainty porcelain cup. She handed one to Amanda and took one for herself.

"I just took these Johnnycakes out of the oven," she said. "Since you didn't touch a lick of my venison stew, I thought you might enjoy one of these." A warm smile crossed her wrinkled, sun-baked face.

The delicious-looking cornbread cakes made Amanda's mouth water. "Thank you, ma'am. I hope you didn't go to any trouble on my account."

"Weren't no trouble at all. Here," Ada said, seizing the plate. "Help yourself."

When Amanda reached for the treat, Ada added, "And don't you go getting all formal on me, what with the 'ma'ams.' I'm Ada, plain and simple."

"Thank you... Ada," Amanda said hesitantly. "Please, call me Amanda. All I've heard since I arrived in Goldsprings is Miss Kennett." She tried to smile, too, but wondered if it looked like her face had cracked instead.

"All right," Ada said before lifting her cup to her lips and taking a sip. "We've established names for one another. Now, let's get to the business of you and David."

Amanda's throat tightened around the Johnnycake she'd just started to swallow. She forced it down with a sip of tea and then set the cup and the plate on the side table.

"I heard him a-bumbling and a-stumbling from the kitchen. He wants to marry you, he does," Ada said.

A tiny spark of hope ignited in Amanda's heart. *He does?*

Ada continued. "He didn't come to a decision lightly, no, he didn't. He worried it around in his mind for a good long time—he just doesn't know what to do."

Her ice-blue eyes pierced Amanda. Ada stayed silent for a few uncomfortable seconds with her drink perched in her lap between her cupped palms.

She said, "David's a good man. He might not be what you were expecting, but you can't go wrong taking a man like that for a husband. He's well-liked in this town, well-respected, and, while he might not be the light-hearted fellow Gabe was, he's hard-working, kind, and sincere." She paused, cocking her head to the side and looking intently at Amanda.

Her kind words and gestures broke the wall Amanda had erected, and her lower lip started to tremble. To her utter dismay, more tears burst free.

Ada sat the tea to the side, leaned over, and gave Amanda a hug.

This gesture made Amanda cry even harder.

Ada continued soothing Amanda, uttering things like, "There, there, child, it's all going to be okay."

But would it be okay, really? Still, Amanda felt grateful for the comfort.

Ada eased Amanda back, placing her sturdy hands on Amanda's slender shoulders. She procured a handkerchief from her sleeve and handed it to Amanda, saying, "Here... it's fresh clean off the line."

Amanda took it and dabbed at her eyes. "I apologize for all my sorrowful behavior, Ada."

"Hush, child," the older woman said with a quick toss of her head. "Me and David have had our share of sorrows of late. You done walked into a house full of sadness. What do you say we put it all behind us and let some light into the house? The good Lord would want no less for us." Her warm, reassuring smile did the trick, bringing a genuine smile to Amanda's face.

"I'd like that, too." But secretly, she wondered if such a thing as light could ever enter her soul again.

"Finish up your tea and Johnnycake, Amanda. Good food and a warm beverage will set your spirit to rights," Ada said, reaching for her own tea. "Then, you can help me clean up the kitchen."

Amanda liked the idea of helping out. She didn't want to be a burden to Ada or to David.

The two women finished their treats in companionable silence.

Amanda felt herself relax, sinking into the plush couch. *What I wouldn't give for a good rest...* As she munched on her Johnnycake, she mused some more on the idea of marrying David. *He's as handsome as can be... plus, he seems to be kind enough.*

As if reading Amanda's thoughts, Ada broke the silence by saying, "I've got a good feeling about you, Amanda. I've been on this earth for far too long to not be paying attention to my heart, and it tells me you and David would be good for one another. He ain't never had a woman that stuck around for him—he's a bit on the quiet side."

She placed the empty teacups and plates on the silver tray and rose to stand. "Even though it weren't what you were expecting, it don't mean it wasn't meant to be. Maybe it could be equally wonderful or better." Her eyes sparkled as she spoke. "Why don't you go check out the room I've prepared for you, think on it a second, and then come on out to the kitchen and let's get these dishes washed? After that, you look like a rest might do you a world of good."

Amanda's heart nearly burst by Ada's kindness. "Thank you, Ada. Which room will be mine?"

"Up the stairs, second door on the right, down the hall." Ada lifted her hand to point before she hefted the tray and strode toward the kitchen.

Amanda sauntered upstairs, fatigue dragging at her limbs. Yet even though she was tired, that spark of possibility she'd experienced hearing David really wanted to marry her burst into a blaze of hope. Perhaps, like Ada said, marrying David might be equally wonderful as marrying Gabe—or even better. There was only one way to find out.

She would say yes.

Chapter Eight

David paused outside the back door, wiping his boots vigorously on the sturdy rope mat so as not to track mud into Ada's kitchen. Kickabilly nickered at him from the pasture, maybe sending him a show of support.

Like a horse can show anything resembling support. You're a fool, you are...

He'd spent the last forty minutes fiddling around in the barn, avoiding heading back to the house. This whole mess stirred by Miss Kennett's arrival didn't sit well in his stomach. And the manner in which he'd handled things, what with his blurting notion to get hitched to the young woman, had turned his cheeks and neck into an inferno of embarrassment.

Secretly, he hoped Ada had sat Miss Kennett down and talked some sense into her, sending her on her way. He had enough to deal with and didn't need any more problems—especially the kind Miss Kennett represented.

But when he opened the door, the sound of ladies' voices forged his jaw into steel. *She's still here.* He clomped into the kitchen, grabbed a glass jar from a shelf, and filled it with water from the pitcher in the icebox. Uncertain what to do now that he stood in the house, he leaned his backside against the counter and glugged the whole glass.

Amanda sailed through the door, a bright smile on her face.

That smile nearly made his knees buckle. But what followed almost had him on the floor in a dead faint.

She pulled up short, and the grin fell from her face. "Oh... David," she said, appearing surprised to see him. "I've decided to marry you, if you'll still have me," she blurted, casting her gaze at the oak floor.

David's knees began to tremble a little bit. "Is that right?" he said, wiping the water droplets from his lips with the back of his hand.

Amanda stood there expectantly, looking like she was waiting for something.

Her beguiling gaze knocked any good sense he might possess from his brain. "Well, then, we may as well go through with it."

Ada strode into the kitchen carrying a basket full of greens from the garden. "Did I hear you right, David? You and Amanda have agreed to be married?"

"I reckon we have," David said, as a strange new feeling wormed its way into his heart, shoving aside his original scheme of revenge. *You're actually starting to like her, ain't you?*

"Well, let's get it done. I can make arrangements this very afternoon, and we can have you married by sundown. Hitch up the wagon for me because I'll be heading into town," Ada said decisively, setting the basket on the counter.

"There sure ain't no reason to rush, Ada," David said as his feet turned into blocks of ice. *Gabe made darn sure the entire town knew of his impending nuptials. What are people going to think if I swoop in and claim his bride?*

He glanced at Miss Kennett, surprised to see the upturned curve of her lips restored.

"Of course there is," Ada said, bustling around the kitchen. "You've both stated your piece, so let's set them to rights. Get on out to the barn and hitch up old Chester for me, will you?"

"Okay, I sure will," he said, eager to get back outside. He needed to stop his heart from hammering inside his chest like a chicken in the sights of a fox.

Out in the barn, Chester stood in his stall, head low, snuffling about, searching for the remnants of his earlier meal of hay.

"Well, Chester," David said, reaching for the harness as Blue stood by his side. "You're to haul Ada into town, it seems."

He got busy harnessing the horse to the wagon, all the while thinking of Miss Kennett being his bride. Every time excitement filled his heart, he kicked those notions straight for the hills. *Don't make no sense getting all full of wonder and joy, you fool. Let's make this a practical arrangement, you know, like I'm doing her a kindness after she came all this way.*

Blue wandered around the Clydesdale and plopped in the dirt, panting hard from the heat.

Again, the ghost of Gabe swirled around David's mind, filling him with guilt. "If you hadn't gone and ordered her up," he said under his breath, "I wouldn't be in this situation, now, would I? I'm just trying to make the best of a bad set of circumstances."

The figment of Gabe laughed. "You think I don't see what you're doing? You think because I'm out of the way, you can have her? Guess again, brother. She won't want the likes of you. She's *mine*."

When Ada exited the house, her hair all bunched beneath a hat to ward off the springtime heat, David stood patiently with Chester, holding the harness. His mood was as sour as the slop he'd fed to the pigs this morning. He helped Ada into the wagon and then stood with his hands on his hips. "Is

Miss Kennett in the house?" *Where else would she be, you idiot?*

"She's taking a rest. She wants to look nice for your wedding," Ada said, the corners of her eyes creasing. "I'm happy for you, David, I sure am."

"Huh," David grunted.

"You'll see. This arrangement will turn out good for everyone."

"We'll see," he said, lifting his hat and smoothing back his thick, brown hair.

***

Several hours later, when the sun hung bloated and heavy in the late-day sky, Ada returned.

Dust billowed from the wagon wheels as Chester slowly clomped toward the house. Blue let out a bark, his black and white ears forward and alert.

David looked up from Kickabilly's right hind hoof, which he'd been cleaning, and rested the horse's leg on the ground.

The entire town seemed to accompany Ada in the form of wagons, men, and women on horseback, and a few stragglers walking along behind.

"Would you look at that? Ada's done brought an entire wedding party for us." He didn't know whether to laugh or sink deeper into his sullen mood. "Let's get this over with."

After Ada parked the wagon, she excused herself with a few female townsfolk who carried baskets, bags, and boxes all packed to overflowing with produce and other goods.

Knowing the moment for getting hitched was on its way, he shuffled on into the house to get himself cleaned up and dressed in a manner fit for a conflicted bridegroom.

When David emerged from his bedroom, dressed in his clean church suit, Ada beamed at him. "Just look at you. You're going to be happy, you wait and see."

"If you say so," David said, unconvinced as he beelined for the front door.

"And you'd best start calling her Amanda instead of Miss Kennett," Ada called after him as he stepped through the door frame.

Outside, he stood around with Sheriff Slinger and a few of Slinger's friends, like Henry Neil and Jim McCarthy. He didn't really know Neil and McCarthy. He'd just seen them around town a bit. But since Ada had probably invited the whole town, they'd tagged along.

David's good buddies, Sawyer Smith and Arlo Roberts, wandered over to join them.

The horses and wagons were gathered beneath the mesquite trees growing near the pasture.

Children of all ages ran around in the garden, playing tag or some such.

Everyone in Goldsprings liked a wonderful celebration—it cut through the hard work and monotony of daily existence.

"What a surprise, David," the sheriff said, hooking his thumbs inside his belt loops. "Did either of you two know he was getting hitched?" he said to Sawyer and Arlo.

"'Bout time," Arlo said through the wide gap between his front teeth. "I reckon he's man enough for the job, though." He and Sawyer let out a chuckle. "My wife's plumb tickled.

She said you could use someone beside Ada out here to keep you company now that Gabe's gone." His expression turned sour, and he shook his head. "What a shame. You have any idea who's responsible?"

"Nope, I sure don't," David said, his heart growing heavy on this most confusing day. He leaned against the fence post and sighed. "You got any suspects, Sheriff?"

Sheriff Slinger spat out a wad of saliva from his chewing tobacco. It landed in the dirt with a soft splat. "I have a couple of people in mind, but I'm not at liberty to talk about it," he said. He rested his elbow on the fence.

David studied his face for a few seconds, wondering who these suspects might be.

"David!" Ada called from the back of the house. "Come on out to the back, we've prepared some lemonade for you all."

David, Arlo, Sawyer, Sheriff Slinger, and the others shuffled around the house, heading for the backyard. They rested their behinds on the stumps placed there for that purpose, and each took a jar filled with lemonade.

Ada turned to David and said, "The preacher will be here soon enough. He had to tend to some church business, but he said he'll be here right quick." She lifted her gaze toward the scrub-covered plains and said, "Oh, look... him and his mule are heading this way."

David nodded. His mouth had suddenly turned dry, so he took a swallow of lemonade.

"All the ladies are making Amanda feel welcome. Wait until you see her. Arlo, your wife is weaving flowers in her hair, and she's doing a great job," Ada said.

Arlo grinned. "And she's probably proud to do that. Betsy likes to pretty things up."

David shifted from side to side as anxiety crept its way into his belly.

When dusk colored the sky in brilliant red, orange, and violet hues, Preacher Bascom called the people to gather.

"You'll join me up here, David," he said, indicating a spot near where he stood, next to a lilac bush bursting with blossoms.

David made his way toward the preacher and stood ramrod stiff, clasping his hands clasped in front of him. He gave a silent prayer to God to bless this moment. After that, he pleaded with Gabe's ghost to forgive him for marrying the woman he'd wanted to marry—especially since David's initial impulse was to get back at his brother. The truth was, he *wanted* to marry her; maybe she'd come to like him in time. And perhaps this might be the only way he'd find a wife, after all. His luck with women hadn't been in his favor.

All these thoughts confused his brain. A woman should be married because she loved a man, not because he was a scheming fool.

When the back door clattered against the wall, his head pivoted toward the sound. He sucked in a lungful of air as Miss Kennett stepped daintily from the house, dressed in an off-white, long-sleeved lace dress that fell to her ankles. A wreath of roses had been placed atop her glossy blond hair, and she looked lovely.

David found himself quite attracted to her. As the preacher droned on with his vows, he kept sneaking furtive looks at his new wife-to-be.

She, too, cast shy gazes in his direction.

With no rings to exchange in this hasty arrangement, as soon as Preacher Bascom pronounced them man and wife, the deed was done. The only thing left to do was to kiss the bride.

David rustled up some courage, leaned forward, and touched his lips to hers. For the briefest of seconds, he lingered, enjoying the press of her soft lips against his. But his ever-present confusion at marrying Gabe's betrothed yanked him backward. *It should be you here, Gabe, not me. I had no right to claim her.*

Numbly, he stared at all his friends as they whooped and cheered.

When Arlo approached and offered him a flask of whiskey, he took it, tipped back his head, and drank a long swallow of the firewater. He handed the flask back to Arlo and noticed that Miss Kennett—A*manda*—was no longer by his side.

She'd been swept away by the women.

Fiddle music began to play and an air of festivity surrounded them, but that same sense of numbness kept David in its grip. The taste of revenge, which he'd imagined a few days ago as bringing a sweet sense of satisfaction, had turned against him like a poison arrow. *You've only gone and betrayed your own flesh and blood, you have. And you're doing Amanda a disservice. Gabe, what have I done?*

The women all disappeared and returned with a feast. Pork cake, venison stew, roasted potatoes, sourdough biscuits, and even railroad cake were laid out on a makeshift plank table, with jugs of hard cider on the side.

Throughout the night, as the dancing and celebration continued, the revelers got louder and louder as the liquor loosened their lips. Yet, as the excitement mounted, David found himself growing quieter and quieter. He kept his awareness of Amanda in the corner of his eye as he chatted with friends and ate the feast the women had prepared. But he made no move to get close to her.

Out of the corner of his eye, movement caught his attention: Slinger, McCarthy, and Neil all staggered toward the barn. *What in tarnation are they doing heading to my barn?*

He popped the last of his cake in his mouth and started to head in their direction when a soft hand landed on his back.

He jumped and turned to see Amanda behind him.

Wisps of her hair had freed themselves from her styled hairdo, and her cheeks looked flushed. But her beauty took his breath away.

"Amanda," he said in a stiff, stilted voice. "What can I do for you?"

"I'm tired, David. I can barely keep my eyes open. It's been a long day, and I want to help you get ready for bed before turning in." She lifted the corners of her lips into a sleepy smile.

David glanced at the crowd.

Several of the participants were saying their goodbyes and departing.

The three men who'd headed toward the barn now veered toward their steeds.

Perhaps they headed out behind the barn to do their business. Slinger has certainly drunk his share of whiskey tonight.

His attention turned back toward Amanda and drifted for a second to her lovely mouth. The implications of the night with its promise of conjugal rights landed heavily in his chest. No way could he further betray Gabe by giving in to temptation. "You go on into my room and wait for me."

A slight wince marred her expression.

I called it my room... well, ain't it? His jaw grew steely. "I'll be along shortly. I have to see to my friends."

"Okay," she said in a small voice.

Can't I just be nice to her? She's come all this way... He placed his hand on the small of her back. "I hope you had a nice time tonight. Ain't Ada a wonder to have gathered all these people at the last minute?" He allowed a smile to form.

She smiled back, rubbing her hands together as if nervous. "Yes, she's a wonder."

"Well..." He withdrew his hand. "Go on, then. I'll come in soon enough."

Her head dipped in a docile nod, and she pivoted to leave.

As soon as she left, his anxiety, which had been dulled to a low hum thanks to the hard cider and whiskey, roared back to life. *She's heading for my bedroom—waiting for me—what am I going to do?* Like a good host, he made his rounds, said his farewells, and the guests began to leave, using lanterns to light their way back to the wagons. His feet seemed to sink into a vat of molasses, making him move like an old man. Slowly, he progressed toward the bedroom, entering the house through the front door.

Pots, pans, tin cups, and glassware banged about, tinkled by the many hands helping Ada in the kitchen.

He tiptoed, not wanting to alert anyone to his presence. Upstairs, when he reached his bedroom door, he paused before entering.

The door lay ajar, and a soft light came from inside the room.

He took a deep breath and pushed gently on the door.

Amanda sat, wearing a long white nightgown, perched on the blue and white quilt his mother had made before she died

For a moment, his gaze stayed fixed to hers. He walked to the opposite side of the bed and sat down, removing his boots and trousers.

"Can I help you with anything?" she said demurely.

"I think I can manage. I've been dressing and undressing well enough for all these years." He lined his boots up next to the oak side stand.

A giggle left her mouth and shot straight through his heart.

He longed to touch her, show her comfort, anything... but his guilt over earlier thoughts at getting back at his brother tightly noosed his desires. *Can't do this... nope.* Without looking at her, he threw back the covers and swung his legs on the bed.

"It's been a long day. Let's turn in and get some rest." He reached over and twisted out the gas lantern, plunging the room into darkness. All he could hear was the steady inhale and exhale of the woman beside him—his right and proper wife.

She seemed to just sit there, not moving.

"Are you going to get in bed, or what?" he said, sharper than he'd intended.

The bed dipped, and her slight form slid beneath the covers.

David let out a long breath and hoped to get some rest tonight. But with her nearness and his refusal to touch her, he knew the night would be a long one.

Chapter Nine

A pale dawn sun brushed its fingers across Amanda's cheeks the following day, rousing her from a tortured slumber. She opened her eyes, expecting to find David clinging to the bed as far away as he could get—because that was how he'd slept all night.

But David wasn't anywhere to be seen.

Last night had been utter heartbreak. Lydia, Julia's mom, had warned Amanda about what to expect on her wedding night, saying, "He'll want you to yield to his desires. It won't be pleasant, but it's necessary to secure your marriage."

But all he did was fall asleep the second his head touched the feather pillow, leaving her with an ache in her chest the size of the state of Nevada. *So, my marriage hasn't been secured...*

Laying on her side, she plucked a blade of straw from a tear in the bottom layer of the bed. A couple strands of horsehair came with it. *Maybe I can be helpful and mend that for him.*

Cheered by the thought of doing something useful, she swung her legs off the side of the feather mattress, which sat atop the horsehair and straw bolster. She tiptoed into the next room, where she'd napped yesterday, and tugged on clean clothes from her suitcase. Brushing out her tangled tresses, she gathered her courage with each brushstroke before facing David and Ada.

Downstairs, Ada buzzed about the kitchen, chopping carrots and potatoes and tossing them in a giant pot. She glanced over her shoulder when Amanda entered the room, with a kind, "Morning, lovey. Did you sleep all right?"

"Yes, thank you, Ada," Amanda lied. "Is... is David around?"

Ada turned back to her chopping. "He's already eaten and has taken off for the day. He said something about needing to do some errands in town."

A stab of disappointment sliced through Amanda's heart. Her lips rolled between her teeth, and she fought the urge to cry. "Can I... can I do something to help you?" she offered in a shaky voice.

Ada lifted her head and looked at her with a frown. "No, thank you, Amanda. You had a big day yesterday. Why don't you relax today and take some time to get to know your new home, inside and out? Chores will come soon enough. There's more than enough work around here to keep us all going from dawn until nightfall. We'll get you to helping out, don't you worry." She returned to her chopping, with the knife making a *clackity-clack* sound as it struck the wood.

Amanda shuffled from the kitchen and headed toward the front room—the same front room where David had deposited her after telling her the news that Gabe was dead. And the same front room where she'd sat last night listening to the townswomen gabbing about their lives—which were far happier than hers was now.

She didn't belong here, plain and simple. This wasn't her home—it belonged to a stranger with whom she had shared vows last night meant to bring them together. Those vows had only gone as far as the lips and no further.

As she wandered through the sprawling ranch, she discovered a small, unfurnished sitting room and a sparsely furnished formal dining room. Hands on her hips, she scrutinized the area before heading up to the room assigned to her yesterday.

It looked rather lonely, with a tiny bed, no dresser, and simple curtains above the window frame. Her suitcase still occupied a place on the oak floor with all of her belongings neatly folded inside. There didn't seem to be an armoire or a cupboard or even a shelf for clothes storage.

So, am I to sleep here at night? Is this to be my room? An awkward feeling—like her clothes were too tight, constricting each breath, or the house was too big and fit to swallow her up—kept her feet pinned her to the floor.

With a sigh, she pried her feet free and exited this small room. From there, she wandered down the hall to David's room, where Ada moved about like a whirlwind, straightening the few books on the bookshelf and folding clothes from a wicker hamper. With a smile, she said, "So how do you like this house so far?"

"It's..." Amanda searched her mind for a complimentary word. "It's... lovely." She stepped toward the bed and rested her hand on the wrought iron frame. "But why are some of the rooms so sparsely decorated?"

Ada plumped up the pillows at the head of the bed. "Well, there's a story to be had here. The family used to live in modest surroundings until Josiah, Gabe and David's father, struck it rich in the gold mines in Grasshopper Creek. They added on to the small house this once was, built with the help of the boys when they were in their late teens."

She patted the pillow and stared into space as if she were far, far away.

"Gabe and David were always hard-working boys." She blinked and seemed to return from whatever memories she'd roamed. "Eileen, their mother, loved this place, but unfortunately, she died before she could finish it. So, Gabe decided to leave those rooms alone—he was hopeful that a woman's touch was all they'd need. He was hoping *you* could turn those rooms into something wonderful."

Amanda sucked in a small breath at the idea of taking on such a project. Her family had grown up poor, barely making ends meet, and, as a result, home decorating had never even crossed her mind. "I'm afraid I don't know much about furniture and the kinds of things we'd need to decorate."

Ada brushed her hands together and scurried out of the room, with Amanda following. "You'll learn. You shan't lack money. You can buy whatever you need to turn this home into a palace, if you choose."

A sense of unease dragged her mood down at the notion of having unlimited funds to do whatever she wanted to create a home here. *I'll bungle it, for sure.* Taking a deep breath, she mumbled, "I'll sure try."

"Good," Ada said, heading toward the kitchen. "Now, why don't you go on outside and explore the outbuildings and such? I've got to get back to preparing food for tonight's supper. Yesterday's partygoers picked everything clean right to the bone."

Amanda made her way outside to begin her exploration of her new home. The moment she exited the house, her shoulders fell away from her ears, and she began to relax.

The yard was a wonder, chock full of plants she'd never seen before. Awe filled her as she gazed at the beauty surrounding her. She wandered past the safety of the yard toward the fenced enclosures holding pigs and chickens.

The pigs all lay on their sides, letting the sun beat down on their thick pink and gray skin. But the reddish-colored chickens busied themselves pecking the dirt and scratching it with their clawed feet to uncover morsels to eat. Amanda longed to find her purpose here, even if it were as simple as scratching in the dirt.

Resting her arms on the fence surrounding the pigs, she gazed out at the structures that made up the ranch.

A few horses grazed in a large pasture next to a gigantic barn. That silly mustang David had saved continued to feed outside the fenced area like it was one of the herd but separate, the same way she felt. Cattle roamed a distance away from the horses.

She didn't know a thing about ranching or caring for livestock—it was a whole new world to her, one she felt ill-equipped to handle.

She pivoted and spied what looked like a sparse vegetable garden. Picking her way across the dirt and pebbles, she made her way toward it. Gardening was something she knew about. As a child, she'd stayed by her ma's side in the garden, planting seeds, picking bugs off the leaves and throwing them to the chickens, and tugging the weeds out of the warm dirt. Gardening filled her with a sense of comfort. While their family had never had a lot of money, they always grew an abundance of food in their garden.

As she stood around the sparse, wire-enclosed patch of vegetables, a measure of cheer filled her heart. Hands on her hips, her mind began to fill with plans. *We could plant some greens over there... beans in that section... and that area over there could be used for corn.*

Excitedly, she turned, taking a last glance at the mustang before heading back to the house to ask Ada if she could take over the garden.

The mustang lifted its head, ears pricked in alarm. It looked around wildly as if sensing some danger Amanda couldn't see or feel. Then, it took off at a gallop.

Her good mood vanished. Something would go wrong in her life—it always did. But unlike the mustang, she couldn't simply turn tail and run. She'd have to live with whatever it was for the rest of her life.

Chapter Ten

Leaving the ranch that morning had torn David's heart in two—he didn't want to leave Amanda's side, no matter how awkward it felt to be in her presence.

The leather saddle beneath him creaked and groaned as he rode Kickabilly along the dust-laden trail toward Goldsprings, lulling him into a drowse. As he rode, he mulled his current circumstance—he was now a married man. Two weeks ago, such a notion was as far from his mind as the distant snow-capped mountains. But yesterday, the preacher had told it true, stating the words, "You are now man and wife."

And then there was that kiss...

Kissing Amanda's sweet, soft lips had surprised him. He'd meant to simply brush his lips against hers in a chaste peck. But the feel of her got the best of him. He'd lingered at her mouth for a second too long.

Clearly, he was tangled in an overpowering attraction to her. Yet he couldn't yield to said attraction—it was wrong, pure and simple. In truth, he'd gone and married the woman meant for someone else: his brother. And for all the wrong reasons, like a foolish desire to prove to his dead brother he was man enough to steal someone away....

The urge to talk to Gabe shot through him with sudden force. Deciding to head back home and visit the laurel tree, directly after his errands in town, he pressed his spurs into Kickabilly's flanks. *I've got to explain myself to my brother—tell him what's going on. That's the only way I can find some peace.*

Kickabilly took off at a canter, surprising a jackrabbit hidden beneath the scrub. The rabbit took off in the opposite direction, zigzagging across the stone-strewn land.

Dust flew from the horse's hooves, billowing around David's face, so he pulled his red bandana over his mouth and nose. He rode at a steady pace until the town appeared, shimmering in the distance like a mirage. Easing back on the reins, he slowed Kickabilly to a walk and headed toward the red-painted church at the end of the street. As the horse clippity-clopped along, a few passersby greeted him from the wooden sidewalk.

"Howdy, David," Arlo called, standing outside the pharmacy with his horse by his side. "How's it feel to be a married man?"

"Not much different than it felt to be an unmarried man," David said with a dip of his chin.

"Kinda surprised you picked up the reins and married the girl Gabe chose for himself," Arlo said with a sly wink.

David stiffened in the saddle. "Gabe's dead, Arlo. And Amanda came all that way. Didn't want her to have made the journey for nothing," he blubbered, his cheeks set to fry with the heat pouring through them.

He urged Kickabilly into a trot, not wanting to make chit-chat with his friend. He had too much guilt swirling through his mind to be cordial.

As he passed the sheriff's office, he spied Slinger, McCarthy, and Neil, all flapping their jaws on the stoop.

You'd think the sheriff has better things to do than stand around lubricating his jaw... things like finding the men who killed my brother.

He brought Kickabilly to a stop at the general store, hurried in, and got his business done. Then, he set off at a gallop for home.

Back at the ranch, he made a beeline for the Texas mountain laurel at the far end of the yard. Leading the horse by his reins, he made his way to the simple stone headstone marking his brother's grave. Tears pricked at his eyes as he stared at the stone, carved with his brother's name—Gabriel J. Brown—and the dates of his short, twenty-six-year life.

Crouching, he touched his fingertips to the stone and shook his head. "I don't know if you can hear me from heaven, Gabe, but...." His throat strangled the words he struggled to say. "I'm a fool, I am. I done went and married your fiancée yesterday. You're probably pitching a fit from wherever you are. I told myself I was just trying to do the right thing, brother, but a desire for revenge got in the way. I just never got over the way you took what I wanted. I was always left with your leftovers."

This thought burned like a brand in his gut.

The grin on Gabe's face when he'd gotten the horses he wanted, or Leslie, or any of the other things he'd snatched out from under David's nose, seemed to leer at David from the grave.

"Why'd you do it, brother? Why'd you always take away my happiness?"

He couldn't come up with an answer to that question.

He held back thoughts of his attraction to Amanda, figuring Gabe didn't need to know the details. "Anyway..." A few tears pricked the back of his eyes. Gabe was his family, not his enemy. So why did David harbor such ill feelings about him?

Using his thumb and forefinger, he wiped the tears threatening to break loose from his eyes. "I'm just hoping you can find it in your heart to forgive me. Or maybe it's me who needs to forgive. You were just yourself—maybe it was all a game to you, and I took it all the wrong way."

A light breeze blew through the leaves, ruffling the hair around David's neck.

David had no idea whether Gabe heard him or not. He only knew the guilt, which was his new constant companion, still occupied a place on his shoulder.

***

Blue raced to greet him as he rode away from the laurel tree. Dismounting from Kickabilly, he ruffled the dog's head and walked the horse to the barn so he could remove his saddle and reins. He glanced briefly at the house and chewed the inside of his cheek as he thought of going inside. Shame heated his face to broiling at his inability to face Amanda. *I've got plenty of things to do out here to stay busy today. Ain't no need to get on back inside and face the mess I made from not doing right by Amanda last night.*

He led Kickabilly inside the livery, removed the leather bridle, and replaced it with a rope halter tied to the fence. He got busy pulling off the saddle and placing it, the padding from underneath, and the reins in his tack room. Striding back to the horse, he proceeded to brush down Kickabilly's sweaty body and pick the dirt from his hooves. Once that was done, he led Kickabilly out to the pasture, noting that fool mustang still lingering outside the fence.

Maybe I can make a good workhorse out of him. That man in town planned on turning him into a domesticated horse when he sold him. Perhaps he could be my domestic horse.

As he shut the gate to the pasture, he looked up to see the two ranch hands he'd hired for the summer moseying down the road in a wagon with two extra horses tied on the cart and trailing behind. They were a welcome sight as he'd need to see to them the rest of the day, keeping David far away from the house.

After sending Kickabilly on his merry way, he strode out to greet them.

Lifting his hand, the squat-looking man called Michael said, "Afternoon, Mr. Brown. Me and Billy brought the supplies you ordered. Where would you like them?"

"You can tie your horses underneath the mesquite trees. Then, bring the wagon around behind the barn, and I'll show you where everything goes. See that building near the barn?"

"Yep," Michael said, pulling back on the reins to stop the horses.

"That's the bunkhouse where you and Billy will stay. Ada, my housekeeper, will see to your meals." His cheeks warmed as the following words tumbled from his mouth. "And, my wife, Amanda..." The term "wife" stuck in his throat like a stick.

"We're mighty obliged to you," Michael said, then clucked and set the horses back in motion.

David followed them toward the barn.

Once they parked the wagon and tended to their horses, they got busy unloading hay and feed, bags of seed stock, and the lumber. David pulled free a newfangled invention called barbed wire meant to repair some of the fences.

The day passed quickly after that. David got Michael and Billy started on fence-mending, which took most of the day.

First, they traversed by horseback along the fence line, finding the places that needed fixing. After that, affixing the end of the wire to one of the men's saddles the way the shopkeeper had advised, Billy urged his horse, Silo, to back up, stretching the wire next to the fence post. They pounded square-headed nails into the fence to hold the wire taut. The work was arduous, lasting well into the afternoon.

By the time the sun started its descent toward the horizon, David realized he'd nearly forgotten about what awaited him in the house—his new wife. As they rode back toward the ranch, his trepidation grew, tightening his belly like the wire they'd stretched around the fence posts.

After telling the ranch hands to wash up for supper using the well behind the barn, he made his way toward the house. Finding no one in the back of the house, he removed his boots. He practically tip-toed across the mudroom, not wanting to alert Ada and Amanda to his presence until he'd had a chance to gather his thoughts.

Their voices came from the kitchen, where they were apparently sitting and gabbing at the table. The smell of whatever they'd cooked for supper tickled his nose, making his mouth water.

David rested his hand on the door jamb and listened like an intruder in his own home.

"You're doing a fine job mending David's socks," Ada said.

"Sewing is one of the things I can manage fine," Amanda said, and her voice sent a thrill through David's chest. "I used to make dresses and such to make ends meet after my ma fell ill. That was after my brother and fiancé got killed in a fire."

"I'm sorry to hear that you've suffered so many losses, lovey," Ada said. "But sewing is a skill that will keep you in good stead for the rest of your life."

Picturing his brother glaring at him with eyes of betrayal, David yanked himself upright and pushed open the door. "Me and the boys are ready for supper," he announced, avoiding eye contact with Amanda.

"I didn't hear you come in, David," Ada said, placing her sewing in a pile on the table. She pushed away from the table and rose to her feet. "Supper's ready as soon as you set yourselves down. Isn't that right, Amanda?" She gazed down at Amanda with a smile. "Amanda prepared the sourdough biscuits."

David afforded his new wife a glance, noting how lovely she looked. *I'm sorry I find her so fetching, Gabe.* "Good, that's good," he said, stepping toward the shelf to grab a glass. He poured some cool water from the pitcher and tipped it to his lips.

Unfortunately, the water did nothing to facilitate further conversation, so he exited the room until called to eat. But the only thing he could think to do was pace about his bedroom.

At supper, David, Billy, Michael, Ada, and Amanda sat around the table, eating in silence. As each second tipped by, David felt more and more tongue-tied. He kept glancing at Amanda, but her gaze stayed fixed on her plate.

When Ada fetched a fresh apple pie for dessert, she finally broke the icy silence by saying, "David, Amanda has some ideas for the garden."

The bite of pie he'd just jammed in his mouth clogged his windpipe. Grabbing his jar of water, he washed down the pie and said, "What kind of ideas?"

"Oh, I'd like to turn it into a proper garden, with green beans and corn. And some ducks might be nice. Duck eggs make for some good eating," she said with a shy smile.

David shrugged. "You can do whatever you like, Amanda. This is your home now," he said gruffly. Abruptly, he pushed aside his plate and said, "I'm full. I'll need to be heading to my room to get ready for bed. We've got a full day tomorrow." He glanced at the two men and nodded. As he rose, he caught sight of the frown tugging at Amanda's mouth. *Put there by me... again.*

He exited the room as quickly as he could to avoid the stares of Ada, Amanda, and the two men. He marched into his bedroom, removed his clothes and donned his nightshirt, and climbed into bed.

As he lay there, his thoughts drifted toward Amanda, her chin quivering from his harsh words at her shy request. *David Brown, you're nothing but a fool. She's done nothing to deserve your cold demeanor.*

With a sigh, he lifted his head and pounded the pillow into submission. He tossed and turned until his body gave up the fight, and he began to drift.

He fell into a world of darkness. Icy fingers clutched at his heart, dragging him into the abyss of a nightmarish sleep. Flailing and kicking, he cried out, unable to surface as the claws pulled him deeper.

When he reached the bottom of the abyss, he landed with a crash in a strange, shadowy cemetery. With a lurch, he scrambled to his feet and peered into his dark surroundings.

A lone figure stood near one of the headstones.

"Who's out there? Is anyone here?" David cried.

The figure lifted a lantern and light spilled across his face, revealing none other than his brother, Gabe. Slowly, eyes fixed on David, he lowered the lantern, casting his face in angled shadows. When he stood, he trained a rifle right at David's head.

"Gabe… what are you…?" David began, but Gabe cut him off.

"You stole my life," he bellowed. "You stole what's *mine*."

David cringed and stumbled backward, holding his arms before his face. "I didn't mean to, honest I didn't. She came a long way to meet you, and when she arrived, I didn't know what to do with her, so I married her," he blubbered, his words sounding like a weak excuse.

"Amanda's *mine*. She's the only woman I ever truly wanted. You'll never get what's *mine.*"

Then, the image of Gabe began to laugh. "You're nothing but a bug, David. I'm the one with all the charm, not you." Gabe held the gun high, peered down the barrel, and pulled the trigger.

David blasted back into the bedroom. He bolted upright, covered in sweat.

Amanda wasn't next to him.

"Thank mercy for that," he muttered, lighting the lantern next to the bed. The rivalry he'd shared with his brother throughout the years flooded his brain. Whether it was a woman or good horse stock, David always seemed to come in last.

She can't sleep here ever again. She can live here, but there is no way this marriage can be anything more than security for her. My brother has made his intentions clear. Not only won't he forgive me, but he'll also never allow me to care for his woman. She is, after all, his.

Makes no mind that Gabe's dead. Even in the afterlife, he'll claim what's his.

And I was foolish to think otherwise.

Chapter Eleven

After cleaning the kitchen with Ada, Amanda walked down the hall, heading for bed. Dawn would come quick enough, and she wanted to help Ada with the daily chores. But, hearing noises in David's bedroom, she paused at his bedroom door.

Lantern light spilled from beneath it, which meant he was awake. Pressing her door to the ear, she caught the sound of David's voice. He seemed to be muttering to himself.

She lifted her hand to the doorknob and paused. *Should I go on in and comfort him? Ask him what might be troubling him?*

Deciding her presence would only agitate him further, she tiptoed past the door. She headed for the small, lonely room next to his, where her belongings still sat unpacked in the suitcase.

Inside the room, she lit the lantern. Then, she carefully lifted out her clean, folded clothes and placed them on the twin bed—she'd find a place to store them tomorrow.

In the bottom of her luggage, she found the parchment, her dip pen rolled in soft cloth, and ink she'd been searching for, as well as her dog-eared copy of *Little Women* by Louisa May Alcott. After setting the ink on the small table next to the bed, she twisted the top off, placed a sheet of paper on the book, dipped her pen in the ink, and began to write.

Dear Julia,

I am embracing a few quiet moments to write you a short letter. We arrived safely; however, an unexpected thing has happened. It seems that Gabe died two weeks ago. I don't know much about his death other than he was shot. So, I have married David, Gabe's brother, instead.

She brushed her cheek with the handle of the dip pen, attempting to gather her thoughts.

This whole situation is unfortunate and strange, but I am making the best of it. David is a quiet man, quieter than Gabe, I think. He keeps to himself a lot or finds chores to do outside. During the day, I rarely see him unless I'm out, and I spot him across the way, in the barn or tending to his animals.

He's taken to breaking a wild mustang. He spends hours outside in a circular pen, riding the mustang as it tries to buck him from his back. He's got another horse named Bueno that is far gentler. And a horse called Kickabilly. Isn't that a humorous name for a horse? It made me smile to hear it. David seems to love his horses. That's all I know for now. Please give Miss Clara a hug from me and take one for yourself.

Her eyes moistened with tears as she thought of living with the Williams family. She'd been happy there.

I genuinely miss you and my home with you in Virginia City. Please write me when you can.

Love,

Amanda

Before ending the letter, she added a postscript.

P.S. David has agreed to let me add to the garden. I'm looking forward to contributing to the ranch in such a manner.

She wiped the dip pen with the cloth, folded the parchment, and set everything to the side. Then, she lay back on the bed and closed her eyes. Enveloped by the darkness, she resigned herself to this sad, loveless life with a husband who barely tolerated her in a community where she knew no one. *I wish I'd remained with Julia. I don't care if I became a spinster—at least I'd be around people I knew and loved.*

She drifted to sleep on a sea of sorrow.

***

The following day, she awoke with a start at the crowing of a rooster. "Oh!" she exclaimed, blinking to orient herself to her whereabouts.

The sun streamed through the window, sweeping the night's chill from the room.

Amanda rose and brushed off her clothes that she hadn't meant to sleep in. She made her way to the kitchen.

Ada stood at the recessed basin, scrubbing a cast-iron skillet. "Good morning, Amanda," she said, glancing over her shoulder.

"Good morning, Ada," Amanda said.

"Did you sleep well?" Ada said, turning back to her dishwashing.

"Well enough. I'm sorry I overslept." Hesitantly, she stepped toward the table.

"Help yourself to some biscuits and gravy," Ada said, referring to the bowl of lumpy brown gravy and one sourdough biscuit on a plate. "I had to claim that last biscuit for you from the clutches of one of the hired hands. I smacked him with my wooden spoon, I did."

A small smile tugged at the corners of Amanda's lips. "Thank you, Ada."

"Weren't no trouble at all. Those boys need to learn some manners," she said, setting the pan down with a clatter.

"Is David out in the barn with them?" Amanda said, perching at the edge of one of the wooden chairs. She seized the plate with the lone biscuit and spooned some of the gravy on top. Truthfully, she wasn't hungry.

"Nope," Ada said, toweling off the pan. "He'll be gone a few days. Needed some supplies in Skullwood Flats, the next town over."

A bite of disappointment took a chunk out of Amanda's heart. *Why didn't he say anything to me? I know he doesn't care for me, but surely a wife should know these things?* She lifted her head to see Ada studying her. Forcing a small smile on her face, she forked a piece of the biscuit, bringing it to her lips.

Ada seemed to sense her sorrowful mood, and her expression softened into one of motherly concern. "Why don't you set to making this house your home? I'll get one of the hired hands to hitch up old Chester to the wagon, and we can head on into town after chores are done." She crossed the kitchen, rested the pan on a shelf, then dried her hands with the same towel she'd used to dry the skillet. "Why don't you make a list of all the things you think you might need?"

A tiny surge of warmth flared in Amanda's heart at Ada's kindness. As she picked at the congealing gravy with her fork, she gave a shy glance in Ada's direction. "Thank you. I'd like that. I'll make a list right now if you don't mind."

"Go right on ahead as soon as you finish your breakfast," Ada said.

So, with a sigh, Amanda finished her food before heading back to her room once more for pen and paper.

***

The trip to town proved uneventful as they wound around the boulders and stones. A gentle breeze stirred dust devils into the air, which whirled along the plains once they descended from the hills. Lizards, awakened from their sunbaths, skittered from the rocks as they passed, and Chester's plodding steps brought a drowse to Amanda, tugging at her eyelids.

"So, what's on your list, Amanda?" Ada said as the town loomed ahead.

Amanda blinked and straightened her spine. "Well..." Excitement bubbled in her chest as she retrieved her list from her pocket and studied it. "I'd like to plant parsnips and carrots together. Then, radishes, lettuces, and onions—those get pulled constantly, so they'll be in their own section. I could put melons, cucumbers, squashes, and pumpkins at the far end of the garden."

"My word!" Ada exclaimed. "You've got quite ambitious plans for that garden, don't you?"

"Do you mind?" Amanda said, hoping she hadn't overstepped.

"Not at all. As a matter of fact, I'm tickled pink. I don't have time to oversee the garden, what with all my other chores. I think David will be pleased." She clucked at old Chester, who gave a half-hearted attempt at a faster walk.

Once Ada let up on the reins, he resumed his slow plod.

A secret surge of joy tugged at Amanda's heart at the thought of doing something that David appreciated. Emboldened, she went on. "I thought we could grow some herbs, too." She began ticking them off on her fingers. "Hyssop, germander, lavender, marjoram, savory, thyme, juniper, yew... and what about some herbs like self-heal, yarrow, red clover, yellow wood sorrel, jewelweed, yellow dock, and narrow leaf plantain?"

Ada let out a laugh. "My goodness, child, your plans sound a lot like David's. Once he sets his mind to something, nothing can stop him. I don't mean no disrespect to Gabe—the boys both worked hard—but David's responsible for most of the structures on the property. He wanted to build another house nearby once Gabe got married and he found himself his own wife. But the good Lord had other plans for Gabe. And apparently, He had plans for David, as well." Ada shook her head. "And, Lordy, the squabbles those two would get into. They always seemed to be going on about something or another. I paid them no mind as long as they kept out of my hair."

Ada shifted on the hard, wooden seat.

"I know Gabe's death has hit us all hard, but that boy was always sticking his nose into places that didn't need to be stuck into. Gabe could find mischief as sure as I'm sitting in this here wagon. He was always ducking out of his chores to head down to the saloon or heading off with a friend to go see to some exciting new endeavor. But not David, no sir. That boy is reliable as the day is long." Ada side-eyed Amanda and her mouth pressed into a firm line as if she'd said too much.

Not wanting to press for more details, Amanda grew silent, stuffing the note back in the pocket of her dress. They continued their journey the rest of the way without another word between them.

***

Amanda was filled with childlike glee at the general store over picking out an abundance of seeds and supplies for the garden. She'd never been able to buy so many things without counting coins to determine if she had enough money to purchase needed supplies. As a child, money had always been tight, especially after Pa decided to use all his earnings to buy liquor and drink away his sorrows. The little money she'd made as a seamstress had gone into putting food on the table. When she moved in with Julia's family, she'd never had money of her own.

Even Ada's mood lightened, perhaps caught up in Amanda's excitement.

Once the wagon had been loaded at the general store, giving Chester a welcome rest, Amanda climbed back on her seat so they could head home. "I can't wait to plant these seeds."

"Dear, your enthusiasm is infectious. I'm even excited for you," Ada said. "I'll help when I can."

"Thank you, but I don't want this garden to be burdensome to you. I'll manage on my lonesome." The word "lonesome" flitted through her mind like a dark cloud, souring her good mood. Once again, she pictured a lonely life at the ranch, with no one to share her excitement over her bountiful garden. *Oh, well, at least I'll have the vegetables to keep me busy.*

A black horse trotted toward them several yards ahead, tossing his head, prancing, and even rearing slightly.

"Whoa, whoa," said the rider, a gentleman bearing a brass star on his shirt. His belly spilled over his fancy silver and brass belt buckle, so only the bottom tips of the engraving were visible.

"Is that the sheriff?" Amanda said, squinting to make out his face.

"Yes, I believe it is," Ada said, adding a tight-lipped grimace.

The sheriff eased his horse to a stop when he was right next to the wagon.

Ada pulled the cart to a stop, staring straight ahead.

"Afternoon, Ada... Mrs. Brown," the man said, tipping the brim of his Stetson.

For a second, Amanda wondered who Mrs. Brown could be. Then, she remembered her new married name. "Hello, Sheriff," she said politely.

"Sheriff Slinger," Ada said, affording him a quick glance.

His shadow-black horse fidgeted and pranced.

"Whoa," the sheriff said. "Easy, boy." He yanked the reins, tugging the bit against the horse's frothing mouth. "You two ladies look quite fetching this afternoon." A grin split his face.

Amanda blushed at the inappropriate comment. Ada frowned but didn't reply.

"I see you've bought some seeds and such," the sheriff continued. "Are you preparing a garden out at the ranch?" he said.

"Yes, it's Amanda's doing," Ada said, having resumed her cold glare into the distance.

"Seems a mighty fine idea," Sheriff Slinger said. "It might help keep your mind off all the nasty business surrounding Gabe's recent demise."

The horse gave a few more head tosses.

Sheriff Slinger grunted and yanked on the reins again. "I was surprised to see David get himself married so soon after Gabe's death. Seemed kind of sudden." His coal-black gaze fixed on Amanda's face.

Amanda's cheeks heated at the comment. She joined Ada in staring off into the distance.

"Gabe had shared his excitement over his new bride not a day before he was killed. Such a shame about his untimely death, wouldn't you agree?" the sheriff continued.

"A tragedy to be sure," Ada said, still not making eye contact.

"Rest assured, I'm looking out for the man who took Gabe's life. Justice will be served," Sheriff Slinger said.

"We appreciate it," Ada said. "Now, if you'll excuse us, we have to get back to the ranch."

"Of course. You take care now, you hear?" he said, directing his gaze at Amanda.

Amanda shivered. The sheriff's gaze felt slimy, like the kind of trail a snail might leave on her skin.

"Sheriff," Ada said, affording him another glance.

"Ada," he said again, adding another tip of his cowboy hat.

Ada clucked Chester into his slow plod as the sheriff sat atop his prancing horse, watching them depart.

All Amanda's earlier excitement over the supplies in the back of the wagon vanished and she rubbed her arms briskly as if chilled. She felt dirty from the exchange, and she didn't know why.

Ada glanced at her. "You stay away from that man, you hear me?"

"Yes, ma'am, I sure will," Amanda promised, nodding. She had no desire to have any contact with him, especially not after this encounter.

"I mean it. I've always gotten a bad feeling from Sheriff Slinger. I don't trust him at all." Ada shook the reins on Chester's back.

The horse picked up his gait to a moderate meander.

Meanwhile, Amanda shivered. She was still convinced that lousy luck followed her like flies buzzing around her head. *Wait—that isn't quite right.* This time, it had just ridden past on a high-spirited black stallion. And its name was Sheriff Slinger.

Something about the sheriff caused her stomach to twist and set her senses on high alert.

Chapter Twelve

Several days after departing for Skullwood Flats, a slightly larger town than Goldsprings, David urged Kickabilly through the shallow stream that flowed past the edge of his land. The wagon was bursting with supplies, and he was eager to get home.

He really hadn't needed to go all the way to Skullwood Flats to get most of the goods he'd purchased. But he'd had in mind to buy a present for Amanda, and that town was the closest place to get her a sewing machine. While he was at it, he'd bought her a book called *Practical Flower Gardening* and another called *America's Garden Book*.

There's no reason I can't show her a bit of kindness and give her something to do that she likes.

When he arrived back at the ranch, he asked Michael and Billy to remove Kickabilly's harness, turn him out, and unload the wagon—except for the gifts he'd bought. He tucked those under his arms and headed for the house, unsure how to present them to Amanda.

He heard the women in the kitchen, so he took his presents into the front room and set them on the sideboard, next to the crystal vase. He placed the books next to the sewing machine, then rearranged them. Finally, he muttered, "That's fine, that's fine where they is. Don't act like an old woman, you fool," and crossed toward the kitchen door.

Ada and Amanda looked up from the counter where they stood, peeling and chopping apples.

"Didn't hear you come in, David," Ada said, wiping her hands on her apron.

"I don't know why," he said, his gaze repeatedly flicking to Amanda's pretty face. "I stomped in the house like old Chester." A slight smile creased his cheeks.

"I guess I was too busy preparing this apple pie," Ada said. "Amanda and I have been cooking up a storm. I thought you might return home today, so we wanted to prepare you a nice meal. Isn't that right, Amanda?"

Amanda stood still, clutching a half-peeled apple in her hand, her gaze fixed on the wooden cutting board. "Yes, ma'am."

David cleared his throat. "Amanda..."

Her gaze jumped to his, and she smiled as if excited to hear her name on his lips. "Yes, David?"

"Would you mind coming with me? I've got something to show you." The words came out all clumsy, like the steps of a newborn colt.

Amanda glanced at Ada, who gave a slight nod. Taking the gesture as approval, she wiped her hands on her blue-and-white checked apron and turned to follow David.

Overcome with awkwardness, he took a couple of steps, opened the kitchen door, then stopped, blocking Amanda's movement. Frozen in place with his back to her, he stammered, "If you don't like it, I can take it back. Or maybe Ada might find a use for it. But the books seemed like a practical decision since you said you wanted to garden."

"Move out of the doorway so she can see what you're talking about," Ada said, chiding him.

He huffed out a sigh, continued through the doorway, and said, "It's over here." His cheeks and neck grew hot as he stood next to the sideboard. "You said you like to sew..."

Her face lit like a sunrise, making his chest feel strange, like someone had poured cake batter in his rib cage.

"Oh, David. What a thoughtful gift." Her eyes shone as she clasped her hands beneath her chin.

"Do you like it?" Averting his gaze, he studied the black metal Singer sewing machine affixed to the mahogany wood.

"Like it? I love it!" she exclaimed, stroking the glossy painted surface. "And books! How wonderful!" She reached for the *Practical Flower Gardening* book, knocking it to the floor.

David leaned over and retrieved the volume, handing it to her.

Cheeks flushed, she hugged the book to her chest. "Thank you so much, David."

He scratched the back of his head and muttered, "You're welcome."

"Did you have a good trip?"

"It was fine," he said, unused to sharing his day.

"Would you like something to eat or drink? I can fix us some tea or sandwiches," she said. She kept her gaze on her shoes as she spoke.

David rolled his lips between his teeth, considering her offer. Finally, he said, "No, thank you. I've got a few chores to see to out in the barn."

He tried to ignore the frown that drew the corners of her mouth down. But her expression hit his chest like a hammer. *Why can't you take her up on her offer?*

Unable to come up with an answer to his question, he whirled and stalked from the house. Blue met him at the front door and wagged his tail.

"Hey, mutt," he said, ruffling the hair on the dog's head. "You been staying out of trouble?"

The dog barked and trotted by his side as he made haste toward the barn. This "wife" business was unsettling. For weeks before her arrival, he'd thought of Amanda as Gabe's.

And Gabe had made sure to tell everyone in town she was his, appearing to take glee in David's discomfort in the mail-order bride plan.

"Just you wait and see, big brother," Gabe had taunted him on his last day on earth. "When Miss Amanda steps off that wagon, she'll be the prettiest woman you'll ever lay eyes on. And she'll be *mine.*" There had been a glint in his eyes when he said that, appearing to dare David to say anything. "What do you have to say to that?"

"I say we'd better feed the horses before sunrise," David had said.

As he strode toward the barn, he thought how right Gabe had been about her loveliness. She was indeed the most beautiful woman he'd ever laid eyes on. But then the nightmare he'd had about Gabe a week ago surfaced, obliterating his appreciation of Amanda's beauty.

"She was the *only* woman I ever wanted," Gabe hissed in his imagination. "And you can't claim her."

"Well, how does it feel to have something you wanted snatched out from under your nose, huh?" David muttered, instantly overcome with guilt at speaking such a thing. He didn't want Amanda to be a tool of revenge. He simply wanted her.

He shook his head, thinking of how much he'd missed Amanda while he was gone.

Thoroughly annoyed with himself for his conflicting thoughts, he walked around the ranch, inspecting everything and making mental notes on what needed repairing. When he returned from the apple orchard, he glanced up at Amanda's window.

She stood brushing out her beautiful golden hair, staring out at the horse pasture.

He ducked behind a tree so she couldn't see him and continued to study her.

The sun shone directly into the window, highlighting her hair into spun gold, making her look like an angelic goddess of some kind.

David's breath caught in his throat. Completely mesmerized, he couldn't look away. Somehow, through some stroke of fate or horrible luck caused by his brother's demise, he'd married an angel.

He must have stood like that for nearly a half-hour until she stepped away from the window.

***

That night, he fell asleep, alone in his bed, while Amanda slept in the bedroom next to his. He longed to invite her to his room—to *their* room. But he couldn't work up the nerve. He fell into a fitful dream in which she lay next to him and they were kissing, clad in nothing but the skin on their bones.

Rage and frustration propelled him out of his dream. He stared at the wall between their rooms, picturing Amanda's lovely body curled up in that small bed.

She could just as easily be curled up next to him.

His conflicted thoughts and unresolved angst with Gabe, even in his death, seemed to trap David in his own prison.

He wanted a proper wife to cherish, but he couldn't get Gabe and the circumstances of his murder out of his head. Nor could he justify his original motivation to "take something from Gabe" the way Gabe had with him.

It had all happened too suddenly—finding his brother's dead body, the funeral, then, David's recklessness by marrying Amanda for his own selfish reasons. And there was no closure with Gabe. His brother had died far too soon.

And yet, rivalry or not, something stank about Gabe's death. It had come too swiftly, without provocation or warning.

David rubbed his jaw as he lay in the moonlit room in this bed that suddenly seemed far too large and empty. He tried to recall anything out of the ordinary on the day of Gabe's death, or anything that had occurred in the days leading up to Gabe's murder. A big fat nothing came to mind.

Except for that last day when he seemed so troubled... And I was still full of resentment toward him. If I can't find justice for my brother's death, I'll never find peace. Despite all the ways he tortured me, he was still my family. And blood is thicker than water.

There had been several sets of boot prints out in the dirt near where Gabe had been found. It looked like a whole mess of bandits had overcome him. He'd probably had no chance of surviving. But still, there were too many questions and not enough answers.

He let out a long sigh and rolled on his side, facing away from Amanda's bedroom.

And the saddest thing of all is I'll never be able to create a good life with Amanda and love her the way she deserves to be loved. Not until I find some answers.

Chapter Thirteen

Amanda fell into an easy rhythm after David had returned bearing gifts. While not what could be called joyful, at least the awkward tension of the first few days had dissipated. Still, it wasn't as if they actually spent time together. She did her chores, and he did his. Occasionally, she'd attempted to get him to sit down with a cup of tea or tell her about his day.

He'd looked at her like she'd grown hooves where there should be hands and exited to the great outdoors, his refuge and preferred place to be.

In a desperate attempt to learn anything about him, she often excused herself from chores in the house to work in her garden. Once outside, she scanned the landscape for glimpses of her husband—the man to whom she was wedded in name only. But that was about as much contact as she got—a visual sighting from several yards away. She'd find him with the horses, herding cattle, or mending fences, or tossing bales of hay as if they were feathers.

More and more, he'd taken it upon himself to spend time with that mustang who kept hanging around. He'd managed to get the horse to trust him enough to dab salve on his sides, which appeared to be covered with gashes. Or he'd throw reins over his head, a blanket on his back, and climb on for a wild ride. So, while he and that wild horse were forming a relationship, she and her husband simply co-existed.

This morning, as Amanda brought in gathered eggs from the chicken pen, Ada stopped her.

"Here," Ada said, reaching for the basket. "Let me put those away. Why don't you go on outside and look for David?

Maybe you and he could see to some chores together. How would that be?" She smiled warmly at Amanda.

"Oh, I don't think—" Amanda began.

"It's worth a try, isn't it?" Ada said, cutting her off. She began stacking the eggs pointed end down in the large ceramic crockpot filled with boiled water and dissolved lime.

"I don't know, Ada... he doesn't—" Amanda said.

Ada interrupted her again. "He doesn't know how to be around you. Is that what you were going to say?" Her smile cut through the frost around Amanda's heart. "You two are new at this. Finding ways to connect might take some work. But David loves being outside with his animals and the fresh air. That might be the perfect place to start."

Amanda chewed on her lower lip. "I guess I can sure try," she said, brushing bits of chicken nest hay from her hands. A warm sensation, like a sunrise, filled her heart.

"That's the spirit," Ada said. "Get on out there and try."

Amanda stepped out the back door and hesitated. *He'll probably say, 'Nope, get on inside and see if Ada needs help.'* But Ada's encouragement bolstered her resolve. So, she wandered toward the barn where he milked the cows each morning.

Inside, her footfalls were muted by the freshly swept dirt in the aisle between the stalls. The smell of hay and cow manure filled her nose. Shafts of sunlight lit the sides of the white and black cows who stood contentedly chewing hay. And, at the end of the aisle, David sat on a three-legged stool next to a cow. He squeezed the cow's teats, sending squirts of fresh milk shooting into the metal bucket beneath the udder.

"Hello, David," Amanda said shyly as she approached.

His head whipped around like she held a rifle in her hands.

"Amanda! What do you need?" he said, eying her with a stern expression.

She wrung her hands together and swallowed her apprehension. "I wondered if you needed any help out here."

He lifted a hand in the air and said, "Nah, I've got..." But then his mouth snapped shut. "What were you thinking?"

She lifted her shoulder in a shrug.

"You ever milked a cow?"

She shook her head.

"Want to learn?" he said.

A slight smile curved her lips. "Yes, I'd like that."

"Okay," he said, rising from his stool. "Sit here." He patted the round wooden seat and stood aside.

She lowered herself to the seat and said, "Now what?"

He bit his lip as he studied her, appearing to be as nervous as she felt. "Now, you grab the teat, like so..." He crouched next to her, close enough for her to sense the warmth radiating from his body. He wrapped his strong hand around the pink and black mammary gland. "Then, you move your hands like you're playing the piano, and the milk comes out."

"Did you ever play the piano?"

"Oh, a long time ago, I played for about a month. I didn't like it, but Mother was trying to civilize Gabe and me." He smiled at the memory.

"Did it work?" Amanda said.

"Nope," he said, directing his smile at her. "Okay, your turn."

A heady sensation spread through her body at the kind way he looked at her. She reached for the cow's udder and did as instructed. Nothing happened.

"You've got to pull it, Amanda," David said. "Pull and squeeze, pull and squeeze."

She tried again. Again, nothing happened.

"Here, it's like this." Reaching for the bovine's mammary glands, his arm brushed against hers, and a thrill shot up her spine. "Grab two of them teats. You get a rhythm going that way."

When she placed both hands on the animal's warm, soft skin, he moved behind her, reached around, and wrapped his hands around hers.

Giddy from the contact, she leaned into his torso.

When he didn't pull away, she took that as a good sign and tugged on the teat. With David's help, fragrant white milk streamed into the bucket. "Oh!" she said, surprised. Her hands jerked away from David's grip and whacked the side of the cow.

The bovine kicked, connecting with the bucket and sending milk all over Amanda's dress. "Oh, my goodness!" she cried, scrambling to her feet, knocking David backward. When she realized what she'd done, she whirled around, pressing her hands to her cheeks. As she was about to apologize, she was surprised by David's response.

He actually started to laugh. It was a rich, deep laugh that warmed her insides from head to toe.

She joined him, exhilarated at their shared enjoyment.

"I think you might want to try another task besides milking," he said, wiping his eyes as he got to his feet. "Let me show you something else, instead. I'll get Michael to finish up out here." He leaned over and righted the now-empty bucket, getting milky mud on his cowboy boots.

"I'm so sorry," she said.

"You're new to this," he said congenially. "It takes practice." He placed his hand on the small of her back and guided her out of the barn.

Elation filled every cell in her body at the contact.

Outside the barn, David released her, placed two fingers in his mouth, and let out a loud whistle.

Michael, who stood several yards away near the pigpen, looked up. "Yeah, boss?" he called.

"Finish up with the milking, would you please?" David called.

"You got it," he said and turned toward the barn.

David replaced his hand on her back and guided her past the fences, heading for the pasture where several horses grazed. "Now, these... these are my pride and joy." His eyes shone.

"Are they?"

"Sure are." He removed his hand from her back and rested his forearms on the fence.

She missed the contact, so she inched closer, standing by his side. "I've watched you out here with your horses sometimes."

His eyebrows rose as if surprised.

She continued, saying, "You look so brave on the back of that mustang. And that other horse—what do you call him? Bueno? It looks like you enjoy riding him."

"I'm training him," David said, his cheeks all flushed.

Kickabilly looked up from grazing in the green grass and meandered toward them.

"My herd started out small. My dad, he gave Gabe and me the funds to get our own horses. We made some inquiries and found this prime breeding stock that a ranch owner wanted to eliminate. Goldsprings breeds some fine stock, it does... and the price was right. My brother..." David's forehead stitched together in a frown. "He just swooped in and claimed the best ones for himself."

Amanda stood stiffly by his side, waiting for him to finish the story. Having just experienced a moment of genuine connection, she didn't want it to stop—but she also didn't know how to soothe away his frown.

Finally, David blew out his breath and continued. "So, I ended up with three skinny mares and one stallion— Kickabilly. He was a young'un, he was... Barely broke... So, I let him sow his wild oats after I fattened up the mares and got their health to rights. Many of those horses...." He swept his arm toward the equines. "Many of those fine horses came from his seed. When I felt like he'd done his job with the ladies, I gelded him and turned him into a working animal. I knew he had more potential than wooing the ladies. He's turned out to be the best horse—far better than my brother's stallion, Amigo." He tipped his head toward a spotted horse in a separate field.

"Why is that horse all by himself?" Amanda said.

David looked down at her with an amused expression on his face. "Girl, don't you know nuthin' about the birds and the bees? Old Amigo there is a boy horse with a mind to do one thing and one thing alone—fill the girl horses with his seed."

Amanda's cheeks flushed with heat. "Oh," she said, staring at her hands.

Again, David laughed. "We've got to teach you some things about running a ranch, don't we?"

"I guess we do," she agreed, smiling.

Kickabilly reached the fence, and he extended his muzzle to David.

David held out his hand and let Kickabilly sniff it. "Good morning to you, Kickabilly," he said affectionately. He kissed the horse's soft nose.

Amanda stared at David's lips for a second, remembering the brush of them against her mouth on their wedding day. That brief contact had felt warm, soft, and inviting. But no more such contact had taken place—until today.

"Now, horses—they have their own set of manners. They sniff each other in greeting. It's usually a three-sniff greeting, like this." He leaned close to Amanda and took three slow sniffs. "They don't skip their manners. We humans just bully our way into their space and go about our business. Kickabilly and his mares had to teach me some equine etiquette. I've spent hours watching them. That's how I learned. They taught me."

Amanda found herself mesmerized as she listened to him. He seemed to be a thoughtful, caring man. And Lord knew David loved his equines. *I'd give anything if he could love me half as much.*

David rubbed his knuckles on Kickabilly's forehead. The horse tossed his head, pushing into the contact.

"Oh, you know you like this," David said to his horse. "This is your favorite spot." He removed his hand and pivoted, resting his elbows on the fence. "What do you say we teach you how to ride. Would you like that?"

Amanda blinked in surprise. "I don't know. Horses scare me."

David's eyebrows flew up, and his gaze sought hers. "Well, we can't have that around here. What if I need help with the herd? They'll sense your fear and take advantage of you. As much as I love these critters, I won't take kindly to them pushing you around."

The tenderness radiating from his eyes took her by surprise, and she found herself all tongue-tied. "Thank you for saying that," she stammered.

This morning had proved a success, and she allowed herself to feel hope about this marriage of convenience. *If we can share warm moments like this every once in a while, it might not be so bad to be married.*

He broke eye contact and gazed off into the distance. "We'll start you off on old Chester. He's my gentle draft horse. He won't hurt you—he's old and kind. Real good around children." David's expression seemed to shutter over, pulling Amanda into her own dark mood.

The memory of seeing Sheriff Slinger several days ago and the slimy way his eyes had made her feel slithered into her mind. Along with that dark thought came the memories of losing John and Jacob, losing her parents and everything that had come after, resulting in Amanda's being in this loveless marriage.

A puff of wind gusted around her head, causing strands of hair to tickle her forehead. As she brushed them away, the warm feelings she'd just experienced with David disappeared. No, she certainly couldn't relax into this moment, as welcome as it had been. Something dark and sinister lurked around the corner.

That was her lot in life. She just had to accept it and carry on.

Chapter Fourteen

The thought of teaching Amanda to ride sent a thrill through David's chest. The next day, he moseyed around the barn, putting a halter on Chester and leading him out into the aisle to prepare him for Amanda.

As he tied off his horse, David reflected on his surprising day yesterday with Amanda. He'd enjoyed her company immensely—until thoughts of Gabe wormed their way into David's brain. Gabe had booted guilt into his head, reminding David that Amanda didn't deserve a man who married her to get revenge on his dead brother. Then, when thoughts of his brother tromped all over his excellent mood, David thanked Amanda for coming out to the barn. After that, he'd excused himself, treating her like a shopkeeper who had brought supplies out to the ranch in her wagon.

He'd kicked himself all day for his off-and-on moods, which were becoming annoyingly consistent. He longed for the days in which he never spoke to a soul, from the minute his boots touched the floor to the second he hung his hat on the bedframe at night. But, although he yearned for the contemplative solitude in which he'd spent many days, he also pined for Amanda.

At the sound of her soft footsteps, he looked up, blinking when he saw her attire.

"What in tarnation are you wearing, woman?" he asked.

Amanda averted her gaze to the ground. "They're called bloomers. Ada found them in a trunk for me to wear. She said they'd be more comfortable for riding a horse."

David lifted his hat, raked his hair with his hand, and replaced the Stetson. "Huh. She did now?"

The "bloomers" were visible beneath Amanda's dress and gathered at each ankle, sort of like full billowing pants.

He'd never seen such a thing on a woman before and wasn't sure he liked it. But, wanting to start the day off right with Amanda, he kept his opinions to himself. If she was comfortable and she never wore the darned garment away from the ranch, he'd tolerate it—for today, at least.

"So, the first thing we do before we ride is we groom the horse. Look in that box over yonder and fetch a bristle brush, will you please?" David inclined his head toward the wooden box of grooming tools in front of his tack room.

Amanda shuffled over to the box and rooted around, procuring the brush which she waved at him. "Is this the right one?"

"Yep," he said. "Bring it on over."

Amanda crossed to where he stood, standing far away from Chester.

David chuckled. "You can't very well groom Chester if you're standing that distance, now, can you?"

She wrinkled up her nose. "Will he bite?"

"The only thing Chester bites is mouthfuls of hay. Looky here...." He grabbed her free hand and tugged her close to Chester's head. Lifting the side flap of the horse's mouth with his thumb, he slid Amanda's fingers into the back of Chester's mouth.

Chester immediately began licking, trying to get her hand out of his mouth.

She let out a gasp and yanked her hand away, wiping the slobber on her dress.

David let out a laugh. "See? He has no teeth in the back."

"Where did they go?" Amanda asked, her eyes wide.

"That's how a horse is built. Equines have these snappers up front to cut the grass. Then, they chomp the grass with their cheek teeth." He lifted Chester's lips, showing her the short teeth used to masticate. "But, no, Chester won't bite. And this was your horse teeth lesson." David grinned, delighting in the shy smile that split her face. "Now we get to brushing. Go on then and run that brush along Chester's side."

Amanda's eyes narrowed as she considered his request.

"Go on then. Put that on Chester's side and brush," he said, flapping his hand.

Amanda lifted the brush to Chester's coat and made a tentative swipe.

Another chuckle left David's throat. "Is that how you brush your own hair?" The memory of watching her brush her gossamer hair in the window a while back floated into his mind. Forcing himself back to the present, he said, "I'll bet you don't. Do it like this."

He stepped behind her, placed his hand over hers, and made slow, sure strokes across Chester's flanks. The feeling of her back pressed against his chest, and her small, soft hand enveloped in his took his breath away. Quickly, he removed his hand and stepped back.

"Go on then," he said, nodding. "You do it."

She glanced over her shoulder at him and offered him a sweet smile. When she turned around, she continued brushing until she came to Chester's rump.

David lunged forward before she stepped behind him.

"Don't go behind the horse unless you place your hand on his back. You might surprise him, and he might kick you."

"Oh!" Amanda exclaimed, stumbling backward, right into David's arms.

He sucked in a breath at the contact. "Easy, girl. Chester's old and doesn't like to lift his legs that fast. I only meant that as a warning," David said, easing her away from him. He took a step back and loosely crossed his arms. "You go on and finish him up. I'll supervise."

Supervising turned into more of a gawking and averting his gaze kind of thing. *She's so lovely.*

Abruptly, as his gaping stirred intense sensation, he moved toward her and took the grooming tool from her hand. "Okay, we're done with this part."

Her head whipped toward him. "Did I do something wrong?"

"Nope. Let's move on in our lesson, okay?" He gave an underhand toss of the wooden brush. It arced through the air and landed on top of the other grooming supplies with a clatter.

"Now, normally, we'd clean his feet with a hoof pick to remove rocks and such, but I already checked them in his stall. So, let's get to riding." His limp felt more pronounced as he hobbled toward the tack room to get the saddle, bridle and reins, and saddle blanket.

After balancing the saddle on the side of the stall, he fit the bit in Chester's mouth and affixed the bridle to his head. Next, he heaved the saddle over Chester's back and tightened the girth. With the efficiency of a soldier, he said, "Let's go." *Why do I become so awkward in her presence? I never got this way with a girl before.*

They strode in silence out to his fenced arena. Noting the bruised expression on Amanda's face when he opened the gate, he said, "You did a real fine job brushing old Chester."

Her face brightened. "Did I?"

"You sure did." He flashed her a smile. "Chester's used to me brushing him. He probably thought it was mighty special to have a woman's hands on his flanks." His cheeks warmed. *Are you talking about you or the horse, you fool?* "Anyway..." He stared at Chester for a few seconds, trying to collect his wits.

"What do you want me to do?" she said, stepping close to him.

Avoiding looking at her, he said, "Well, you're going to ride side-saddle. Do you know what that is?"

"Sure. It's the way my mom used to ride. She hooked her knee over that part, there," Amanda said, pointing to the front of the saddle.

"That's right. That's called a horn. So, I'm going to lift you up and place you in the saddle, and you're going to hook one foot here...." He pointed to the stirrup. "And hook that knee of yours over the horn. Ready?"

"I guess so." Amanda stared at the horse with wide, fearful eyes.

"You'll be all right. Chester and I won't let anything bad happen to you," he promised with a smile.

Her face furrowed into a frown.

"Really," he assured her.

"I don't know, David. Unfortunately, bad things always follow me around."

Her expression looked so sorrowful that he wondered if she meant Gabe's death or her marriage to him. He scratched the back of his neck. "Ain't nothing going to happen to you in this here arena, Amanda, I promise. Chester's going to take real good care of you, isn't that right, Chester?"

The horse turned to regard David, then turned back around, patiently waiting.

"Okay, up you go." David placed his hands around her petite waist and lifted her high onto Chester's back.

Amanda squealed and clung to his wrists.

"You got to let go of me, Amanda," he said, straining from the awkward angle of her weight pressing down on his arms. "Settle in the saddle. Just sit, and we'll get your legs situated."

She took a shuddering breath and did as instructed, clinging to the horn with a tight grip.

"That's it. You're doing fine. Now, I'll steady you, and you just swing that leg of yours over the horn you're holding onto, okay?"

She shook her head.

"Amanda. I'm not going to let anything happen to you." He reached up to grab her waist. "I've got you. Swing your leg."

She swung, clocking him in the ribs in the process.

He let out an "oof."

Chester shifted side to side.

Amanda yelped and seized Chester's mane. "I'm so sorry," she said.

"I'm a cowboy. I've endured worse," he said, plastering a smile on his face to cover the stinging sensation spreading through his ribcage. "Are you steady?"

"Kind of..." She pried her fingers from Chester's mane and clutched the horn so hard her knuckles were white.

He took her booted foot and placed the toe in the stirrup. "Steadier?"

"Kind of..." she said again.

"Take a breath, Amanda." He filled his lungs with air, lifted his arms, and let them float down as he exhaled. "Like that."

She let out a shaky breath.

"Good. Another one, ready?" He inhaled, lifting his arms as her ribs expanded. Then, he let out a big sigh as she let out her air. "There you go. Now, just hang on, and we'll take a little stroll around the arena. Ready?"

"I guess so," she said in a quavering voice.

"Either you is or you ain't, Amanda. 'Guess so' is somewhere in the middle." He looked up at her.

She took another deep breath and said, "I'm ready."

"That's my girl," he said.

The words floated effortlessly off his tongue, but she wasn't his girl... not really. He stepped to the side and led Chester in a slow plod in the dirt.

"How's that?" he said, not turning to look at Amanda. "You doing all right?"

"I don't think so," she said, a twinge of alarm to her voice.

When David looked over his shoulder, Amanda clutched the saddle as she teetered to the side. He dropped the reins and lunged for her before she toppled to the ground.

She let go and landed in his arms.

"Whoa!" he exclaimed, losing his balance, stumbling backward. He managed to right himself as he set Amanda on her feet. For one sweet second, she lingered in his embrace, close enough to kiss. He released her, backing away as if his hands were on fire, and said, "That was a good start. Want to try again?"

She shook her head and stared at her boots.

"You did real good, Amanda. You just need practice, is all."

"I did terribly," she said, lifting moist eyes to him.

"No, you didn't." He thumbed away a tear with his callused thumb. "Don't you be going on about it. You did fine—this is new to you. You'll get the hang of it. Let's head back to the barn. I think Chester is plumb worn out from all the excitement," he said with a smile.

"Really?" she said, blinking away her tears.

"Really. Isn't that right, Chester?" He cupped his hand around his ear. "Did you hear that? Chester said you did good, and now he wants to go back to the barn."

Amanda giggled, and it was the sweetest sound he might ever have heard.

Ada emerged from the house as they headed back to the barn. She stopped on the porch, ringing the clanging bell outside announcing lunch.

"You go on in the house and wash up. I'll be in shortly," he said.

"Are you sure? I could help you put Chester away," she said.

"Nah." He patted the horse's neck. "Chester and I have a routine." He kept his gaze on her as she departed, enjoying the view of her lovely figure. The last couple of days, he'd been enjoying Amanda more than he had a right to do. With a sigh, he set his legs to walk to the barn before heading into the house for the midday meal.

Inside the house, Ada served up venison stew in the kitchen to Michael, Billy, David, and Amanda before sitting down to her own bowl.

"Did you two have fun?" she said to David, flicking her gaze between him and Amanda.

"Amanda's got the potential to become a real horsewoman," he said, winking at her.

"No, I don't," she said with a scoff.

"Okay, not yet, anyway," David said, reaching for a sourdough biscuit.

Michael snorted. "It looked like you was going to strangle that old horse, Mrs. Brown."

Her cheeks reddened, but she grinned. "He's a mighty big horse."

"That he is. He's a big one. At least you tried," David said, dipping his biscuit in the stew. He took a bite, enjoying the easy banter around the table.

"That's all any of us can do is try," Ada said, scooping some stew onto her spoon. "I'm right proud of you, Amanda."

"Are you?" Amanda beamed at the praise.

"I am. You're getting on out there and trying your best," Ada said, dabbing at her face with her napkin. "Remember when you and Gabe learned to ride? It came to you so easy, David. But, Lord, what a time your brother had. And I never believed the stories he told about you spurring your horse on your first ride—not one bit."

David frowned at the memory. They were just a couple of kids when they first rode horses. Father had lifted David into the saddle, handed him the reins, and he took right to it.

But Gabe had been as scared as Amanda, seizing that horse's mane so hard David thought he'd pull the hair out by the roots.

To cover up his shame, once Gabe had "found his seat," he'd pulled up beside David and swatted the rump of the horse David rode, sending the animal into a mad gallop across the plains.

David had come off the saddle, landing hard on the ground. When he'd managed to round up his horse, he'd limped back to the ranch. There, David overheard Gabe telling some cockamamie tale to his parents about how David didn't know a thing about riding. He went onto say how David had spurred the horse and couldn't hold on, so he'd fallen.

David had been mad at Gabe, but he didn't defend himself since Gabe was being patted on the back by Father and told how good he'd looked in the saddle.

Gabe, of course, had eaten it up. After that, the rivalry began in earnest, with Gabe always trying to "one-up" David.

Unable to stomach his lunch any longer, David pushed away from the table. "Will you excuse me? I forgot to take care of something important in the barn."

And then, without waiting for a reply, he limped away from the pleasant moment at the table, turned sour with his thoughts of Gabe.

Even in death, Gabe always had to get his own way. And that way meant never letting David have a lick of fun.

Chapter Fifteen

Life at the ranch proved lonely and unfulfilling with small dabs of happiness. It was all so confusing.

Amanda sat on the bed in her room, her eyes filled with tears, reading the post she'd just received from Julia in response to her letter.

"Dear Amanda," she read under her breath. "It gives me joy that you've managed to find happiness in a difficult situation. You've always been so strong. As your friend, I wish you all the best. But don't despair—life might turn out the way you want it to, or even better."

Julia went on to share details about Marshall, her upcoming wedding, and the arrangements she'd been making for her wedding day.

Amanda clutched the letter to her bosom. *Oh, I'm so happy for Julia. Finally, she's getting the kind of marriage I would have liked.*

Deciding to reply to her friend while she had a moment to spare, she retrieved a piece of parchment paper from the small stack on the side table, as well as her dip pen. After opening the ink bottle, she proceeded to write.

My dear Julia,

It is with fondness that I write you, sending you well wishes for your upcoming nuptials. You will make a fine wife to Marshall, and he shall make an excellent husband. You have forged a strong alliance that will withstand the tests of time.

She paused, unsure how much of her up-and-down marriage with David she should share.

I've started a garden. Ada, David's housekeeper, and I rode into town to purchase supplies for the garden. Would you believe I was given unlimited funds with which to make my purchases? Can you imagine having unlimited funds? It seems David is quite wealthy. But you'd never know it. He's a kind and quiet man. Oh! And he bought me gifts—a sewing machine and two books! How thoughtful of him! How is it that I have managed to marry someone good, kind, and handsome with all my bad luck?

Just writing the words caused her to tense.

I keep waiting for the other shoe to drop. I am quite pessimistic, and I fear losing David in some manner. For this is how my life has become since losing John and Jacob. It seems to be one upset after another and one loss after the next, with no let-up.

Amanda frowned, not wanting to leave Julia with bad news or sorrow.

Guess what? I got to ride a horse a couple of days ago. It was kind of scary, but David said I did okay. Chester, one of David's horses, is a giant of an animal. I looked down and thought it to be a long way to fall, so I got scared. But, at supper, David gave me compliments, and so did Ada. The ranch hands teased me good-naturedly. So, perhaps we'll do it again.

That day was better than acceptable. David had touched her many times, making her entire body tingle. And they'd laughed and seemed to enjoy one another. *Until the end, when he retreated into his own thoughts...*

She tapped the end of her pen against the paper, unable to think of anything else to say.

I miss you with all my heart. Please give my kind regards to your parents and Clara, and thank your father for taking me on this long journey. Do, please, continue to write to me.

Yours in friendship,

Amanda.

Satisfied with her letter, she folded it in two and placed it on the side table. Remembering Ada's support in taking chances with David, she decided to fix him lunch.

As she entered the kitchen, she said to Ada, "Would you mind if I take a lunch out to David so we can eat outside?"

Ada turned from the stove, where she stood stirring a pot of salted pork and beans. "Kind of like a picnic?"

"Yes, that's right—a picnic of sorts," Amanda said, twisting her hands around and around. *Is this really a good plan? What if he sends me back into the house?*

Ada nodded, adding a secretive smile. "I think that's a wonderful idea, Amanda. Let me help you prepare some plates."

She grabbed a couple of sturdy plates from the shelf next to the stove. After placing them on the counter, she spooned some of the pork and beans onto each one. Next, she cut two pieces of cornbread out of the cast iron skillet and set them on the plates. Lastly, she added a slice of apple pie to each dish.

Handing them to Amanda, she said, "You take this outside into the backyard. I'll fetch you some lemonade and utensils. They'll be right here when you return." She patted the counter and resumed her stirring.

"Thank you, Ada," Amanda said.

"I'm pleased as punch you and David are getting on so well," Ada said, winking.

Amanda blushed as she carried the food outside. *Are we getting along so well?* Truthfully, their relationship seemed like a wagon lurching across a stream. There were never any assurances whether they'd make it across intact.

She set the plates on the stumps beneath the trees the guests had sat on at her wedding, then headed back inside for the other items.

When she returned to the kitchen, David strode toward the backyard, frowning.

Oh, dear. He's not going to like my picnic plan. Amanda stood nervously, clutching the utensils and the glass jars of lemonade.

"What's this?" he said.

"I thought you and I could have a picnic."

"Out here?" he said, his eyebrows stitching together.

Yes, I thought it might be nice," she said, her anxiety spiking. *He's unhappy about eating outside.*

David shrugged, perched on one of the empty stumps, and reached for the plate with the most food. He began to shovel it into his mouth nonstop. Finally, after he'd finished the pork and beans, he said, "This was nice—to eat outside, I mean."

"Was it?" She nibbled on the cornbread.

"Yes, it was. It must be ninety degrees outside today. But it's pleasant out here in the shade." He lifted his arm and wiped the sweat from his brow.

"Yes, it's rather warm." She sat her plate of nearly untouched food to the side. "Have you eaten many picnic meals?"

"Not really, no," he said, forking a bite of apple pie. "Matter of fact, this might be my first one."

Amanda brightened. "Really?"

"As sure as I acknowledge the corn," David said. "I'm telling it true."

Amanda smiled. "My brother Jacob and I used to take a pail of fried chicken down to the river, sit on the bank, and eat it."

David nodded, chewing his food. "That sounds nice. Fried chicken is one of my favorites."

"Is it? I'll have to make some for you sometime. My ma had a good recipe for it."

"I'd like to try it," David said, forking another bite of pie. "This pie's real good—did you make it?"

She nodded, her cheeks flushing.

David smiled at her. "Real good," he said again, using his hand to pick up the remaining pie, which he shoved into his mouth.

She returned the smile then frowned as thoughts of her family tugged at her heartstrings. "I really loved my brother. It broke my family when he died."

David washed the pie down with some lemonade. Lowering the glass, he said, "I'm sorry to hear that, Amanda. No one should lose a sibling—not through tragedy." A distant look replaced the warm gaze he'd just given her.

Amanda studied his face, wishing she hadn't brought up the topic of brothers.

His lips parted as if to speak, then they snapped shut.

She cocked her head to the side.

Out of nowhere, he blurted, "Did you love my brother?"

"Gabe?" she said, her head jerking back in surprise.

"I don't got any other brothers, Amanda," David said. "Did you love him?"

She huffed out a breath. "Honestly, no."

"Then why'd you want to get hitched?" He set his empty plate to the side in the grass.

Her eyes rolled skyward, seeking answers. When she met David's gaze, their eyes locked. A tingling sensation rocked through her, and she had to look away.

"Gabe seemed nice enough... and funny."

"Oh, he was a real cutup, he was," David said, frowning. "The life of the party, always having a hog-killin' time of it." His expression grew dark and guarded.

"He also seemed like a gentleman and..." Her shoulders rose and fell.

"Yes, Gabe always seemed to be a lot of things," David said.

She glanced at him, wondering what he meant, and added, "I had no other options. So, here I am." A wan smile briefly curved her lips.

"Here you are." He nodded, appearing satisfied with her answer before he drifted off into his own brooding thoughts, staring at the horizon.

As Amanda studied him, she wanted to ask him if she could try horseback riding again, if only to feel his arms around her.

David stayed silent for a long beat, leaving Amanda to wonder what she'd done or said that might have upset him.

Suddenly, he rose to his feet and propped his hands on his trim hips. "Tomorrow, I have to head over to Redlake, the next town over. There are some supplies I need. Won't take more than a day to get there and back."

Her stomach slid to her feet. *He wants to get away from me again.* "I see."

"What's the glum look about?" he asked.

"I don't know," she said, not knowing what else to say.

"I was going to ask if you wanted to accompany me but, seeing as I've put a frown on your face...." His voice trailed off.

"You were going to ask me if I'd accompany you to Redlake?" she said in a somewhat squeaky voice.

"Yes, ma'am," he said, rubbing his jaw with his palm.

"Yes! I'd love to go," she said, clasping her hands over her bosom.

"That's good, then. That's settled." He lifted his hat in a now-familiar manner and raked his hand through his hair. "We'll be heading out at dawn." His eyes twinkled with what appeared to be mirth.

"I'll be ready," she said. "Thank you for the invitation."

David didn't reply. Instead, he turned and strode in the direction of the barn, whistling.

Amanda stayed glued to the spot, watching him walk away. *We're going to travel together!*

She hoped she wouldn't do anything or say anything to upset him. As far as she could tell, his mood could head south at the slightest provocation. And she seemed to always be the one doing the provoking.

Chapter Sixteen

The sun seemed to yawn its way over the horizon as Kickabilly meandered across the plains, pulling David and Amanda in the wagon. David stayed silent for the most part, sneaking furtive glances at the woman by his side.

With each passing day, his enjoyment of Amanda increased. And each time he relaxed into a pleasurable appreciation of her, his unresolved guilt and conflicted emotions toward his brother seemed to grow like an invasive weed. In fact, this morning, he'd woken before dawn in a state of panic. *What in tarnation was I thinking? I shouldn't have invited her on this trip.*

The decision had been an impulsive one that could only lead to trouble. David needed to be very careful to keep his attraction to Amanda in check.

The cart squeaked and jostled as they rumbled over a patch of rough terrain. One of the wheels seemed to get stuck, and David leaned over the side of the wagon to find it struggling over a boulder. *The last thing we need is for a wheel to break.* He clucked at Kickabilly and the horse dug in his hooves, leaned forward, and pulled. The wagon lurched over the stone, landing with a groaning thud.

Amanda lost her balance, toppling into him.

He steadied her with his hands, sucking in a breath at the warm contact. Pushing her away from him, he settled back into silence. *I've still got no answers for Gabe's death and no peace in my heart for marrying her. What am I going to do?*

The journey into Redlake proceeded without incident, save for the awkward silence that stretched between them. David's mood soured with each turn of the wagon wheel until he was spitting mad. More than anything, he wished he could just hold her hand and enjoy the day like any other married couple. But he couldn't get Gabe out of his mind any more than his guilt at his original motivations for revenge. *Am I that namby-pamby of a man as to seek revenge on a dead man because I couldn't set it to rights when Gabe was alive?*

He felt ashamed for even wanting to be a "normal" married couple when his wife was his brother's fiancée. Anger ripped through his heart at the injustice of Gabe's death, as well as his inability to stand up to his brother when he had a chance. *He's the one that should be here on this trip with Amanda, not me. I'm nothing but a coward.*

Instead, Gabe was dead and his murderer out there somewhere, living life as a free man.

The man who murdered my brother needs to be behind bars. And I need to set right my motivations for marrying Amanda. She deserves no less. Only—I don't know how to do that. Not with all this shame and guilt in my heart.

Kickabilly picked his way down the town's main dusty street, lined with an assortment of shops. A few townsfolk ambled along the sidewalk in the midday heat, but, for the most part, the road was empty.

When they arrived at the blacksmith's, next to a general store at the far end of town, David reined his horse to a halt next to a flatbed cart full of baskets of apples.

The wagon driver was nowhere to be seen.

"Stay here," David snapped to Amanda.

She looked at him with these wounded eyes, so he amended his sentiments. "Or, come in if you like. I need to see to some metalwork for the horse stalls. You can do what suits." Then, he hopped from the seat and stalked toward the smithy's building, heedless to whether Amanda followed or not.

Black smoke billowed from the chimney at the back of the blacksmith's shop.

David stepped onto the wooden sidewalk and made his way through the door to a brick-lined interior. Fire spewed from beneath an iron cauldron at the far end of the building, sending sparks shooting into the air.

A blacksmith clad in a leather apron and a simple shirt, opened at the neck, stood before an anvil. He hammered a red-hot iron rod of metal held in his ungloved hand.

The hammer echoed with a metallic clang each time it struck the metal rod. The blacksmith's bare forearms bulged with muscle as he worked. His cheeks were covered with soot and sweat poured from his body. He looked up when David approached.

"The name's Elgin," the blacksmith stated, extending his palm.

"David Brown," David said, shaking the blacksmith's hand.

"What can I do for you, Mr. Brown?" he drawled.

David looked out of the corner of his eye at Amanda, who stood meekly by his side. He wasn't sure how he felt about her seeing this sweat-covered giant of a man.

"Amanda," he hissed. "Wait outside for me."

She frowned but then turned to leave. Instantly, he missed her.

"I'm fixin' to put metal doors on the horse stalls in my barns. I've heard you're one of the best blacksmiths in these parts."

Elgin nodded. "I stand by my work, that's for certain." He wiped the sweat from his eyes with his massive forearm. "How many doors will you need?"

"Eight for the mares and seven for the geldings and the stallion," David said.

"It'll cost you," Elgin said.

"How much are we talking?" David said, well versed in the art of haggling.

The men dickered back and forth until they agreed on a price. Then, they decided on a date for David to pick up the finished product and shook hands again to seal the deal.

When David exited the store, Amanda stood balanced at the sidewalk's edge on one foot, her arms extended wide. Her eyes were closed, and her face was tipped toward the sun.

For a second, he got lost in her beauty. Reining himself in, he scanned the road, hoping no one saw her foolish behavior. "What in tarnation are you doing?" he snapped.

Startled, she lost her balance and tumbled from the sidewalk, catching herself against the horse with the apple cart.

The horse whinnied, lurching away. A basket of apples fell from the bed of the wagon, rolling into the dusty street.

David hustled into the road, snatching up apples. As he worked, his gaze flitted back and forth, searching for witnesses to Amanda's bumbling behavior.

Amanda scurried about near him, gathering apples in her arms.

Once they each had an armful of fruit, they both hurried toward the felled basket.

David righted the wicker, and they dropped the apples inside before anyone saw what had happened.

"I sure hope none of those apples got bruised," David said, depositing the receptacle in the back of the wagon.

Amanda simply stood there, her cheeks as rosy as the apples, eyes wide.

David studied her for a few seconds. *She's a clumsy one, my Amanda is.* He couldn't help himself and started to laugh.

"What?" she said, her eyebrows stitching together.

"You're like a foal who can't keep her legs under her," he said through his hilarity.

"I know," she said, staring at her feet. "I've been this way for a long time. I can't seem to help myself. It's like once I grew up, my body didn't match my mind."

"You just need more hard work," David said, smiling. "You probably ain't used to using your body. We can set you to rights."

"Can we?' she said, with the most beguiling expression he'd ever seen.

David swallowed as he realized he was smitten with the lovely woman before him. *David Brown, you're a besotted fool.* He lifted his gaze to the sky.

Dark clouds hovered ominously on the horizon, rolling in their direction.

"Let's get ourselves some refreshments, get Kickabilly some water, and head on back. What do you say?" He wanted more than anything to pull her into his arms and kiss her.

"All right," Amanda said. "I brought some boiled ham and eggs. We can eat in the wagon, if you like."

David's eyebrows rose. His mood had been in such a twist this morning, he hadn't noticed when she'd packed the food. "Well, aren't you a clever one?"

They climbed into the wagon and set off toward the livery to water his horse before proceeding on their way.

He kept glancing at the sky as they headed back. So far, the clouds stayed high and kept their rain to themselves. But as the sun slid toward the horizon, the clouds darkened, bloated and threatening. Distant thunder rumbled, followed by a few bursts of lightning.

David glanced at Amanda. "I think we're going to be hit with a storm."

"What should we do?" she said. "Do you think we can find shelter?

"Let's see how it goes before making a decision," he said.

A few minutes later, fat droplets landed on his Stetson. Then, the droplets became a drizzle, and then the rain turned into a downpour. The lightning continued with the cracks of thunder occurring almost instantaneously.

Amanda quickly became drenched. Hugging herself, she shivered.

"I see a farmhouse ahead." David lifted his arm and pointed.

Amanda nodded, gritting her teeth.

"Let's see if we can get shelter there," he said, raising his voice over the pelting rain.

"Okay," Amanda said, her teeth chattering.

David reached behind him and pulled his long leather coat from the back of the wagon. "Here." He thrust it at Amanda. "Wrap yourself in this."

She took the coat and wrapped it around her, pulling it tight. "Thank you."

He urged Kickabilly into a trot. As the horse surged ahead, David could barely make out the landscape through the pouring rain.

When they arrived at the farmhouse, David reined the horse to a halt, leaped from the seat, and said, "Wait here. I'll go ask permission to shelter here." He raced toward the farmhouse and knocked on the front door.

No one answered.

He rattled the doorknob, intending to push the door open and shout for assistance.

The doorknob was locked.

Walking around the house, he peered in the windows, spying no one.

With a sigh, he raced back to the wagon and hopped in the seat. "Let's head to the barn. There's nobody home. If they return, I'll explain to them what happened."

"Okay," Amanda said, her teeth clacking together.

David glanced at the sky.

Light still shone through the clouds near the horizon, but soon they'd be engulfed in darkness. They had to move quickly as they had no lantern.

"Hurry," he said.

Inside the barn, he helped Amanda from her seat, removed the harness from Kickabilly, and unhitched the wagon. He led his horse into one of the empty stalls and fastened the latch. Inside the stall sat a bucket half-filled with water, which Kickabilly sucked into his mouth.

Next, David borrowed some hay from the back of the barn and tossed it into the stall for Kickabilly to munch. Then, he searched for a place to rest until the storm passed. "Are you okay?" he called to Amanda, now huddled on the floor.

"I'm glad to be out of the rain. I'll be okay," she said.

Inside one of the stalls, fresh hay had been spread. "Come here. I found a place for us to hunker down and wait it out."

A few seconds later, Amanda shuffled toward him, swallowed up in his coat.

"Here," he said, indicating the straw. "Let's spread the coat on top of the hay and take a rest."

"Okay," she said, removing the coat from her shoulders and laying it out on the dried grass. Then, she lowered herself onto the leather coat, pulled her knees toward her body, and hugged them tightly.

Her hair coiled in wet, dripping ringlets around her face, while her clothing looked soaked clean through.

David stood over her for a second, considering his next move. "You look cold," he said, stating the obvious.

"I'm freezing," she agreed.

"Wait here. I'll be right back." He pivoted and headed out of the stall, searching for a horse blanket or anything that might warm Amanda.

In the dimly lit barn, he had to feel his way around, but finally, he found something that felt like wool.

"Let's get you warmed up," he said when he returned. "I'll hold this blanket up, and you peel off some of those wet outer clothes. Ain't no sense in you trying to warm up with them things stuck to your body. They'll suck the heat right out of your skin."

Amanda hesitated.

"Don't worry, I won't look." He lifted the blanket and turned his head away.

A soft rustling came from where Amanda undressed.

"Okay," she said.

"Okay," he said, still staring into the shadows. "Wrap yourself in this here blanket, and I'll drape your garments over the stall to dry."

"Thank you," she said, seizing the blanket from his grip.

He retrieved her soggy clothes from the clean straw and draped them over the stall door. He removed his sopping shirt but left his woolen pants on. He lowered himself next to her, pulling her back into his front, with his arms wrapped around her. "How's this?"

She snuggled into him like a wet kitten. "This feels nice," she said. "Thank you."

He said nothing, unable to reply. As he held Amanda tight, her shivers gradually subsided, and her breathing became deep and even. Before he drifted off to sleep, his last conscious thought startled him. It felt so right to cradle her in his arms.

Could she ever indeed be his?

Chapter Seventeen

The whisper of dawn gently tugged Amanda out of her deep slumber into a state of lingering drowsiness. She'd slept soundly, and now, as she came to, she knew why.

David lay next to her, breathing slow and deep, with his arm wrapped around her.

I'm in David's arms! Heaven! He felt so warm and solid next to her. She held her breath, not daring to move.

Squeezing her eyes shut, she imagined what it would be like to wake up like this every morning, madly in love with one another. Together, they'd work the land. Ada would remain with them, and Amanda would alternate between helping her in the house and joining her husband outside to work by his side. She'd even learn to ride a horse, and they'd go for long rides in the summer sun. And then they'd have children—Amanda wanted three or four little ones.

She pictured David playing with their children, teaching them to ride and catch fish in the stream. The children would laugh as he scooped them into his arms, swinging them round and round.

Or he'd enter the house after a trip to town, lift the children who were overjoyed at seeing their daddy, and carry them into the kitchen for supper. Then, he'd kiss her soundly and ask about her day before telling her about his.

She'd serve him fried chicken and mashed potatoes, and he'd tell her he was a lucky man to have such a fetching wife who cooked such fine chicken.

I'd be the happiest woman in the world.

For a few minutes, the fantasy delighted her like colorful butterflies fluttering over her head, making her almost giddy. But then the reality of their relationship nudged its way into her mind, replacing the cozy feelings with a cloak of despair.

He'd barely spoken to her when she arose yesterday before dawn. And, once they'd set off, David had shunned her the entire ride to Redlake. For hours, she'd endured the loneliness of being with someone who didn't want to be with her. And then, when they'd arrived, he'd told her she could go into the blacksmith's—but when she did, he'd rudely ordered her out.

And yet, when she'd tripped and fallen, spilling apples all over the road, he'd shifted into the warm-hearted person she'd glimpsed in the last few weeks. He'd transformed into the man she wanted to be with, body, heart, and soul. After that, they'd enjoyed a too-brief moment of warm connectedness.

But were his constant mood swings really a surprise? David was a handsome and capable man. She doubted she could ever be what he wanted. *Does he find me unattractive? Is my clumsiness off-putting to him? I'm probably not the pretty, capable wife he envisioned for himself. He probably pictured himself with a swan who could ride horses and milk cows—and all he got was an ugly, ungainly duckling who spills apples and runs into horses.*

What could I do to make myself more appealing to him? Work harder, like he suggested?

She sighed, knowing there wasn't anything she could do— she was who she was, and she wouldn't change. David would be stuck with her and all her unattractiveness. He'd have to endure her in this loveless marriage for the rest of his days.

David's arm tensed around her midsection, interrupting her gloom-filled musing.

She held her breath, not wanting him to know she was awake.

He rolled away from her, leaving a chasm of cold stretching between their two bodies, popping her earlier fantasies like a delicate soap bubble.

He cleared his throat and aloofly stated, "We need to go. The people that live here might be back soon."

She made a show of rolling her shoulders and stretching, as if she'd just awoken, before saying, "Okay, of course." What she wanted to do was turn to face him, ask him how he slept, and start the day with a good-morning kiss. Anything but the brusque manner with which she'd been greeted by him.

Not wanting to see the disappointment in his face when he looked at her, she waited, facing away from him, until he left the stall. Resigned to her fate, she rose, lifted her clothes from the stall, and donned the still-damp attire. She emerged from their shelter and kept her head down as David harnessed Kickabilly and walked the horse and the wagon out of the barn.

"Are you coming?" he called. "No one is about. Let's get a move on."

With a sigh, she shuffled from the barn. Life, it seemed, insisted on passing her by when it came to good luck.

With a bruised scowl on his face, David helped her into the wagon.

That was when she resigned herself, yet again, to a life of misery. She was cursed, through and through. She couldn't seem to find happiness anywhere, and that was the way life would be—unless something significant changed her and David's lives.

Chapter Eighteen

David kept his eyes glued to the horizon, unwilling to glance at Amanda's beautiful face. Last night's storm had left the land scrubbed clean, with the promise of a glorious day of sunshine and clear skies ahead. Tiny birds flitted about the grass-lined field beside them while cattle grazed in the distance. A jackrabbit scampered across the dusty road, zigging and zagging its way to its destination.

Usually, he'd appreciate the beauty of nature, but not this morning—thoughts of Amanda moved through his mind like marbles on fire, scorching the surface upon which they rolled. He'd awoken with his arms wrapped around a woman who didn't belong to him.

She'd felt great in his arms. He hungered for her, and he wanted to wake like this every day. As usual, though, his guilt had steamrolled past his brain, making him feel unclean, lying next to her.

He didn't deserve to be with Amanda—she wasn't his, and she never would be. Not with the ghost of his brother still lingering in David's mind, screaming that she was the only woman he'd ever wanted. And not with the burden of guilt he carried over his thoughts of getting back at his brother.

No, the woman by his side was meant to be his sister-in-law, not his wife.

Wanting to get home as quickly as possible, he clucked to the horse and shook the reins. He had to get Amanda out of his field of vision, as well as his mind. Once they got home, he'd work like the Devil was at his tail if he had to, if only to tire out his restless mind.

Hey-ya," he said to Kickabilly. "Get on now."

Kickabilly lifted his head and increased his pace.

Amanda raised her hand and pointed in the distance. "Look, David. It's a pretty little lake. Can we head that way and take a look at it?"

Sure enough, a body of water, sparkling with sunlight dancing on the surface, sat to his right. It would be lovely to savor the view with Amanda by his side. But that thought was nothing but a useless fantasy, sure to drive him to madness. *So stop your nonsense, David Brown. She ain't yours to enjoy.*

He barked out a gruff, "No," and urged Kickabilly on. Out of the corner of his eye, he noticed the frown marring her features—as usual, put there by him. Clearing his throat, he added, "There could be Indians out there. I don't want to tangle with no Indians."

"But Mr. Williams spoke to some Indians—" Amanda began.

"Or there could be cougars," David said, cutting her off. "Kickabilly's scared of cougars, and I can't protect the both of you at the same time."

She turned her head to look at him with a slight smile on her face.

What in the blazes is she smiling about? His frown deepened, and he said, "It's just not safe to be wandering out here alone."

Her chest rose and fell, and she looked away from him.

David lapsed into broody silence again, well aware he wasn't behaving like the gentleman he knew he could be. *She deserves someone so much better than me.*

About an hour from the ranch, a wail drifted into earshot, coming from a wooded area up ahead. David frowned but didn't stop. Another cry—the distinct sound of a child—pierced his heart.

Kickabilly's head perked up, and his ears swiveled forward to listen.

"Oh, David!" Amanda cried, reaching out and squeezing his forearm. "Listen!"

Her touch ignited his soul. "I heard it," he grumbled, clucking at Kickabilly and shrugging out of her grasp.

"We've got to stop!" Amanda said. "We've got to help."

David gave her a side-eyed glance. "I've seen Indians in this neck of the woods. If it's an Indian child, there are other Indians around, I guarantee it. I told you, we don't want no trouble from them. Besides, they take care of their own," he added, trying to rationalize his behavior.

The child screamed and sobbed, making a caterwaul.

"David, please," Amanda pleaded, touching his arm again.

With a sigh, David reined Kickabilly to a stop. "Stay here, and I'll suss it out." Feeling torn about staying here and protecting Amanda and helping a stranger's child, he grabbed his rifle from the back of the wagon. He headed in the direction of the cries.

But Amanda hopped off the wagon and followed him, both annoying him and pleasing him. *It's better if she stays close so I can see to her safety.*

"If there's trouble ahead, stay out of my way," he said gruffly.

"The child could be in danger. So I want to help," she said.

159

"Suit yourself," he groused. "But stay out of harm's way, you hear me?"

Amanda said nothing as she moved further away from him.

Ahead, two bleating bear cubs clung to a branch high in a tree. Their plaintive cries tugged at David's heart.

A bronze-skinned child of around seven years old clutched a small bow and arrow, sobbing and crying. Snot streaked the boy's dirty face.

A large bear, presumably the mother, frantically tried to climb the tree.

But the boy waved the arrow at the mother bear's face, screaming in his native language. As his limbs flailed, he managed to jab the sharp arrow tip into the snout of the bear.

The bear grunted and growled, waving her foreleg savagely.

"Oh, boy," muttered David. "Stay back, Amanda. That mama bear's mad that she can't get to her cubs. And a mad mama is a mean mama. So, let's crouch behind this tree and come up with a plan." He lowered to a crouch, tugging at Amanda's skirts until she joined him.

With her hands on his shoulders, she snuggled into his back.

The sensation reminded him how good it had felt to wake up with his body pressed against hers. Chiding himself for his foolish thoughts, David peered around the trunk of the tree. He kept a steady grip on the rifle by his side.

The mama bear repeatedly lunged at the tree trunk, growling and snapping her massive jaw.

The sobbing kid cried and battered the wild animal with his weapon.

The baby bears called to their mother, shifting side to side on the branch they occupied. Finally, one of them put his paws and sharp claws on the trunk of the tree in an attempt to climb down to his mother.

Amanda whimpered, pressing her face against David's back.

David reached behind him and placed his hand on her leg, through her skirts. "Stay calm, Amanda. We don't want to spook that bear." He wanted to comfort her and take her fear away, but he also wanted to save the child. "The best thing we can do is stay calm. That mama bear only wants to get to her children and make them safe."

"But that bear—what will she do?"

"She wants her kids, that's all." He kept back the part about how that mama would do anything she could to get to her children, including killing the boy. Lowering his voice, he whispered, "Stop your whimpering, Amanda. You'll only agitate the bear more. We need to stay real quiet. I'm going to handle the situation and free the child."

Slowly rising, David lifted his rifle to his face and slid his finger over the trigger.

"What are you doing?" Amanda hissed. "You'll leave those baby bears without a mama."

"I'm only going to scare her a bit so the child can climb free," David whispered.

The mama bear tipped her head in the air and sniffed. Then, she whirled and charged him.

Amanda screamed.

David's knees grew weak as he aimed the rifle at the bear's head. In two seconds, if his aim wasn't true, either he or Amanda might be dead.

Chapter Nineteen

As the massive black bear charged toward them, Amanda bolted out from behind David, assuming he'd pull the trigger and chase the beast away while she raced for the tree. *I've got to help that child.*

"Amanda! No!" David shouted. The sound of his rifle ricocheted past her ears.

She didn't look back, desperate to save the little boy. When she stood near the tree, she lifted her arms to the sobbing child.

He dropped the weapon he'd been using to scare away the bear and scrambled down the trunk. When his feet landed on the forest floor, Amanda scooped him into her arms. She hurried away from the tree and glanced over her shoulder.

David and the bear stood in a standoff, with his rifle pointed at her massive head. "I don't want to shoot you," he said in a soothing voice. "But I'll do it if I must."

Amanda's heart swelled at his bravery. Yet, at that moment, she realized how devastated she'd be if anything were to happen to him.

The baby bears continued to bleat in the trees. Finally, one of them put his paws out, crying out when he began to slide down the trunk.

"Oh!" Amanda exclaimed.

The mother bear pivoted away from David and charged toward Amanda.

"Amanda. Don't run!"

Swiftly, Amanda ducked behind a tree, holding the boy close and peeking around the trunk.

The baby bear caught himself before falling to the ground and called to his mama in terrified bleats. The mother bear stopped charging Amanda, whirled, and raced toward the tree and her kids.

With his arms wrapped around Amanda, the little boy clung tightly and buried his damp face in her neck.

"Shh, shh, shh," Amanda soothed, patting his sweaty back. "Where are your parents?" she asked.

The child blubbered something to her in his native language, which Amanda, of course, couldn't understand.

With the bear occupied with her cubs, David lowered his gun, flicking his gaze between the bears and Amanda. "Stay right there, Amanda," he softly called. "Stay right there until this mama has freed her children."

She nodded and hugged the child even closer as the babies all scrambled toward their mother. The rustling of nearby trees caught both her and David's attention, and their heads swiveled at the same time.

Half a dozen Indians, dressed in deerskin and armed with spears and bows, stepped through the trees.

The mama bear's head whipped toward the Indians. She let out a sort of woof and raced away with her cubs following her.

The Indians surrounded David and lifted their spears.

David dropped his rifle and raised his hands, palms out. "I don't mean you no harm," he said. "We only wanted to help."

The native people probably didn't understand what he said, so they continued to point their sharp spears at David's chest.

Oh, no! Amanda feared the worst. Those savages were going to kill her David.

The little boy gave a shout and pushed away from her embrace, dropping to the ground.

"Wait!" she cried, but his tiny bare feet powered him in the Indians' direction.

Once the boy reached the native people, one of them, the tallest of them all, scooped the child into his arms.

The boy chattered excitedly to the tall man, patting his cheeks and chin. The tall man turned toward his people and said something, and they all lowered their weapons.

Turning toward David, the tall man said, "Thank you." Wordlessly, he inclined his head to the others, and they all disappeared into the shadows of the forest.

Amanda let out a cry of relief.

David crouched to retrieve his rifle. His shoulders slumped as he faced her, saying, "Let's go before more trouble finds us."

When she scurried toward him, he said, "You all right?"

"Yes, I'm all right."

"Thank God for that," he said with a long sigh. And then he turned to trek toward the wagon.

The rest of the journey home was made in silence, but it wasn't that stiff, stilting silence of the day before or this morning. Instead, it seemed to be one born of facing an experience and coming out to the other side unscathed—and still together.

***

That night, as Amanda lay in her tiny bed, she mused on the last two days of their journey together. She'd seen a different side of David when he'd gone to help the child despite his initial protests. In her heart, she knew he only wanted to protect her and keep her safe... but he'd also wanted to save the child. She could see it in his eyes. And his bravery in facing the bear was commendable. He'd never looked frightened the way she had felt. Instead, he had just done what he thought was best in the situation.

That David was a far cry from the David who kept his distance or acted irritated by her presence. And when he'd uttered the words, "Thank God for that," he'd shown her that maybe, just maybe, he liked her a little.

She rolled onto her side and pulled the bed covers up to her chin. *I'll bet David would make a wonderful father.* She let out a shuddering sob at her following thoughts. *How could I have fallen in love with someone who doesn't love me back?* Because she knew it, in her heart. She'd been trying hard not to feel it—every time the notion arose, she pushed it away. But honestly, she loved the man.

David's regard for her, though?

He had married her out of obligation. For the rest of her life, she'd be his responsibility, nothing more. And that thought was too heartbreaking to bear.

Chapter Twenty

Tossing and turning in his bed that night, David replayed the scene with the bear over and over. *What if that bear had killed Amanda? I never would have been able to live with myself. Why did I hesitate in shooting the beast?*

Amanda had been both brave and foolish to race to that tree when the bear charged him. *What was she thinking, running off like that while a wild animal charged us?* He rubbed his chin. *She probably thought she'd better go protect that little boy the same way I wanted to protect her and keep her safe. She's got a good heart. So how did she end up with a wretch like me?*

He pitched his body to the other side, wondering what it would be like to have children... wondering what it would be like to have children with *Amanda*.

Caught up with building the ranch and dodging the rivalry between him and Gabe, he hadn't thought about it much when his brother was still alive. *I always figured I'd be an uncle to Gabe and Amanda's kids, not the father to our own. And now, if I can't see myself as Amanda's husband, how can I see myself as our children's father?*

With a groan, he heaved himself back to the other side. *Why didn't I write to her first? Was ordering up a bride via the mail really such a stupid idea? I chided Gabe all those weeks, but maybe, secretly, I was jealous that he'd found something I hadn't—a real wife. But it didn't work out that way, did it? I didn't order a bride, she's not mine, and she'll never be mine.*

He lifted his torso with his forearm and pummeled the pillow into shape with his fist. Satisfied he'd punched the pad into a comfortable shape when he lay back down, he managed to fall into a fitful sleep.

Sometime later, he shot awake at the sound of whimpers. Thinking it was his mind re-imagining the child's wails from today, he closed his eyes again.

Another cry split his heart. Throwing back the covers, he leaped to his feet, clad only in his nightshirt. *It's Amanda! Good Lord, what's wrong?* He raced out the door and headed toward her bedroom.

Amanda writhed on the mattress, tangled up in her bedding.

David rushed to her side, calling, "Amanda! Wake up! You're having a nightmare!"

Her eyelids flew open, and she stared at him blankly. She blinked, and her eyes focused on his face.

"Oh, David," she cried, hugging him to her. "I had the most awful dream!"

"There, there," he soothed, patting her back. "It weren't nothing but a dream. Dreams ain't nothing but ghosts."

Hearing himself talk about ghosts, he winced. *Why do you listen to spirits, then, David Brown? You've been obsessed with your brother's ghost.*

Amanda clutched him closer, saying, "It seemed so real."

David eased her away, grabbing her shoulders. "Look at me, Amanda. It was only a dream. You're with me, now, see?"

When she met his gaze, his heart stopped beating. *Good God, she's beautiful.*

Her lips parted, and her breath touched his face.

His lips parted, and he inched closer. Unable to stop himself, he closed the gap and pressed his lips to hers.

Amanda let out a moan.

The feel of her mouth on his was like nothing he'd ever felt—not with Mary and certainly not with Leslie. A torrent of passion poured between their mouths and carried them away. And her warm body pressed next to him...? Divine.

Within seconds, though, the ghost of Gabe—the very thing he'd assured her wasn't real—swooped into his mind, staring at David with accusation and betrayal.

She's mine! Gabe hissed. *You can't have what's mine.*

David wrenched away from Amanda, staring at her shocked expression. "I can't do this," he said before wiping the taste of her from his lips with the back of his hand.

"Why can't you?" she pleaded, clutching his nightshirt.

"I just... I just can't." He pried her fingers from his clothing. "It ain't right."

Cursing, he fled from the room.

He rolled back and forth on his mattress in his bedroom, which now seemed as stiff and unyielding as the wrought iron doors he'd purchased for the horse stalls. He knew, technically, he hadn't done anything wrong. On paper, at least, Amanda had pledged her life to him, and by rights, he could kiss her. The kiss had started out so right—it seemed natural, like they were doing what was appropriate for two married people. But then, when guilt overtook him, it felt so wrong.

But why? She never even met Gabe! It's not like I swooped in and stole her the way Gabe had done with Leslie and the way I wanted to do when I met Amanda. I wanted to take her as an act against Gabe—my dead brother! What kind of chicken fool am I?

The morning Gabe died came rushing into his head. He'd played that day over and over since the day of Gabe's death, wanting to suss out any details that might be clues.

That day, Gabe had been out of sorts. And on the days leading up to the murder, he'd been moody, much like David had been acting of late. On one occasion, David had caught his brother brooding in the barn, dark shadows etching lines into his face. Or Gabe would excuse himself from the table before finishing a meal, claiming he wasn't hungry.

His brother ate like a wolf. Since when did he not finish one of Ada's meals?

Or, when Arlo asked Gabe and David to head downtown to the saloon for a night of drinking and carousing, Gabe had declined.

Gabe? Decline a night of fun and foolishness? His brother was always the center of attention, the life of the party.

David had brushed it off as nerves over Amanda's impending arrival. But that morning, Gabe had been incredibly dark. David had asked him about it, wanting to help if he could. Gabe had practically snarled at him, the same way that mama bear had growled when they'd faced off near the tree. So, David had pursued it no more.

David rolled onto his back and folded his arms, resting his head in his hands. Staring at the shadows on the ceiling, he murmured, "Just let it go. I couldn't save him, and I can't bring him back from the dead. So, why in tarnation do I think I can ever find happiness with the woman Gabe wanted to marry?"

Another chilling thought rocked him to his core. *I wanted revenge on Gabe by marrying his woman when I should have focused my attention on getting revenge for his murder.*

With a forceful exhale, he vowed to find whoever killed Gabe and make him pay. Only then would he be able to let things go.

Chapter Twenty-One

Before Amanda even awoke the following day, the kiss she'd shared with David in the night replayed in her mind. It had been so passionate, so caring... it spoke to a hunger she certainly felt for him. But then he'd wrenched his mouth away from hers, muttering something about how "it ain't right." He'd only been torturing her with his desire until he realized he didn't want that with her—he never would. She was his responsibility, nothing more.

And, sadly, now she knew she loved David without reciprocation. *So, I'd better learn to make the best of things out here on the ranch without pining for something I can never have.*

Yet, with this awareness of newfound love came a profound sense of loneliness. *How can I survive this unbearable isolation I feel when I'm around him?* For that, she had no answers.

Before heading to the kitchen to help Ada with chores and breakfast, she wrote a letter to Julia. *Maybe if I tell her of my feelings for David... perhaps that will ease the ache in my soul.*

She swallowed before putting pen to paper. *Oh, this is so hard. How can I confess what I don't want to admit I feel?*

Finally, she summoned some courage and began to put words to her thoughts.

My dear Julia,

I have re-read your last letter many times. It always gives me pleasure to hear from you. Perhaps you think I do not mean that, that I am caught up in this new marriage of mine. But I really do! You must know that.

We have had very warm weather here. It is enjoyable most days, which is a boon to my flourishing garden. It is not yet producing, but soon I believe it will yield a bounty of vegetables.

I am helping Ada with chores whenever I can. She has taught me to bake with sourdough starter, preserve eggs with lime, and put up jams and jellies. I've learned to make Johnnycakes and Old Comstock raspberry cream tarts, too. The latter is most delicious, especially when served with sweet cream. Oh! And there are two men, ranch hands, who work out here with David, so we must prepare much food to sustain them.

But now I must confess to you a situation of torment for me. I have fallen in love with David, though I'm afraid he does not share such feelings with me. I was taken with a nightmare last night, and he came to offer me comfort. Then, he kissed me with bold passion. Oh, Julia, it was beautiful! For a moment, I felt so loved. But then he wrenched himself away as if he realized who he was with and that I am not the one who holds his heart. He made it clear he does not want to be with me.

How I wish I were the one he wanted! At times, we share laughter and companionship. He finds my clumsiness quite funny, and not in a cruel way. He says it is a delight to behold, and he will teach me how to work hard and gain some grace. I sure hope so. At those times, I find myself feeling like the Amanda I once knew, who possessed a carefree attitude and a measure of joy.

But then he withdraws and will not speak to me. He finds reasons to get away from me to be with his horses or perform chores I know he has already done. You can see, can't you, how much he must dislike me?

I wish you could come to visit me, but I know you will soon be busy with your upcoming nuptials. I wish you all the best in your union with Marshall. You are so fortunate to be marrying out of love instead of duty. Now I think my notion of being someone's mail-order bride was foolish. The curse of bad luck that befell me when John and Jacob died continues to plague me. But we all make mistakes, and this one is mine to bear.

Please hold me in your prayers that I find the strength to endure this loneliness. I hope you will excuse me for not writing more, but I do not always know what to say. I hope I will hear from you soon.

Your friend,

Amanda

She folded the paper in half and then in half again, effectively shutting away her feelings. But still, she wondered if her luck would ever turn for the better.

A knock at the door startled her out of her musings.

"Yes, what is it?" she said, pulling her nightgown tightly around her neck.

"It's Ada. Did you forget that we have church this morning?"

"Oh! I'm sorry. Let me make haste to prepare! I'll be out shortly."

"You're fine, dear. The men have already eaten and are out with their chores. I've saved you some breakfast, but we haven't much time," Ada said.

"Thank you, Ada. I'll be out soon."

She quickly dressed in her Sunday clothes, consisting of a corset and a petticoat beneath a blue calico dress with smocking along the bodice. She'd fashioned the lovely garment with her own hand. It had a white lace collar and lace at the end of the sleeves, and Julia had told Amanda it "brought out her eyes." After she finished dressing, she brushed her hair until it shone and then twisted it high atop her head.

Once dressed and groomed, she hurried down the hall toward the kitchen.

Ada looked up from the counter where she stood washing dishes. "I managed to save you some Johnnycakes and bacon. Go on and eat it right quick before one of them boys get a notion for a third helping."

"Thank you, Ada. I'm sorry I didn't help you with breakfast. It won't happen again." She poured the last of the bitter coffee from the pot in the center of the table and hurriedly consumed her meal.

When Amanda rose to help finish with the cleaning up, Ada said, "We'll get to this when we return. Let's head on out to the wagon." She paused and appraised Amanda with a sweeping gaze. "You look lovely, dear. David will be so pleased."

Amanda blushed despite what she knew to be true—David didn't want her at all.

When she stepped from the house, the wagon was ready to go. Ada strode by her side as they headed toward their transportation.

David sat on the buckboard holding the reins, staring straight ahead. He'd dressed in a clean blue shirt and trousers, and his hair had been combed back from his handsome face.

Amanda made her way around to the opposite side of the wagon, with Ada trailing behind her. When they reached the cart, Ada said, "You get on up there next to your husband."

David gave her a side-eye, and for a second, their eyes locked. But then, as usual, he looked away, and his lips pressed tightly together.

Amanda climbed on the buckboard and sat as close as she had to, with as much space as she could manage. On her other side, Ada pressed close to Amanda.

David clucked to Chester, and away they went.

Dew clung to the few plants lining the wagon trail, and the sweet fragrance of wildflowers tickled Amanda's nose. A cloudless blue sky stretched in all directions, from mountains to plains.

Well aware of David's every move, pressed as she was against him, Amanda tried to keep her spirits high by enjoying the beauty all around her. Ada kept her mind occupied with a conversation about some recipe or another she wanted to try.

Amanda responded politely. But the entire journey, she kept her attention on David, hoping he'd tell her she looked nice or maybe offer to give her another lesson with Chester.

However, he stayed mute, as usual.

As they approached the town, her spirits began to lift. Increasingly, she looked forward to church. It gave her a chance to socialize with some of the other women from town. It also gave her something to think about other than her loveless marriage.

When they arrived at the whitewashed church, she brightened. Seeing the church, with its single spire towering over the building, warmed her heart. Already, several families and their children were making their way toward the entrance.

I so wish I could have children one day.

David pulled the wagon to a stop beneath a tree, next to other wagons and horses. And then he stepped from the buckboard. After securing Chester, he made his way to the other side of the wagon and helped Ada from her seat, and then lifted his hand to Amanda.

When they touched, Amanda felt a jolt of electricity pass between them, making a small gasp escape her lips.

David's eyes raked her body briefly, and then he glanced away.

Everything was so confusing about David. Especially when he placed his hand upon Amanda's back to guide her toward the church. She imagined his hand as a gesture of ownership—that by placing it at her back, he was telling everyone that she belonged to him.

But she knew this to be a foolish idea.

Inside the nave, they took their seats in the polished wood pews. Sitting between her husband and Ada, Amanda once more imagined herself to be a part of a happy family with an adoring husband. She clung to this idea throughout the entire sermon as Preacher Bascom delivered his message.

But when the enlightening talk ended, David excused himself, saying he needed to speak with the sheriff. He exited the pews and quickly departed, leaving Amanda to face the truth about their relationship, not the silly story she'd concocted about how much he adored her.

She followed Ada out to the lawn, where they stood with a group of women.

Ada and the others engaged in a lively conversation while Amanda simply observed. She kept glancing toward her husband, who stood several yards away, involved in what looked like a heated discussion. *What's he talking about? Why does it look more like an argument than a conversation?*

Her attention was yanked away when someone interrupted her. Amanda turned to see a woman she'd never met before.

"Oh, hello," she said to the beautiful, dark-haired young woman. "I haven't seen you here before. Are you new to the area?"

The thought of meeting someone her age who had only recently arrived gave her a thrill. *Maybe we can be friends? Oh, how I'd love a new friend in this town.*

The woman eyed Amanda with a cold glare.

For a second, Amanda was taken aback. *I don't know you, and you're looking at me like I've done something wrong.*

But then, the glare disappeared, her eyes softened, and the striking woman's lips curved into a smile. "Hello," she said, extending her hand. "I'm so pleased to finally meet you. I heard about your marriage to David, and I wanted to introduce myself. I'm afraid I've been away visiting relatives."

Amanda shook the woman's hand, eager to make her acquaintance. "Hello! Yes, we married several weeks ago. I'm from Virginia City. And you?"

"Oh, I grew up around here," the woman said coolly. "How long have you known David?"

Amanda's cheeks and neck grew warm. *How much should I tell this woman? Do I say I arrived as a mail-order bride?* Deciding against that idea, she said, "Not long. But he's a wonderful man."

"He is," the woman said, and her gaze slid past Amanda.

Amanda's head swiveled to see what had caught her attention. *She's looking at David. Why?* When she pivoted her head to regard the woman again, she paused. *Are those tears in her eyes?*

"Oh, I apologize. Where are my manners?" The lovely brunette retrieved a fine handkerchief from her sleeve and dabbed at her eyes. "This dust..." she said, waving the handkerchief back and forth. She tucked the soft cloth back in her sleeve. "Allow me to introduce myself. My name is Leslie."

"Leslie! I'm Amanda. I'm so pleased to meet you. Perhaps we can be friends." Her heart surged with hope.

"Perhaps," Leslie said. She reached up to pat her glistening hair, smoothing a few stray hairs away from her face. "I'll be seeing you," she said before casting her gaze over Amanda's shoulder.

Amanda was left with an unpleasant feeling churning around in her insides. *Leslie seems to already dislike me... could this be more of the bad luck that follows me around like a stray dog?*

Chapter Twenty-Two

As David was heading back to gather Amanda and Ada for their departure, he pulled up short to see Leslie standing with Amanda. *What in tarnation is she doing here? I told her I never wanted to see her again after Gabe stole her and she came crawling back to me.*

When he stood in front of Amanda, he ignored Leslie. "Let's go," he said, reaching for Amanda's arm.

"David," Leslie said in that too-charming, snake-oil-like voice of hers.

"Hello, Leslie," he said without making eye contact.

Amanda's gaze flickered between him and Leslie.

"Go get in the wagon. I have chores to get to," he snapped.

"All right. I'm going to go get Ada and say goodbye to Preacher Bascom," Amanda said, a frown creasing her lovely face.

"Fine," he said, pivoting to make a beeline to the wagon and get away from Leslie. "Go on then and get Ada."

Amanda departed, and he made haste for the wagon.

As his footfalls landed, he heard lighter footsteps coming up behind him. He glanced over his shoulder to see Leslie following him. Head down, he sped up.

When he arrived at the cart, he unwrapped Chester's reins from the railing he'd tied him to. "Ready to go, Chester?" he said, patting the horse's neck. "Did you have a good nap?"

"David!" Leslie called.

He ignored her and ran his hands along Chester's side. "You're a good old horse, Chester."

When her hand landed on his arm, he whirled around. "What in tarnation are you doing?"

"I can't believe I returned from my trip to find you *married*," she said, her eyes moist.

His stomach tightened. *She's probably faking her tears.* "What I do or don't do is none of your business. Don't you remember I told you to stay away from me?"

"I knew you didn't mean it. I thought you just needed time, and we'd reconnect when I returned. My grandmother's doing better," she said. "She's well again."

"Good for her. Now, if you'll excuse me, I need to get back to the ranch." He started to climb onto the buckboard, but Leslie scooted in his way.

"David, don't. I know you still love me. We had a good thing." She placed her forearms on his chest, clutching his collar with her fingertips.

Even the smell of her rankled his nose. He took a step back, and her hands fluttered to her sides. "We had no such thing. We courted for a bit, that's all. And then you left to be with my brother." The memory stabbed his heart with bitterness.

"Yes, but I came back to you. Gabe never wanted me the way you did." She retrieved a handkerchief and dabbed at her eyes.

"And I never wanted you, so, there you go. Now, would you please get out of my way so I can get to my business?" He checked the back of the wagon for no reason other than to distract himself from Leslie's presence.

"You can't mean that," she cried, tears tracking down her cheeks.

"I can, and I do. We were trying things out, is all. And it didn't work." Since he couldn't get to the buckboard, he began fussing with the harness, ensuring the tracer was snug and the belts all adequately secured.

"Then why were you so furious with your brother?" she said.

"That's personal. It had nothing to do with you." *And everything to do with our rivalry.*

"Didn't it? I overheard you having an argument about me."

David's nostrils flared as he glared at Leslie. "And I just got through telling you my business was with Gabe, not with you."

"I'm sorry to hear of Gabe's death," she said, her tone softening.

"Me, too," he said. But a disturbing thought burrowed into his brain. *At least I have Amanda. No way I would be with her if Gabe were still alive. Those two would be happily married, and I'd be on the outside, as usual.*

This thought sent his guilt about marrying Amanda to spinning. At this point, his motivation for marrying her was all murky. *Did I marry her out of revenge to get back at my brother, who couldn't even defend himself? Did I marry her out of obligation since she'd come so far? Or did I marry her because she's so pretty and I'm lonely?*

The whole thing was so confusing, he couldn't wrap his head around it.

"How did it happen?" Leslie said, her voice all low and soothing.

He afforded her a side-eye.

"Gabe's death... how did it happen?" she said again.

David stayed mute, still fussing with the harness, not wanting to discuss anything with Leslie.

She sidled toward him and reached for his hand.

He snatched it away from her and moved toward Chester's rump.

"I'm the one who can make you happy, David. *Me*, not your frumpy wife."

Bile shot into the back of his throat as he whirled to face her. "Now, you look here. Amanda is anything but frumpy. She's got more gumption than you have in your little finger. And I'm in love with her."

Surprise shot through him at his confession. He blinked a few times before shaking his head.

Leslie's expression turned cruel. "You're always taking your brother's *leftovers*, David."

That sentence landed like a hammer in his gut, leaving him speechless. *My brother's leftovers...* The thought tied his tongue in knots.

He lifted his gaze over the top of Chester's behind to see Amanda and Ada approaching him.

Both wore the same concerned, eyebrows-furrowed expression.

Can you blame them when I'm in the middle of an argument with a woman I never truly cared for? "Are you ready to go?" he called to them, brushing past Leslie to round Chester's rump.

"Yes," Ada said. "Are *you?*"

"I'm fine. Ready to head back, that's for sure." He strode toward the buckboard and helped Amanda into the wagon.

Her eyes bore signs of hurt and betrayal as she lifted her skirts and settled into her seat.

Ada regarded him with a sympathetic gaze.

Well, at least one woman isn't angry with me, he thought as he assisted her onto the seat. Not caring to offer any explanation, he strode around the front of Chester, hopped onto the buckboard, and never bothered to spare a glance in Leslie's direction. Instead, he shook the reins, adding a cluck, and urged Chester into his slow plod.

No one spoke as they lurched down the dusty road, heading through town. David nodded to a couple of people passing in the opposite direction by wagon or horseback but made no effort to say anything. When they passed the pharmacy, he thought about stopping to get something for some aches and pains he'd been experiencing but then changed his mind. *Leslie will probably follow me there.* He wanted to get back to the safety and comfort of his own ranch and put this confrontation with Leslie behind him. Besides, he had other things to think about.

His conversation with the sheriff had gotten him nowhere. When he'd asked if Slinger had any news, the sheriff had said no. In fact, he'd seemed altogether disinterested in the case, saying some nonsense about trouble to the south with the Indians or something. After that, he mentioned hiring a new deputy sheriff to help him see to all the trouble the Indians were causing. David hadn't paid it no mind since he'd been focused on news of his brother. *Slinger's answers seemed so vague... it's almost as if he's hiding something.* He'd left the conversation with the sheriff with a bad taste in his mouth.

Once they left town, his hackles rose and a sense of unease overtook him as if something, or someone was following him. He continuously looked over his shoulder and scanned his whereabouts for signs of danger.

The wagon shook and jostled across the plains, leaving clouds of dust in its wake, obscuring his vision. Chester's ears pivoted back and forth, hearing things David couldn't hear.

As they climbed into the hills, surrounded by trees, his anxiety increased. He tugged on the reins and they stopped.

Amanda looked up at him, questions in her eyes.

Ada said, "Is everything all right?"

"I ain't sure. I'm a little spooked, is all. It's probably nothing. I didn't get much sleep last night." His gaze slid toward Amanda and quickly flitted away.

"Yes, that can change one's disposition," Ada said soothingly.

As they approached the shallow creek bed that crossed the trail, he thought he heard a branch snap. *It could be anything. Could be a bear or a cougar... even a deer. Or maybe it's them Indians we saw when we rescued that little boy.* His hands tensed around the reins.

Chester picked his way through the brackish water lined with stones to get to the other side. The wagon lurched and creaked but then sought purchase on dry land again. David stayed alert, watching, listening for signs of danger. When they left the trees and entered a less forested area, he relaxed somewhat, and his thoughts drifted back to the conversation with the sheriff. *I got a whole lot of nothing from that bit of jaw wobbling. If I'm going to find out anything about Gabe's death, I will have to do it myself—I sure can't count on the sheriff.*

As they approached the ranch, David again cast his gaze to and fro. *Something's not right. I just know it.*

Beside him, Amanda worried her hands round and round.

David wanted to soothe her, to tell her everything was all right, that he'd protect her. But what was he to protect her from? There was no evidence to support his unease.

However, he'd lived too long on this earth to not trust his instincts. Something terrible was about to happen. So, he vowed to make sure everything was locked tight and put to bed right before he turned in tonight.

And then he'd head to bed himself, with a rifle by his side.

Chapter Twenty-Three

The entire ride home from church, Amanda replayed the image of Leslie and David in a heated conversation. *They looked altogether too familiar with one another. Why hasn't he mentioned Leslie to me?*

Yet now she knew why the woman had looked at her with such a glare. It was clear something was going on between Leslie and David.

But what? Amanda's brain ached as she tried to sort it out.

As usual, David stayed silent by her side. His moods were becoming just a part of who he was; she was beginning to see him as a thoughtful, caring person—just not caring about her. When he spoke to Ada or even his hired hands, he seemed cordial, warm even. But with her, it was as if blocks of ice fell between them.

As they trekked across the dry plains, dotted with low-growing shrubs, a realization formed. *Oh, I'm so stupid. Leslie and David must be in love! Why didn't I see that? It has to be the answer.*

Leslie had touched him with an intimacy Amanda had never presumed with David. *She'd instantly moved closer to him and expected to resume the kind of relationship she probably shared with David before I arrived. Oh, I'm such a fool. Why didn't I consider this before?*

Amanda couldn't be jealous or upset—she'd been the one to bungle her way into his life. But her sorrow deepened.

I'm sure he didn't plan on marrying me. He probably thought to ask Leslie for her hand in marriage when she returned. And then I stepped in and spoiled his plans while he'd done what he thought was proper. He took it upon himself to make right on something his brother had initiated—he'd gone and married me. But he couldn't love me--he's in love with Leslie!

As the horse plodded along, carrying them back home, the loneliness inside her grew. A vast chasm of sorrow formed between her and David. She'd never be able to connect with him. Now she truly knew she'd carry this unrequited love with her for the rest of her days. And any musings she might have had when she arrived to birth her husband's babies would never come to pass.

I'll be just like Ada, toiling away on the ranch with no children to teach, to keep company with, or to share the companionship of family.

As they entered the woods, David's demeanor changed. His posture stiffened, and he clutched the reins as if they might escape from his hands. As a result, Amanda fretted, wringing her hands over and over the entire journey home. Only when the wagon came to a stop near the barn was she able to relax.

David helped Amanda and Ada from the wagon and led the horse and cart toward the barn.

"Let's finish our clean-up and set to making supper, shall we?" Ada said to Amanda.

After giving a longing glance at David's back, she turned her attention to Ada. "Of course."

After removing her Sunday best clothing, Amanda dressed in her usual work clothes consisting of a slightly shorter dress with weights fitted into the hem. She made her way down the hall to help Ada.

Inside the kitchen, Amanda scrubbed the dried food on the pots, pans, and dishes. At the same time, Ada bustled about the kitchen preparing the meal.

By the time Amanda got the last pot clean, the kitchen was filled with the fragrant scents of baking sourdough bread, side pork, and bubbling hot gravy.

Ada set a pie tin in the oven, filled with apples and cinnamon and covered with a lattice crust. When she closed the oven door, she turned to Amanda and said, "Why don't you go take a rest while our supper is cooking? I'll come to get you when it's time to set the table."

"Thank you, Ada," Amanda said before heading back to her room.

There, she retrieved her trusty pen and paper and set to writing another letter to Julia.

My dear Julia,

Today, we went to church. I am meeting more ladies at church and forming connections, which, as you know, is a balm to my heart. I look forward to Sundays as it gives me a chance to escape my tiresome thoughts.

Our preacher gave a lovely sermon today about the benefits of forgiveness. I'm afraid this is a topic I must embrace for reasons I shall soon reveal. Oh, Julia, today it was made clear to me why David can never love me—at church, I was approached by a lovely young woman, similar in age to me. Of course, her beauty was exceptional, leaving me to feel as if I am quite plain. And I caught her arguing with David--they were arguing, Julia, and it was quite clear to me that they are in love. She holds the key to his heart.

How can I be upset or angry with him? Instead, I am filled with sorrow for what I cannot change and did not intend.

He did not plan for my arrival. I came here on the heels of his grief for his brother, Gabe, who had been so cruelly taken from his life. After seeing David with Leslie—for that is her name—I am confident she was his intended betrothed, and she arrived to bring him joy.

Let us not speak of this anymore, for I know I shall not. Instead, I shall tuck this tale into the bosom of our friendship, never to speak of it again. My pride will not allow me to. Rather, I shall live out my days here, knowing that I have brought sorrow into this household when there should only be happiness with Leslie's arrival.

Pray for my strength and endurance, as I shall pray for your happiness.

Your friend forever,

Amanda

After folding the letter, she placed it carefully on the little table where she kept her writing implements. With her head held high, she exited to the kitchen, determined to not be more of a burden to David than she already had become. She would strive to make him happy, even if it meant letting him go.

Chapter Twenty-Four

That same sense of unease that had followed him home in the wagon today, with Amanda and Ada by his side, lingered as David did his chores in the barn. He removed the harness from Chester, brushed him down, and shut him in his stall with fresh water and hay. After that, he set to cleaning and polishing the harness, halter, and reins. Using a cloth and some castile soap, he carefully wiped down the leather, making sure to remove all traces of dust and grime from their travels. Neatsfoot oil, a yellow oil manufactured from the shin bones and feet of cattle, was applied next. As he worked, he meticulously buffed the leather with a cotton rag until it shone all over.

All the while, he kept looking over his shoulder and jumping at random sounds.

When Michael came into the barn, David said, "You seen anything suspicious around here today?"

Michael leaned against the wooden wall, scratching his head. "Suspicious like what?" He spat a mouthful of brown phlegm from his mouth onto the wooden floor and used his tongue to reposition the wad of chewing tobacco in his cheek.

"I don't know... suspicious like anyone ride past on horseback in the distance, or did the horses seem off?" David felt like a fool for even asking.

"Nope," said Michael, spitting another wad of phlegm. "Can't say that I have. Want me to keep an eye out?"

"Sure, you do that. I came home feeling spooked about something and can't quite reckon what." David hung the reins on the peg affixed to the tack room wall, wiped his hands with the cleanest place on the rag he could find, and exited the room, closing the door behind him. "It's probably nothing. I ain't been getting much sleep lately."

"That'll do it to a man," Michael commiserated. "You reckon supper's ready?"

"Ada will let us know," he said. "You finish with that fencing?"

"Yep," Michael said. "That's what I came to tell you. We finished it up and wonder what you want us to do next."

"Why don't you and Billy finish up for the day and head on inside. You have the day off tomorrow, and we're all caught up, so…"

Michael nodded and turned to exit.

When David stepped outside the barn, long shadows stretched across the land. He scanned his surroundings, finding nothing out of sorts. The horses grazed in the pasture, the cattle rested beneath a tree, and chickens clucked in the henhouse yard.

His gaze lingered on Amanda's garden.

She spent her days out there toiling, all by her lonesome. He'd thought to help her a time or two but never got up the nerve. She'd done a fine job of making neat rows, already flourishing with life.

A surge of pride filled his heart for her handiwork before pivoting to head inside.

When he entered the kitchen, Billy and Michael sat around the table, helping themselves to jars full of fresh milk.

Ada turned from the stove and said, "There you are. I was just going to go fetch you. Supper's ready."

"I can see that," he said, taking his seat. "Where's Amanda?"

"Oh, she's feeling poorly. She asked to be excused from supper. I sure hope she's not coming down with the consumption." Ada spun around with a platter of pork and set it in the center of the table.

Fear lanced David's heart. "Why would you say that?"

"Poor dear looked awful when we arrived home from church," Ada said, retrieving the sourdough bread she'd baked.

David scratched the side of his head. Amanda had every right to look awful, what with seeing him and Leslie arguing. "She'll come around. Just needs a rest, is all." He cut a slice of pork and heaped it on his plate.

"If you say so," Ada said, lifting an eyebrow in a knowing look. She knew full well how much he despised Leslie.

David shook his head and set to wolfing down his meal.

After supper, he made his way down the hall to check on Amanda. He turned the doorknob, only to find it locked. Like a lovesick idiot, he pressed his ear to the door, listening. When he heard nothing, he eased away from the door and headed for his own room to turn in.

***

The following morning, he awoke at dawn, dressed, and headed for the kitchen.

Relieved to see Amanda bustling around the kitchen, he said, "You feeling all right?"

She smiled at him and said, "Yes, David, thank you. I just needed some rest."

David nodded and turned to Ada. "I'm thinking of heading back into town today. I'm fixing to talk to that new deputy sheriff."

"Oh? I didn't know there was a new deputy sheriff," Ada said, flipping the flapjacks in the griddle.

"Slinger let me know yesterday when I spoke to him," David said.

Ada met his gaze. "Did he now? Any other news?"

"Nope." David shook his head. "That's why I thought I might go have a conversation with the deputy."

"I need some things at the general store," Ada said. "Mind if Amanda and I tag along?"

"Suit yourself," he said, his gaze sliding toward Amanda.

Sorrow flickered across her face, as sure as he was standing here. But it was quickly replaced with a smile that didn't quite meet her eyes.

"Yes, I need some more supplies for the garden, if you don't mind," she said.

"I don't mind. I'll drop you and Ada off at the general store and return to fetch you when I'm done with my conversation," David said.

"All right, then," Ada said.

***

After dropping the two women off in town, David strode down the wooden sidewalk, heading for the sheriff's, which sat down the road apiece on the other side of the feed store. He peered in the window before entering, but the room inside looked empty.

Behind him, a man's voice said, "Can I help you?"

David whirled around to find a uniformed man with a shiny star affixed to his shirt, identifying him as the deputy.

"I'm David Brown," David said, extending his hand.

"Deputy John Angus," the man said, shaking David's hand.

His handshake felt sure, and he looked David right in the eye when he spoke. He stood a mite taller than David with broad shoulders and an ample belly hanging over his belt.

"Aren't you the owner of that ranch several miles yonder in the hills?" Deputy Angus inclined his head in the direction of David's home. "Past that little spit of a creek?"

"That's my home, yes, sir." David nodded.

"I've heard you raise some mighty fine horse stock. I was talking to a fellow named Arlo who told me as much."

David's chest puffed with pride. "I reckon I do."

The deputy nodded. "I'm fixing to get another horse as soon as I'm settled. Maybe I'll come out and take a look."

"I've been working a couple of geldings that I'm thinking to sell soon. They're fine horses. Real stable temperaments. Come on out as soon as you're ready." David smiled.

"I'll sure do that. So, what can I do for you?" Deputy Angus said. He reached past David and opened the door to his and Slinger's office. "Would you like to come inside?"

David nodded and followed him into the building.

Inside, a large wooden desk and sturdy wooden chair occupied a space in the center of the room. Another smaller desk sat in the corner. An oil lantern glowed in the middle of the desk, surrounded by several pieces of parchment. A gun rack hung on the wall next to the desk, holding several rifles. At the back of the room, past a potbelly stove, stood two empty jail cells.

Deputy Angus perched his behind on the edge of the desk, loosely crossed his arms over his chest, and said, "What's on your mind?"

"My brother was shot and killed several weeks ago. I found him with a bullet hole clean through his head." David filled in the details, then added, "And I don't think Slinger's taking it too seriously. I've asked him to look into the case, but when I spoke with him yesterday, he seemed more concerned with some Indian trouble."

Angus's eyebrows shot up. "This is news to me—both the death of your brother and the Indian trouble. I've heard no such thing."

David shifted where he stood. "Not a thing?" *That sounds mighty suspicious. Why wouldn't Slinger have informed his deputy if there's trouble? And why hasn't he mentioned anything about Gabe's murder?*

"Nope. And we sat down at length just this morning to go over my duties. Tell you what... I'll ask around and make some inquiries. I'll follow up with you next time you're in town."

"I'd appreciate that, Deputy," David said. He made his farewells and exited the building, heading back toward the general store.

Amanda and Ada stood outside the store, overseeing the young lad who loaded the wagon with their supplies.

Amanda's eyes sparkled with excitement as she chatted with Ada. "These seedlings will make a fine addition to the garden."

"I believe you're right," Ada said, lifting her gaze to David. "How did your meeting go?" she said.

David glanced at her, and then his attention fixed on Amanda. Her excitement seemed to blow away as if buffeted by a gust of wind when she looked at him.

He frowned and turned back to Ada. "Well enough, I suppose. He's going to look into something for me. He seems like a good, honest man."

"That would be a change," Ada said with a sniff.

David helped the women back in the wagon and set off toward the ranch.

When they arrived home, the women headed for the house while David set to unloading the wagon and seeing to Chester's care. Leading Chester, he entered the barn, unhooked the wagon, and removed the harness and fittings. As he crossed the barn, harness in hand, he noticed the tack room door was ajar. *I don't recall leaving it open.* Frowning, he opened the door wider and peered inside.

A set of reins had fallen from one of the pegs and lay in a heap on the floor. Nearby, one of the saddles sat askew on the saddle rack. *This don't look right. Could the ranch hands have done this?* He shook his head. *Nope, they have the day off and said they were headed into town.*

After hanging the tack, he stooped to pick up the fallen reins and righted the cockeyed saddle before exiting and closing the door. That was when he noticed a bale of hay had toppled from the stack in the corner. No way could a bale of hay have fallen unless someone had shoved it.

What in the world is going on here? He crossed toward the corner, hefted the bale, and pitched it on top of a lower bale. Then, he scrutinized the building and the stalls, looking for something else amiss. Finding nothing, he rubbed his jaw. The hairs on the back of his neck prickled. Someone had been snooping around here today while he was gone. He just knew it. He didn't have the proof other than the reins, the saddle, and the bale of hay.

Blue trotted around the corner, limping, to greet him.

"Hey, Blue," he said, frowning as he patted the dog's head.

Blue licked his hand in greeting. He kept lifting and lowering his rear leg as if unable to bear weight on it.

"Yeah, I missed you, too," David said, crouching to examine Blue's hind leg. "What's gone and happened to your leg?"

Blue whined and whimpered when David touched the dog's stifle.

David's eyes narrowed. "Did someone land a kick on you with his boot?"

Blue licked his hand again.

"Well, let's get you into the house and let Ada fix you up. What do you say?" David scratched the back of his head and gritted his teeth.

He'd found his proof. Sure, one of the horses could have kicked his dog, but Blue knew to stay away from the horses' hind end. And the prickles rolling up and down his spine told David different—someone or several people had violated his property.

And he was determined to find out who.

Chapter Twenty-Five

All day, as she'd helped in the kitchen and changed linens in each bedroom, a niggling thought worried Amanda's brain. Something was bothering David. He'd been spooked when they'd returned from church two days ago. And last night, when he'd come in from chores, he'd brought in the dog who had a lame leg.

Amanda had overheard Ada and David as they tended to the dog's wound saying something about "things amiss in the barn" and "Old Blue's too smart to get in the way of a horse's hoof."

She wished he'd confide in her someday, but, even more, she hoped no one was lurking about outside. That notion had her glancing out the window and looking over her shoulder.

And that whole situation with Leslie kept resurfacing in her mind. *What should I do? Should I try to talk to David about it?* She shook her head. Since David barely talked to her at all, what chance of success did she possibly have talking to him about his love life with another woman?

"Amanda," Ada called from the kitchen as Amanda tucked clean linens onto David's mattress.

"Yes, Ada?" she called back.

"Can you come into the kitchen, please?"

"Yes, of course, I'll be right there." She smoothed the bedding on David's mattress and gave his room one last appraising glance before exiting. As she strode down the hallway, a thought occurred to her. *What if I ask for Ada's advice about Leslie?* Thinking that might not be a bad idea, she entered the kitchen.

"Let's make some corn dodgers as a midday snack. What do you think?" Ada said, reaching for a tin of cornmeal.

"What are corn dodgers?"

"Oh, they're delicious," Ada said. She retrieved a large ceramic bowl from a shelf. "We make a batter of cornmeal, boiling water, and salt and fry it in pork fat."

"That does sound good," Amanda said, reaching for her apron, which hung on a peg on the wall. As she tied it around her waist, she was just about to ask Ada about Leslie when a knock sounded on the front door.

Ada frowned. "Who could that be?" She exited the kitchen to answer the knock.

Amanda crossed the room to see who'd come over. When Ada opened the door, Sheriff Slinger stood on the porch. Recalling the conversation she'd had with Ada about avoiding Sheriff Slinger, Amanda shrank back, out of eyesight.

"Afternoon, Miss Ada," the sheriff said.

"Hello, Sheriff," Ada said, her tone of voice becoming icy. "Can I help you?"

"I sure hope so. I've got some business to talk about with David. Mind if I come in?"

Ada hesitated, then said, "Why don't you wait on the porch? I'll call him in from the barn."

The sheriff tipped his hat and said, "I'd be much obliged to have a drink of water if you don't mind."

Ada called into the kitchen. "Amanda, get the sheriff a jar of water. I'm going to fetch David, and I'll be right back."

"All right," Amanda called back as a shiver cascaded down her back. She didn't want to even be near the man, let alone fetch him some water.

After grabbing a jar from the shelf, she filled it with cold water from the pitcher and sauntered toward the front door.

Thankfully, Sheriff Slinger's attention was fixed on David, who strode from the barn with a frown on his face.

"Here's your water, Sheriff," she said timidly, extending it to him.

His head swiveled, and he cast a lazy eye up and down her body.

Her free hand lifted to her chest protectively.

"Afternoon, Mrs. Brown," he said with a leer.

The sheriff took a step in her direction when David said, "Amanda, just leave it on the railing and head back in the house."

Warmed by his apparent concern, she did as asked, leaving the front door ajar so she could listen.

"Do you have some news about Gabe's death?" David said.

"I do. We may have found a clue." The sheriff took the jar from the railing and lifted it to his lips.

"What's the clue?" David said.

Sheriff Slinger tipped his head back and drained the jar before replacing it on the railing. "You know I want to do right by you and your brother's death."

David scratched the back of his neck. "So you say."

"It's important to me that the people of this town are well cared for—that their requests are taken seriously." Slinger hooked his thumbs in his belt loops. "If you or anyone has a problem, you know you can come to me for answers."

David frowned as he listened.

What's the sheriff going on about? Amanda wondered.

"I've told you before how I grew up poor," the sheriff continued.

"Yes, you have," David said, lifting his hat, smoothing his hair back, and replacing the Stetson. "Many times."

"And I've worked hard to make a name for myself in Goldsprings." Sheriff Slinger crossed his arms over his chest.

"Did you come here to hang fire, or is there a point to your story?" David said. His expression looked spitting mad.

"I just want you to know you can trust me," the sheriff said.

"And I'd like to be able to do just that," David said, appearing perplexed.

The sheriff shifted side to side on his booted feet. "Did Gabe give you some sort of pouch or something like that before his death?"

David frowned. "No, sir, he did not. Why?"

"Mind if I check his room?" Sheriff Slinger said.

David's frown deepened. "I told you he didn't give me no pouch."

"This could be important, David. It might help us solve the whole case. Isn't that what you'd like to happen?" Sheriff

Slinger said congenially. "You were asking about your brother at church the other day. I thought in as much as you're so eager, you'd be happy to let me look around."

David's eyes narrowed as he regarded the sheriff. "I suppose there's no harm." He glanced toward the front door and spied Amanda, huddled just inside. He gave a subtle shake of his head before inclining it, indicating she move away from the door.

She scurried away from the entrance and began fussing with the sofa cushions, patting and plumping them.

Before tromping inside, David said, "What might be in this pouch that's so useful?"

"I'm afraid I can't say, David," Sheriff Slinger said. "This whole case is complicated. It might compromise things if I tell you too much."

He's lying. Amanda glanced through the crack in the door. The concerned lines on David's face indicated he didn't believe the sheriff any more than she did.

"Come on in, then, and have a look around," David said, his jaw rigid as he pushed open the door.

Amanda quickly exited toward the kitchen.

"What's the sheriff going on about?" Ada whispered once Amanda stood beside her at the counter. "His jaw's a' wobbling, but he ain't making sense."

"Something about a pouch Gabe might have given David before he died," Amanda whispered back.

"A pouch?" Ada said as she stirred her batter.

"That's what he said." Amanda crossed to the stove, adjusted the damper on the stovepipe, and lifted the iron lid on the range to check the wood fire Ada had prepared this morning. Satisfied with the heat, she retrieved the cast iron skillet and placed it on the stove.

"That don't make no sense at all. What would a pouch have to do with Gabe's death?" Ada said. She rested the spoon inside the bowl full of batter and removed the tin of pig lard from one of the shelves. Using a different spoon, she scooped several spoonfuls of the grease into the pan.

The semi-solid white pig fat immediately began to turn translucent as it melted in the pan.

Ada used the tip of the spoon to swirl the lard around.

"I don't know. It all sounded suspicious. David looked like he didn't believe what the sheriff said, especially when he mentioned something about how he couldn't say what was in the pouch because it's a complicated case." Amanda picked up the bowl of batter and brought it over to Ada.

"Sheriff Slinger's a snake-oil peddler for sure," Ada hissed. She scooped the batter into her spoon and dropped it in the pan. "I guess we'd best leave David to deal with the sheriff. David's got a good head on his shoulders. If something's amiss, he'll get to the bottom of things."

The batter sizzled in the hot fat.

Amanda hoped Ada was right.

Once the pan was full of corn dodgers, Amanda got up her courage and said, "Ada, if you don't mind, I'd like to ask you a question about something of concern."

Ada's worried glance slid toward Amanda then back to her cooking. She wiggled the tip of the spoon beneath a corn dodger and carefully flipped it. "What is it?"

"You remember that woman from church? Leslie? And David was arguing with her? He's in love with her, isn't he?" Amanda blurted, her cheeks and ears becoming hotter than the frying pan. She retrieved a platter from a shelf and laid a cotton towel over it to soak up the grease from the cooked corn dodgers.

Ada started laughing. "Oh, child, the last woman you need to worry about is Leslie. She's nothing but a hussy, and, no, David doesn't love her. They courted for a bit, and then Gabe stole her away from David. I think his ego was bruised, but not because he loved Leslie. Quite the contrary. He found her shallow and rather vindictive." She finished flipping the rest of the corn dodgers. "Is that what's had you so quiet in the wagon on our rides to and from town?"

"Yes, ma'am, I'm afraid it is."

Ada flashed Amanda a warm smile as she lifted the corn cakes from the hot oil. "I know David isn't acting like a proper husband around you, Amanda. I've watched him. I'm sure he's sorting things out in his own mind. You've got to trust in fate and in David. I've got a good feeling in my bones that things are going to turn around, and everything will work out well."

"Really?" Amanda said.

"Yes, really." She shook her head and chuckled. "David, in love with Leslie... that takes a mighty long stretch of the imagination." She began dropping more batter into the frying pan. "I don't know what it was with Gabe and David, but they always had some sort of competition between them. Gabe didn't fancy Leslie any more than David did. I think it was his competitive spirit that made him take her away from David. But I always thought he did David a favor. David can be too nice—I always wondered if he was worried he'd hurt Leslie's feelings if he cut things off."

A massive chunk of ice inside Amanda's chest began to thaw at Ada's kind words. *So he doesn't love Leslie! I'm happy I didn't get my letter to Julia in the post. She'd worry about me and my happiness.* And the thought of "everything will work out well" stirred hope in her heart. *Could Ada be right? Could I get out from underneath the curse of bad luck?*

David strode into the kitchen, deep lines of concern marring his expression.

"What was the sheriff doing in our house?" Ada said as if she knew nothing. She placed the last of the corn dodgers onto the plate.

"Oh, no good, I reckon," David said, fetching a jar from the shelf. "He was telling me one yarn after the next, beating around the bush. Once he gets his jaw to wobbling, it's hard to get it to stop." He crossed to the icebox, retrieved the pitcher, and poured himself a tall drink of water. "Gabe never gave you no pouch of something to store away, did he?"

"A pouch? Not that I recall. And why would he give me something to store away? He'd most likely give it to you." Ada handed the platter to Amanda. "Place these on the table and head outside to ring the bell for the ranch hands, will you, please?"

Amanda nodded.

"Yes, I thought as much, too," David said. "But Slinger insisted there's something on the property that Gabe must have given to us. You should have heard him go on in Gabe's bedroom." He removed his hat and raked his hair. He glanced at Amanda, and his gaze seemed to soften.

A thrill raced up Amanda's spine as she crossed to the table.

"And then, all of a sudden like, he remembered some meeting or another he had to get to straight away. I don't know, Ada. I think he's up to something." David tipped back his head and drained the glass of water.

A feeling of dread replaced Amanda's last jolt of excitement. If Sheriff Slinger were "up to something," as David had suggested, what could it be?

And, worse, what kind of havoc would it wreak upon their household?

Chapter Twenty-Six

Days passed with no sign of trouble on the ranch, making David feel like he'd been spooked over nothing. So, his thoughts turned back around to Amanda. *She deserves so much better than me. Why can't I just be nice to her?*

Riding the fence line on Kickabilly while Blue trotted next to him, he checked on the repair work Billy and Michael had done. *What could I do for Amanda that's nice?*

He glanced at Blue, who barely limped now. "Glad you're feeling better, Blue. Glad it wasn't no bone break."

The dog looked up at him, tongue lolling.

Around the bend, he came across a field of wildflowers. On impulse, he dismounted from his horse, ground-tied him, and picked a bouquet, intending to give them to Amanda.

"You won't tell, will you, Kickabilly? We'll have Ada give them to her."

Kickabilly said nothing.

"And not a word from you, either, Blue."

Blue sat and scratched at his neck with his hind foot.

"I knew you could keep a secret," he said, sliding the toe of his left boot into the stirrup, grabbing onto the saddle, and swinging his other leg over the horse's back. "You two are loyal to a fault," he added before urging Kickabilly on.

When he returned to the ranch, Amanda was out in her garden, picking weeds. Flowers in hand, he stared at her for a long moment before fear got the best of him, forcing him to head inside the house.

When he crossed into the kitchen, Ada was bustling about with meal preparation, as usual. He cleared his throat and said, "I picked these for Amanda. Will you see that she gets them?"

Ada stopped moving and turned to stare at him. "Will *I* see that she gets them? You've got legs that work as well as mine do."

David's throat tightened around his words. "I don't..." he began but couldn't think of an ending to the sentence.

"David," Ada said, shaking her head, "what is it with you? Why can't you just love your wife?"

"I..." he tried but, again, couldn't finish his thoughts.

"Dear boy... living your life and allowing love in doesn't take anything away from Gabe's death."

Her open expression made him feel all strange, like someone just lassoed his insides.

"I'm serious, David. Why do you keep on punishing yourself? I see the way you look at her when you think no one's watching." Ada's lips pressed together and she turned back to mixing whatever it was she was making—something with meat and vegetables.

"Never mind, Ada," David said, his cheeks ablaze as he set the flowers on the counter. "It's personal."

At this point, he wasn't even sure why he kept Amanda at a distance. It was like fear kept him from getting close. But didn't seem like he could do anything about it, so he pivoted and strode back outside.

He made his way into the barn, intending on cleaning any tack that needed attention. When he stepped through the doorway, however, he came to a stop.

Amanda stood in Chester's stall, feeding him sugar cubes.

A lump formed in David's throat. *She's gone and worked through her fear of horses... why can't I work through my fear of her?*

Amanda spoke to Chester in low tones, telling him what a good horse he was and "so pretty."

You're the one who's pretty, Amanda. Right now, you look as beautiful as an angel. David's heart pounded erratically in his chest as these thoughts floated through his mind. He resumed walking and cleared his throat when he stood outside the stall. "Hello, Amanda."

She turned and gave him a smile as bright as sunshine. "Hello, David."

For a second, his tongue got all tangled in his mouth. He worked it around the inside of his cheek and said, "What do you say we go for a ride again?"

"Right now?" she asked, looking up at him in such a beguiling manner all sense fled from his brain.

"Now's as good a time as any, don't you think?" he said, feeling as awkward as a teenager who'd never spoken to a girl. He continued, "I know you're no expert, but Chester, here, will take good care of you, won't you, Chester?" He patted the horse's nose.

"I'd love that, David. Let me head back inside and change my clothes." She brushed her hands off.

He frowned. "Into them bloomer britches?"

"Yes," she said, casting her gaze at the ground. "Is that okay with you?"

"Go on, then," he said, swallowing back his distaste of the strange garment. *If it makes Amanda feel better about getting on a horse, then who am I to argue?*

After she left, he saddled up Chester and Bueno, the gelding he'd mentioned to Deputy Angus, since Kickabilly had just had a workout. Bueno, a black and white Paint, had a lovely spring to his step and a smooth trot, so David looked forward to taking the horse out with Amanda.

As he led both horses out of the barn, Amanda emerged from the house. And, bloomers or no bloomers, she looked so darn fetching his knees nearly buckled. There was a new lightness to her carriage when she walked, as if a burden had been lifted. He couldn't imagine what had produced the change, but he liked it.

"So, here's Chester, all ready for you," he said, averting his eyes from her lovely face.

He placed the reins over Bueno's neck and stood by Chester's side to help Amanda into the saddle. "Here," he said, lacing his hands together so she could use him as an assist to mount Chester. "Put your foot right here, and I'll help you up."

Her shy smile melted any lingering ice in his chest.

Placing her hands on his shoulders, she fit her foot in his clasped hands. Then, reaching for the saddle horn with one hand, she gave a push to stand upright.

Chester tried to stay steady but moved to the side. Amanda yelped and nearly toppled both her and David over, but he grabbed her by the waist before she fell.

"I'm sorry," she said, her cheeks all flushed, with his hands still on her waist.

David chuckled and reluctantly let her go. "Let's try 'er again."

They exchanged a soft look before moving away from one another.

"Okay," she said, fitting her foot once again in his hands.

"Steady, now," David said.

In one smooth movement, she got herself situated in the saddle.

"I did it!" she said, grinning.

"Yes, you did. Now, here... take the reins while I mount Bueno," David said.

Whatever lightness she now carried seemed to pass into him. He swung into the saddle, feeling a kind of ease he hadn't felt in a long time—maybe ever. "Now, you know Chester takes his time to get from one place to another. He's not in a hurry. But Bueno, here, being young, gets a mite impatient. So, he might inspire Chester to speed up a little, but don't worry—Chester's the safest horse on this ranch. He takes good care of people he likes."

"And you think he likes me?" Amanda said, her lashes fluttering.

"I do indeed," David said, swallowing.

They headed down the road, talking about little nothings like her garden and his ranch chores. For the first time, David felt like they behaved like a proper married couple, sharing joy over daily life occurrences.

"How would you like to see a lovely little lake up yonder?" he said, inclining his head to the right.

"Oh, I'd love that!" she cooed.

The horses climbed up the forested hill. Chester moved with slow, elderly grace while Bueno moved with the enthusiasm of the young, as if eager to get to the top. When they stepped free from the trees, ahead lay the lake, sparkling in the sunshine.

"Oh, David! What a wonder!"

"Let me dismount and help you down," David said as he swung his leg over the saddle. He rested the reins on Bueno's neck and crossed to Chester. Then, he held his arms up high to Amanda.

She leaned forward, grabbed his shoulders, and slid to the ground, brushing across his torso as she did.

The contact sent a jolt of pleasure humming through him. For a second, he let his arms linger around Amanda's waist before releasing her. Their eyes locked, and her mouth parted, and, for a few tender moments, he considered kissing those sweet lips.

Instead, he backed away, saying, "You did real good on old Chester. I told you he'd treat you right."

"He did. I felt safe on him. Your horse seems more spirited," she said, clasping her hands in front and swaying side to side.

"Oh, he's young, is all. I've only been working him a short time, but he'll be a real fine horse. The deputy wants to come out and take a look at him." David's gaze kept darting to her lips.

"Does he? You're a good horseman, David," she said.

This sentiment set his cheeks ablaze. He shifted back and forth and said, "Let's go take a gander at that lake, shall we?"

213

She smiled and started to sashay toward the water, moving in a carefree manner.

The lake was surrounded by trees on the opposite side. Rocks, sand, and dirt circled the lakeside where they stood. When Amanda got close to the water, she sat on a rock and carefully untied her sturdy shoes.

"What in the dickens are you doing?" he asked, propping his hands on his hips.

"I'm going to wade in the lake. Take your boots off." She smiled again, and her face lit up with mischief.

"I ain't going to take my boots off, girl," he said.

"Come on, David. Wade in the water with me." She dropped one shoe in the dirt, then the other, and then removed her socks. Then, she hiked up her skirt in her hands and picked her way into the water.

David stood mesmerized on the shore, unable to tear his gaze away.

Once she stood up to her ankles, she pivoted and taunted him. "Take your boots off."

"No, I ain't going to do it," he said.

"Chicken." She leaned forward, scooped up a handful of water, and flung it at him.

The water splashed his face with a shocking jolt.

He sucked in a gasp, then chucked his boots one at a time and hurriedly peeled off his socks. As he raced into the lake, Amanda squealed and began splashing him with handfuls of water. He reciprocated, using his feet, hands, even his cowboy hat to get her good and wet.

When they were both soaked, David took her hand and led her from the lake. Thankful for the blazing sun, he sat on a rock and pulled her to a rock next to his. "We'll need to sit a spell to dry off."

She grinned. "We will."

"You're a hoot, Amanda."

Her grin turned shy.

On impulse, he said, "Tell me what you were like when you were a little girl."

She seized her long ponytail, which had fallen from her up-do, and wrung the water out. "I was mostly happy. I used to play and do boy things with my brother Jacob and John, Julia's brother. We'd take off into the woods and play cowboys and Indians or wade through the stream by our house. Sometimes, we'd use sticks to make rivers at the edge of the stream. Or we'd climb trees and get into all sorts of shenanigans." A wistfulness made her voice all soft and sweet.

"Did you now?" David picked up a stick and handed it to her. "Show me how you'd make a river."

A shy smile crept across her face. "Oh, those were silly kid's games. I'd place the tip of my stick in the stream, like so..." She reached past David toward the edge of the lake. "And then dig a line like this." Her stick dragged through the mud, creating a tiny stream for the water to flow. "I'd imagine weensy little animals sipping from my tiny river, or bitty moms heading down to the stream with their wee buckets...." Her cheeks grew flushed as she spoke.

David eyed her, mesmerized. Her expression looked so soft and pretty. *I ain't never seen no one as beautiful as Amanda.*

"But Jacob and John would stomp all over my little village." She tossed the branch into the lake. "I used to be good at climbing a tree. I'd climb as high as I could and shimmy out along a branch to dangle like a raccoon. You ever seen coons hang from trees?"

"All the time," David said. "I can just imagine you up there. So, why'd you stop?"

Her shoulder rose and fell. "I don't know. I guess I got older, and Mama said I needed to behave. And then Jacob and John died, and Mama and Papa died, and I got despondent. I've been sad ever since." Dark clouds flitted across her face as she spoke.

"I'm sorry so much has happened to you," David said, boldly pushing a strand of wet hair from her face.

"Thank you, David," she said, looking at him with a gaze that turned his insides into corn mush.

"You can climb a tree on the ranch any old time," he added with a chuckle.

"You mean that?" Her eyes sparkled.

"If it makes you happy, then I sure do."

Once again, their eyes locked, and it seemed like volumes were spoken in the silence.

"What about you?" Amanda said, breaking the spell. "Were you and Gabe close growing up?"

David pursed his lips and looked at the cloudless sky. "I reckon we were as close as any two sons. But there was always this rivalry between us. It's like if I wanted something, Gabe went out of his way to get it. And it wasn't like he was homely or unfriendly or anything. More like the exact opposite—my brother could charm the feathers from a crow.

216

And he was a good-looking man, too. Always getting in trouble with the ladies..." He frowned and picked at his thumbs.

"Doesn't sound like I'd get along with Gabe."

David turned his head to see a frown on her face. "Why's that?"

"That's what John was like... a charming, handsome man. Our families decided that he and I would get hitched someday. We grew up together... we climbed trees and played in the river. That doesn't mean I loved him. I was just doing it because I thought it was the right thing to do." She let out a long sigh and then cocked her head, studying him intently. "Do you miss him? Gabe?"

He chewed on his lower lip, gazing out at the lake. Spying a flat rock, he picked it up and flicked it into the lake, where it skipped a few times before sinking. "I do. I'm surprised to say I miss him a lot. We had our rivalry, and I've been bitter about it for a long time. But he was family, you know? He was all I had left. I reckon my bitterness needs to be buried, too."

"Oh, David," Amanda said, her eyes moist.

He rolled his lips between his teeth. "Gabe was my blood relation. I can't seem to find any peace in my heart about his death. I can't seem to move forward until I find out what happened to him. Then, I'll be able to move on..." *With you...* Although he couldn't say the words, he hoped the meaning came through.

For a second, it felt like he and Amanda had fallen into their own personal world, where no one else existed but them.

Then, she reached out and put her hand on his arm. "I promise you, David. We'll find justice and put this whole thing to rest."

For the first time in forever, hope bloomed in his chest, telling him that maybe Ada had been right. Maybe, God willing, everything would be all right. But, life being the way it was, they might have to face more trouble before they got there.

Because as lovely as this day had been, once they returned home from their excellent outing, he still had to find out what Sheriff Slinger was hiding.

Chapter Twenty-Seven

Amanda practically floated to bed that night. *What a wonderful time I had with David today at the lake.* They'd conversed, even laughed... for a moment, Amanda felt like a proper married woman. She twirled like a schoolgirl as she entered her bedroom, considering how lovely it would be if she were to enjoy life the way she used to. *I felt so free at the lake... so happy.*

But then, on the ride back, David had sunk into his moody, quiet self. The only saving grace had been that this time she knew what it was about.

David wanted answers about Gabe's death—he'd at least shared that much with her.

And she was determined to help him. *I'll be a better wife to him. I'll do what is asked of me and maybe... if I'm lucky... one day, he will love me back.*

Even if he didn't come to love her, today, he'd shown her that he could be her friend. And having a friend was worth its weight in gold.

Buoyed by positive thoughts, she drifted to sleep.

***

Sometime later, she awoke with a start. Outside her window, horses screamed, pigs squealed, and chickens squawked. Inside the house, windows shattered in an explosion of sound, and footsteps pounded.

Hurriedly, she scrambled from her bedding, tugged her robe around her, and raced into the hallway.

David, fully dressed, bolted from his bedroom, carrying his rifle. Spying Amanda, he tossed her a small handgun.

With fumbling fingers, she caught it. "What do you want me to do with this? I don't know how to use a gun, David."

"It's for your protection. If anyone attacks you, point it and pull the trigger. It's loaded."

Ada burst into the hallway from her room, a few doors down. Dressed only in her nightwear, with a scarf wrapped around her head, she looked wild-eyed. "What's going on?"

"You and Amanda—stay inside. I'm going to go find out what's going on." He turned to race downstairs, but Amanda stopped him with her hand on his shoulder.

"Wait. I'm coming with you," she said with fierce determination.

"Well, then, by golly, you keep that gun close and don't hesitate to use it." His head whipped around toward Ada. "You stay put. Get back inside your bedroom and lock the door."

Ada disappeared, and David headed toward the stairs. Amanda scrambled to keep up with him as he hurried down the narrow steps, taking two at a time.

Two men bolted from David's study right as Amanda's foot landed on the floor.

David lifted his rifle and pulled the trigger, aiming at one of the men. The bullet missed, blasting through the wall in a burst of noise and splintered wood. The men sprinted toward the front door, with David on their heels.

He lifted his rifle again and shot.

One of the men jerked and clutched his shoulder but kept on running. With a mighty tug, he threw open the front door. The door whacked against the wall with a thundering resonance, sending the lovely crystal vase tumbling from the sideboard to crash to the floor.

David bolted through the door and clattered onto the porch.

One of the men shouted, "Get the horses, get the horses!"

The two men leaped onto shadowy shapes, shouting, "Heya, heya," spurring their steeds into action.

Another man raced from the barn, leading one of David's horses. He bounded onto his waiting horse. Five horses, three with riders on their backs and two secured with ropes to the other horses, took off at a mad gallop, heading for the dawn horizon.

David cursed as he came to a stop, trying to catch his breath.

Amanda ran across the front lawn in her bare feet to be by his side.

"Lord help me. They took off with Bueno and one of my mares." His breath emerged in ragged pants.

"Oh, no!" Amanda cried, placing her hand on his arm.

He didn't pull away, saying, "Go on inside and get some shoes on your feet if you're going to be out here. I've got to check on the damage. I know those were the bandits I sensed a few days back, I can feel it in my bones. They've been watching us for days."

Amanda nodded and turned to head back inside. Upstairs, she knocked on Ada's door. "They're gone, Ada."

The older woman opened her door, her face the color of ash. "Good heavens. What did they want?"

"I don't know, but they took two of David's horses—a mare and Bueno. He's outside checking for further destruction." Amanda panted as she spoke, her heart beating fast.

"Oh, dear. David was getting ready to sell that horse. He's put hours and hours into Bueno. And one of the mares?" Ada bustled about her bedroom, grabbing her robe and lighting her lantern. "Let's head downstairs and see to the house."

Amanda nodded, heading for her bedroom for shoes.

As dawn bloomed in the sky, Amanda and Ada made their way to the bottom floor. The sight that greeted them made Amanda's heart sink like a stone.

Tentatively, she entered David's study. Papers lay scattered everywhere, his books were strewn all over the floor, shelves had been knocked over, and his desk drawers lay wide open.

The library looked much the same, with books and papers everywhere.

"Good lord, what on earth were they after?" Ada exclaimed. "Could it be they were after that so-called pouch the sheriff asked about?"

"I don't know," Amanda said, making her way into the kitchen to retrieve the broom made from broomcorn tied to a smoothly hewn branch. She also snagged the metal dust bin before making her way back to the front room to begin sweeping up the debris.

"What a sorry mess this is," Ada said, joining her a few minutes later. She gripped a bucket full of water with several rags draped over the edge.

While Amanda swept up the porcelain vase, Ada set to scrubbing the wall where the bullet had exploded.

The sound of a rifle outside near the barn had Amanda racing to the window.

A few seconds later, David staggered from the barn with what looked like his dog in his arms.

"Oh, no! It's Blue!" she cried.

"What?" Ada exclaimed, hurrying to be by Amanda's side.

Tenderly, David strode toward one of the apple trees several yards from the house and laid the dog near the tree trunk. Amanda raced outside and stood on the porch as David disappeared into the barn.

When he returned, bearing a shovel, he called, "Get back in the house, Amanda. You don't need to see this." His voice emerged thick and husky, like he'd been crying. "Those bandits broke both of Blue's hind legs. I had to put him out of his misery."

"Oh, David, I'm so sorry!" Amanda exclaimed, pressing her hand to her mouth.

"You didn't have anything to do with it," David called. "No sense getting sorry. Go on now and get back inside."

"What else did they do?" she said, her feet glued to the porch floor.

"Looks like they only took Bueno and Calico, my prize mare. Thank the lord Kickabilly and Chester are okay. The barn's a shambles. Those bandits were searching for something mighty fierce."

"Your study and the library are a mess, as well. Books, papers, everything is on the floor. Ada and I are working to clean it all up."

David nodded, wiping his mouth with the back of his hand. "All right, then. Get on back in the house while I lay my dog to rest." He continued to stand where he was, rooted to the spot as was Amanda.

"All right," Amanda said, without making a move. She met her husband's gaze, and the world seemed to close around them both. Finally, she said, "Do you think they were searching for whatever the sheriff thinks Gabe had? That pouch?"

"I sure don't know, but I reckon. I'm sending Michael straight away into town to fetch the sheriff. Michael and Billy said they heard a commotion outside. They both came out with their guns, but they couldn't see anything or anyone until it was too late. They said they tried to calm all the horses, knowing they're my pride and glory, but there was only so much they could do."

"You'll find them, David. You surely will," Amanda said.

"I sure hope so. I can't afford to lose anything else." He gave her a long, lingering look that swept through her like a strong wind, rocking her soul. "Now, get on inside the house so I can finish my business. I'll be in shortly."

"Okay," she said, turning to leave.

The bad luck continued to follow her, it seemed. But this time, it came with a thread of connection to something precious—her newfound friendship with her husband, David.

If they could nourish this connection, they might find the answers David needed.

Chapter Twenty-Eight

The sun already blazed in the sky by the time Sheriff Slinger and Deputy Angus arrived with Michael.

Slinger rode a stallion as black as the sheriff's soul. The horse pranced and shifted side to side as if even it didn't like to be near Slinger.

From where David stood in the pigpen, he watched as the sheriff tried to get his horse to mind him without much success. It was like watching a badger with a bear—neither would win, and both would end up bloody.

He hefted the pig slop bucket over the fence with a sigh and then climbed out of the pen.

The pigs made grunts of satisfaction as they consumed the leftovers Ada threw in a bucket for them each day. Two of them began to squeal over some tasty morsel each thought they deserved.

David wiped the sweat from his brow as he set aside the bucket and strode in the horsemen's direction. The entire morning he'd been consumed with cleaning up the mess left by those two bandits and making sure the animals were fed and cared for. He could use a few more hours sleep, but that would have to wait until nightfall—there was still too much to do.

"Afternoon, Sheriff. Deputy Sheriff," he said, as the three men reined to a halt a yard or two away.

"David," the sheriff said, swinging his leg over the saddle and landing on his booted feet on the ground.

Deputy Angus dismounted, as well.

Michael said, "I'll take over the chores you started."

David nodded and said, "Much obliged. Billy's in the barn, still putting it to rights."

"I hear tragedy has fallen on your ranch again," Slinger said, crossing his arms over his chest. His gunmetal-colored gaze flicked at his surroundings before landing on David.

As Michael and his horse trotted toward the barn, David said, "Yes, you got that right. Tragedy arrived last night in the form of three bandits. They took two of my horses and killed my dog, Blue." His eyes blazed as he studied the sheriff's response. *I think he knows more than he's letting on.*

"Your ranch hand filled us in. Mind if we look around?" Slinger said.

David's eyes narrowed. "Suit yourself. But can't think of what you'd find if you didn't find nothing the other day. I've been going through the damage all morning, Sheriff," he continued. "They tore through my study, my library, and my tack room. As far as I can tell, nothing's missing."

"Just trying to be thorough," Slinger said. "Maybe those bandits left behind something of importance."

David cocked his head and regarded the sheriff. Again, his suspicions arose that the sheriff knew more than he let on.

From the narrow-eyed way Angus studied Slinger, it appeared he felt the same way. "We won't be taking much of your time, David," the deputy said. "Just a little look-see, then we'll be on our way."

David accompanied them, showing them around the barn, then leading them into the house to look through the library and the study. As they examined each room, David filled them in on what happened in the night.

"I woke up to rustling in the house. They weren't a bit careful with their actions—they plowed through my rooms like a couple of cows. When I came downstairs, they fled from the house. I got one of them in the shoulder with my rifle, but that's it."

Angus met his gaze. "That's good, that's good, David. That might help us find them. I'll check with Doc Stevenson when I head back to town."

"Ain't no reason to do that," Slinger said, moving aside David's compass and his pen set on his desk. "Bandits like that—they're likely gone for the next county over by now. I don't think they would simply saunter through town and head for the doctor's, do you?"

Both Angus and David exchanged a look.

"Just trying to be thorough," Angus said, echoing the sheriff's earlier words.

"You can suit yourself. I just don't want you to waste your time. We've got to find these culprits." Slinger slapped David's back a few times with his pudgy hand.

David stepped away. Even the touch of the sheriff set his teeth on edge. "If you'll excuse me, I'd best be getting back to my chores," he said, ushering the two men toward the front door.

He glanced around at the now-tidy house. Amanda and Ada had managed to set things back to order. All he'd need to do was repair and re-paint the front room wall where the bullet had struck, and the house would be as good as new. A flush of pride filled his chest over his wife's hard work.

"We're going to find these bandits," the sheriff said again.

That's what you said the first time you stopped by... and the second time... and then you forgot about the whole case. David nodded his head woodenly.

"I'll make sure to follow up with you, David," Angus said. "It's a shame about your horse, Bueno. I was looking forward to checking him out."

"He was a right fine horse," David said. "I've got another one that might suit you, but Bueno was special."

"Good, good. As soon as things settle, I'll be out again, and we can see to the horses."

David watched them depart as they strode down the porch steps, crossed the front yard, and headed for their horses. Only when they appeared as specks in the distance did he look away.

Footsteps overhead let him know Amanda was upstairs. He headed for the staircase and climbed it, finding her bustling about in his room, wiping the dust from his dresser with a rag.

"Can I talk to you for a moment?" he asked, standing in the doorway. Ever since their time at the lake yesterday, a newfound connection stretched between them.

"Of course, David." She dropped her hands by her sides and looked at him expectantly.

The sun cast light on her hair from the window behind. She once again looked like an angel sent from heaven. He crossed the room and leaned against the dresser, close enough to touch her. "I'll be leaving guns around where you and Ada can find them easy enough if I've gone into town. And I'll start teaching you how to use a gun straight away."

She nodded, her expression somber. "All right. I think that would be best, too."

He reached up and scratched his stubble-covered cheek. In all the commotion of the morning, he hadn't had a chance to shave. "I have this niggling feeling that this is somehow connected to Gabe's death and that nonsense Slinger said about him leaving me with some sort of pouch."

Amanda clutched the cleaning rag in her hands, worrying it around and around. "You're probably right. You have a good head on your shoulders."

The compliment pleased him. "We have to solve this straight away. I'm afraid of what might happen if we don't. I think Angus is on my side. He didn't say as much, but he looked at the sheriff with the same suspicion as I did."

Amanda stared at his arm.

"What?" he said.

"You're bleeding." She pointed to his sleeve.

Sure enough, when he glanced at his shirt, he saw a stain of crimson. "It's probably nothing."

"Wait right here. I've got a healing concoction Ada taught me to make." She scurried from the room before he had a chance to protest.

When she returned several minutes later, she carried a basin full of water, a couple of rags, and a jar of some yellow-green goo. She dropped a couple of the rags near the hearth, and the others went into the basin. "Sit," she said, indicating David's mattress.

Moved by her concern, he sat.

She perched next to him and proceeded to roll up his sleeve, revealing a bloody gash. "Oh, my," she exclaimed. "How did this happen?"

"Who knows? I think I scraped against a nail in the barn. My mind's been preoccupied with the mess those bandits left." David reveled in her warm, caring touch as she retrieved a clean cloth from the water, wrung it out, and wiped it carefully across his skin.

Amanda continued to cleanse the wound as he studied her, transfixed by her beauty.

I don't deserve her. It's as simple as that.

When she'd finished cleaning his arm, she set the basin and the wet rags on the floor beside her and unscrewed the jar. "Ada and I picked all these herbs a month or so ago. It's got self-heal, yarrow, red clover, yellow wood sorrel, jewelweed, yellow dock, and narrow leaf plantain—all said to heal a wound such as you've got here."

"I see," David said, barely tracking her words. *What if I'd lost her? What if those rascals had injured her or killed her?* The thought seized his heart and yanked.

"She had me soak the herbs in oil, and then we mixed it with beeswax to make this salve," she said, gently dabbing the concoction on the cleansed wound.

"Okay," he said, utterly mesmerized with her. *I couldn't bear it if I lost her, too. I'd have lost my mind.*

Without thinking, he hooked his hand behind her neck and pulled her lips to his. He kissed her tenderly, sensing her yield to him. Then, he deepened the kiss, losing himself in the thrilling sensations coursing through his body.

When he eased away, her cheeks looked flushed, and she regarded him with a tender, soft-eyed gaze.

"I could have lost you, Amanda. Those bandits could have killed you and taken you away from me. I couldn't bear if it that happened—I'd have wanted to follow you wherever you went." He brushed his knuckles against her silken cheek.

Amanda stroked her swollen lips with her fingertips. "Oh, David. I... I thought you didn't even like me."

"Why on earth would you think that?" he said, surprised by her confession.

"You..." She cast her gaze at her lap. "Sometimes, you're nice to me, but then you get all cold with me and shut me out. You're like the well out back that doesn't always want to pump water."

He let out a chuckle and considered her statement. "I guess I am." Then, he grew thoughtful. "I do like you, Amanda. I... I..." He swallowed back the words he longed to say.

"What? Please say it, David, whatever you were going to say," she said to him with pleading eyes.

"I..." he said again, the words lodged in his throat. "I care for you." He couldn't seem to allow the word "love" to cross his lips. "But I ain't been able to do right by you."

Eyes shining, she clapped her hand over her mouth.

"I told you yesterday... Gabe and I... we were rivals throughout our life. I..." He looked away from her, unable to meet her gaze. Feeling bold, he turned back to meet her gaze. "Gabe was plumb excited to meet you. You were all he talked about. And I married you as if I had a right to do it when you came all the way out here to meet my brother."

"Oh, David, I..."

"Hold up. I ain't finished. I married you for all the wrong reasons. At first, I told myself I was doing it out of respect for Gabe, to make sure you were cared for after traveling all that way to get hitched to my brother. Then, each time I looked at you, I'd feel a stab of guilt, like I was betraying my own flesh and blood by claiming what was his by rights. Each time I was near you, I pictured my brother, angry, looking down from heaven with an accusatory glare. But the deeper truth is, I did it out of revenge."

He grew silent, rolling his lips between his teeth.

When he continued, he said, "I'm sorry to admit it, but a part of me married you to get back at my brother and tell his ghost, 'Hey, I got the girl you wanted.' I'm so ashamed by my actions...." His throat got all choked up. "He wasn't no enemy to carry a rivalry with to the grave any more than you were a prize to be snatched away. You deserve better than the likes of me, Amanda."

"Don't I get a say in all this?" she said, her gaze fierce. "From what you told me, I wouldn't have liked Gabe. I'd have married him, sure; I'd have followed through with my obligations the same way I would have followed through to marry Jacob. I didn't love either of them, David. But I've grown to love you."

As their eyes locked, his breath flew from his lungs. "I don't deserve you."

"Yes, you do. From what I've seen since I arrived, you're a good and caring man. You're honest, you're hard-working, and I'm honored to be your wife."

Unable to stop himself, David reached for her again, pressing his mouth to hers. He set free some of the passion he'd kept locked inside for all these weeks. But then another nagging thought crept into his brain. Reluctantly, he eased away from her.

"I told you I can't find peace with Gabe until I avenge his death and find out who killed him. I can't do right by you, either, until I get that done. Gabe was all out of sorts the day he died. He was dragging around the ranch like he carried his horse on his shoulders." He reached around and squeezed the back of his neck. "And I was still mad at him for stealing Leslie, so I let him stew. And here I didn't even like Leslie..."

He shook his head, then stroked the corners of his mouth with his thumb and finger.

"I'm having a hard time forgiving myself for not checking in with Gabe that day. I should have inquired. I should have asked him about what was bugging him because I knew his mind was in a knot about something. Had I done that, he might be alive today. So..." His gaze tangled with Amanda's, and for a few precious seconds, all thoughts escaped him. "I just can't move ahead until we solve his murder."

Amanda reached out and stroked his cheek with her palm. "Then, let's solve the murder, David. But let's do it together as husband and wife."

Chapter Twenty-Nine

David's face carried so much pain, Amanda could barely breathe. All this time, she'd thought he didn't like her. And the truth was he was tormented about loving her—he didn't think he deserved her. And he carried grief and confusion about the whys of marrying her.

Her heart broke into a million fragments as she studied him. There were no words that could reach him in his torment... none that came into her mind, at least. So, feeling a sudden need to be busy, she leaned over and picked up the basin holding the water and the now dirty rags.

"Where are you going?" David asked.

"I'm just going to take this down to the kitchen, and I'll be right back," she said, feeling shy and confused. So much had happened in a short time—David had *kissed* her. And he seemed to be okay with it as he still sat here in this room with her. Also, he'd confessed his care for her. *So, even if he doesn't love me... at least he cares for me.*

Her gaze landed on the cloth she'd set aside near the fireplace to wrap his wound. *I'd better dress his injury first.* She rested the basin back down on the floor and crossed to the hearth. Her foot caught on the edge of the braided wool rug, and she tripped. Frantically, she reached for the wall to keep from tumbling to the floor.

David bolted to his feet and raced to her side. Seizing her elbow, he steadied her and helped her upright.

"Oh, my! I'm so clumsy. I think I need to work harder outside," she said, her cheeks warm with embarrassment. "That's what you keep telling me."

"Don't you worry about it. I've tripped on that rug a time or two." His forehead creased as he stared at something behind her.

Her head whipped around. "What are you looking at? Oh!" She turned and stooped to study a loose brick in the mantel. Using her fingers, she tugged at the brick, and it popped free of the wall. Peering inside the hole left behind, she said, "My goodness. There's a whole compartment back there."

David chuckled. "That's where Gabe and I used to store our secret treasures. When we were younger, we felt like we needed a secret spot to hide things we didn't want our parents to find. I forgot about that hidey-hole."

"What kinds of treasures?"

"Oh, let's see," David said, scratching his stubble-covered cheek. "I think he hid some tobacco back there, as well as Father's pipe. We smoked it one day, and I got sick as a dog. He didn't, and he made sure to taunt me about it. Then, there was the time we stole a bottle of whiskey from Father and stuck it back there."

He let out a laugh.

"But you can't hide the effects of alcohol, so when we drank it one night, we got our behinds whooped. We started laughing and goofing around, and then Gabe stumbled down the stairs. Mother caught us, and she turned us over to Father. He was none too pleased we got into his liquor." His expression fell. "I guess Gabe and I didn't always behave as rivals. We could have some good fun occasionally, too."

"I'm sure you did, David," Amanda said, as her heart broke into bits. *David's carried so much pain for so long...*

"Let me see your hands—are you okay?" he said, reaching for her.

She lifted her hands, and he held them in his large, warm palms. "Just a little scraped up. Nothing to bother with," she said, withdrawing from his touch. She felt all flustered by this new connection they'd forged. "Let's see if you left any treasures in there," she said to change the topic.

"Oh, ain't nothing in there, Amanda. We stopped storing things in there a good while back—after Mother and Father died." David frowned as he looked at the opening in the wall.

"Maybe you forgot something," she said, peering inside the dark hole. She couldn't really see anything but a shadowy outline. "I think I found something."

She worked her slender fingers inside the wall and touched a soft object.

"Yes," she said excitedly. "There's something in there!"

David crouched next to her. "What is it?"

She wriggled her fingers to get a good grasp and tugged.

A fold of burgundy-colored velvet protruded from the opening.

"That's as far as I can get it," she said.

David grabbed the fabric and gently tugged it. "There's something big back there. I sure don't recall putting anything in there of late." He met Amanda's gaze.

For a few seconds, they simply stared at one another.

"Do you think this is the pouch the sheriff was after?" Amanda whispered.

"We sure won't know until we pry it out of here," David said. "Here... you work it from your side, and I'll work it from mine."

Together, they dug and tugged at the velvet until they'd managed to work it free without ripping it.

David unwrapped the shiny cord that had been wound around the neck of the pouch. He reached his hand inside and slid out the contents, consisting of a stack of money, silver and gold coins, and a folded piece of parchment. His face blanched as he stared at the money pile. Then, with trembling fingers, he unfolded the parchment.

For a few long seconds, he stared at it with glistening eyes.

"What is it, David?" Amanda said, gently placing her hand on his forearm.

In a strangled voice, choked with emotion, he said, "It's a letter, Amanda. It's a letter from Gabe."

Chapter Thirty

David rose from his crouch next to the fireplace mantel in his room, clutching Gabe's letter in his shaking hand. Unable to move, he simply stood in place for a few moments, staring out the window at the ranch he and Gabe had worked so hard to develop.

In the distance, the horses grazed.

There was a hole in his heart for the two he'd just lost— Bueno and his mare, Calico. He loved his equines with a passion that made no sense to him at times; he cared for them and trained them with satisfaction that touched him deep in his soul. Those animals had never given him any grief the way Gabe had done. But he and Gabe had gone on many a trail ride, side by side, in easy companionship, mending fences and searching for lost cattle. At times like that, he and Gabe were the best of friends.

And his buddy Blue was no longer out there—Blue had been a steadfast part of David and Gabe's life since they got him from a neighbor as a wee pup. Blue used to try to herd Gabe and David until they reminded him that his job was to herd cattle, not humans. They used to laugh when the dog would nip at their heels and bark, urging them on.

His gaze flitted to the pigpen.

The plump pink animals lay on their sides in the sun, the same way they did every day until they were moved to get up and root around for food.

David got a kick out of the pigs. They squealed and hollered when he fed them the pig slop, as if they were dying. A chuckle erupted from his mouth as he recalled the time he and Gabe had tried to ride to race while riding the pigs.

The porkers had squealed and run around in circles until Gabe and David fell off, landing in the mud. And then, with mud plastered to their faces and dripping from their hair, they'd laughed until their sides split.

The chickens pecked and scratched in their pen. They left their eggs in the little nests David and Gabe had built. Ada and Amanda retrieved the eggs every morning, preparing the fine food they nourished their bodies with.

And to the left lay Amanda's garden, already abundantly green with life.

Yep, Gabe and I made the start of what we hoped would sustain our families and us for the rest of our lives. Only his life was cut short, and the family I never dreamed I'd have has only just begun.

He turned to regard Amanda, who sat on the edge of the bed, studying him with a soft-eyed expression. Tears pricked at the back of his eyes as he considered her. She'd arrived here to be Gabe's wife. He'd married her to teach his brother a lesson and to show Gabe that he could get what Gabe had wanted. David had gotten no satisfaction from his foolish move. And the lesson had been his to live and learn from, not Gabe's. *Family is family. You can't go carrying a grudge toward a family member who's crossed to the beyond and can't speak up for himself. And, Lord, help me, but I've grown to cherish Amanda.*

As he plodded across the room to sit by her side, his body felt as heavy as a horse. "May as well get this over with. Might as well see what Gabe had to say."

Amanda rested her hand on his thigh.

In a choked voice, thick with emotion, he read:

Brother,

I've wondered how to tell you what I've found out by working in town as the deputy sheriff. I thought to write it all out, hoping that I might soon share it with you and, together, we might find a way to get out of this tangled mess.

If you're reading this letter and I'm not by your side, I'll assume I'm dead. I put my life on the line to do what I'm about to tell you.

Sheriff Slinger is a corrupt man. I had my suspicions, so when I heard the job of deputy sheriff was open, I seized it. You see, I was out drinking one night when I saw him take a bribe from some people I know to be bad—Henry Neil and Jim McCarthy. If you ever see them in town, turn around and walk the other way.

David stopped reading and frowned, recalling Slinger, Neil, and McCarthy heading for his barn the day he and Amanda got hitched. *I'll bet they were snooping around to search for this pouch.* He lowered his gaze and continued to read.

I heard tell of Neil and McCarthy stealing cattle from a ranch in Virginia City. Then, they went on to perform bank robberies. And I heard them talking to the sheriff about some money they stole from old Frank Parson at the general store. Slinger said he wouldn't take them in if they gave him a cut of what they stole. As deputy sheriff, I managed to get my hands on the money—it's the cash in this pouch. But Slinger has taken many bribes. I sneaked into the office at night and removed some of his bribe money. It's in my desk drawer, unless he's found it. I've been witness to most of his transactions, although Slinger was none the wiser. I managed to overhear him on many occasions while I pretended to be snoozing at my desk or heading off to buy a round of drinks for us at the saloon.

I didn't want to accuse the sheriff without proof, so I waited and watched him more closely. It's worse than I thought. The sheriff isn't just taking bribes no more—he's working with Neil and McCarthy and a whole mess of bandits, giving them information on who to target and who to rob. Then, they split the money. Like I said, what I've managed to get my hands on is in the back of my desk. I think I have the proof, and I'll be going to the marshals over in Skullwood Flats to give them the information they need to put Slinger behind bars.

David paused his reading. Anger flared inside him at the information Gabe had revealed. *Why did he keep it from me? Why did he wait to tell me? I could have helped him, and he could be sitting here today.*

"David, are you all right?" Amanda said softly.

"Huh?" he said, coming out of his fog. "This is a lot to take in. Why in tarnation didn't he tell me?"

"Well, maybe he was trying to protect you," she offered.

"I didn't need protection. I'm a grown man who's older than Gabe." David blew out his breath from between pursed cheeks, cast his gaze at the letter in his lap, and continued to read.

If you read this letter following my passing, I'm sorry, brother. I'd hoped to tell you in person. And, if something happened to me, please take care of Amanda. She will have no other family besides us when she arrives. Her family was taken from her through tragedy. I know you will do right by her, David. You were always a better man than me.

A brick-sized block clogged David's windpipe, and he found himself unable to speak. *He thought I was the better man?*

Right here, ten feet from where he lay his head every night, lay the absolution for the guilt he'd carried all these weeks. Amanda had never deserved his cold demeanor.

But his brother didn't deserve to be dead, either. Right then and there, he vowed to come up with a plan that would put Slinger behind bars.

Sheriff Slinger would never see daylight again.

Chapter Thirty-One

David sat on the bed, stunned, with Amanda by his side. Gabe had proof of Sheriff Slinger's corruption, and he was making a plan to take the man down. The evidence sat in David's lap in the form of a letter. *Why didn't he talk to me? Why did he think it a good idea to keep this important news from me?*

Unable to process or even think a helpful thought, he bolted to his feet. "Want to take a walk with me?"

Amanda's eyebrows rose in apparent surprise. "You want to take a walk with *me*?" she said in a high-pitched voice.

"I don't see anybody else in this room, do you?" he said.

"No," she stammered.

"Then, let's go." He started to turn, intending to tromp out of his bedroom the way he usually did, but he paused. *I've got to consider Amanda, now. I can't go rushing off like I'm in charge of the world, and she ain't a part of my life.* He glanced over his shoulder. "You coming, or what?"

"I'm coming!" she said and rose from the bed, all wide-eyed and eager.

David's heart began to pound as he watched her. *She's so dang pretty—how did I end up with such a lovely gal?* He stepped aside for her to exit and then followed her down the stairs.

Once he stepped onto the landing, he called to Ada, who he heard clattering in the kitchen. "Ada, can you come out here for a moment?"

"Sure, David," she called back.

When she appeared in the front room, wiping her hands on her apron, he waved Gabe's letter. "Amanda found this. It was stuck in the hidey-hole that Gabe and I used to keep our business out of our parent's noses."

Ada's mouth curved in a playful smile. "Like the time you stole your father's whiskey?"

"You knew about that?" David said, his neck, cheeks, and ears starting to blaze with heat.

"It was hard not to know, what with the caterwaul you two was making after the whooping your dad gave you." Her expression grew somber. "But what did Amanda find?"

David's voice got all choked up again. "It's a letter—from Gabe." He thrust the parchment toward Ada.

She held it and lowered her gaze to scan the letter. When she was finished, her hand flew to her mouth. It took her a few seconds to compose herself before she said, "Gabe knew! He knew it! I always suspected that sheriff of foul play. Didn't I tell you to stay away from him, Amanda?"

"Yes, ma'am, you did. But I already had my own suspicions," Amanda said, standing stiffly next to David.

"So, what are you going to do, David?" Ada said. She handed him back the paper.

He carefully folded the letter and rested it on the sideboard where the crystal vase once stood, intending to put it somewhere secure when he returned from his walk. Then, he thought better of it and deposited it in his pocket. "I ain't got a plan yet. I thought I'd wander about outside for a bit... you know, to sort my thoughts. I always think better when I'm away from the house." He cast a hesitant gaze toward Amanda. "Amanda's agreed to join me."

Ada's lips curved in a lightning-quick smile that disappeared in a flash. "That sounds good. Real good. Well, you go on outside and get to sorting. I've got to get back to supper preparation." Her gaze slid to Amanda, and she gave a quick nod before disappearing into the kitchen.

A sudden wave of awkwardness overtook David, effectively gluing his limbs to the floor. Finally, he said, "Well, let's get to it," and turned to walk out. The same as when he hesitated upstairs, he paused, opened the door, and stood aside for Amanda to exit first.

In the yard, he said, "Let's walk beneath the trees. It's a mite warm out today."

"All right," Amanda said.

She seemed pleased to merely be in his presence, which made no sense to him at all. She'd been right when she'd said he was like the well out back that didn't always want to pump water. He'd shut her out on many occasions when overcome with guilt and his own consternation over their marriage.

They strode in silence beneath the mesquite trees that lined the yard. As he walked, David pondered the letter. *What in tarnation am I going to do? I'm not like Gabe, who swirls through the world like a windstorm.*

Without thinking, he took Amanda's hand in his. It felt comforting to be walking by her side, having her here with him, offering quiet support. But when he glanced at her, tears tracked down her face.

"What's wrong?" he said.

"Nothing. Nothing's wrong. It... it just feels nice to be holding your hand," she said.

All he could think to do was nod.

He continued to hold Amanda's hand as he wandered aimlessly around his property. Finally, they stopped at her garden. He eyed the neat rows planted with leafy green vegetables. "This here garden is real nice, Amanda."

"I'm glad you like it," she said, casting her gaze to the ground.

"I'm proud of you for all the effort you've put into this plot of land. You've turned it into something real nice. Ada never has much time for the garden. She's got too much to do in the kitchen. I know she appreciates you, too."

Amanda lifted her gaze to meet his eyes. "Really? That's kind of you to say."

His heart caught in his throat when he witnessed her bright eyes shining as she gave him her soft-eyed regard. "Have you always been interested in growing things?"

He released her hand and turned to face her, leaning against the garden fence post which held the poultry netting in place. Already he missed the warmth of her touch.

"I used to help Ma out in the garden." She began to wring her hands as if she didn't know what to do with them. "She'd tell me, 'That little plot in the corner is all yours, Amanda. See what you can do with it.' So, I worked it, digging it with the little shovel Pa had fashioned for me. And, by golly, I got things to grow." Her rapid blinking shook tears free. "I loved my ma. I loved my whole family. I don't know why they were taken from me. And, until you told me you loved me, I thought I'd have to live the rest of my days in sorrow. What did I do to deserve such a life?"

His heart seemed to break into a million pieces. Reaching out, he wiped her tears away with his callused thumbs. "You didn't do nothing, Amanda. Life is sometimes cruel. We just got to deal with it and find solutions to what ails us."

She sniffled and wiped her eyes with her sleeve. "So, what will you do about Gabe's assertions? How will you catch the sheriff?"

"I don't rightly know." He pivoted and rested his back against the fence post. "I've been turning it over and over in my head as we've been walking. As far as I can tell, Slinger don't know what I know. He hasn't given any indication that he knows anything about my suspicions. Last I saw him when he came to see to the robbery out here, he spoke all smooth-like, like a rattlesnake trying to convince you it ain't no rattlesnake. Oh, sure, he said all the right things—about justice being served, and we'll find the bandits who stole my horses, but now I'm thinking it was that gang Gabe spoke of. And Slinger knew..." He paused to gather his thoughts. "He's in cahoots about the loss of my horses. And, he might have been in cahoots about harming you."

That snake he'd just spoken about wrapped itself around his neck, making it hard to talk or breathe. He glanced at Amanda, noticing a few strands of hair flying about her beautiful face. A soft breeze billowed about his head, cooling his heated body.

"But I'm okay. And now you've got to figure this out," Amanda said, nodding. She reached out and hooked one of her fingers with one of his, then withdrew her hand.

The sweet little gesture warmed his heart.

"So, if he doesn't know, then what?" she said.

"I don't want to head into town, guns blazing." David ran his palm over his mouth and jaw. "I'm thinking we need to get some assistance to trap him. We need a foolproof plan. He's been pulling the wool over the eyes of the townsfolk ever since he took his oath. A lying rattlesnake, he is. All his talk about how he grew up poor and had to make a name for himself by doing right by the people of Goldsprings was just that—talk. He's a greedy, conniving, power-hungry son-of-a-gun, nothing more." His stomach tightened into a knot.

"Slinger's jaw used to get to wobbling down at the saloon when he had a few pints down his gullet," he said. He pushed away from the fence post and propped his hands on his hips. "He'd go on like he was sitting at church, and we were all his preachers. He went on about how he had no money growing up, like I said. He wanted to go to school in a bigger city, but it weren't possible because his family had no money. He wanted to buy a farm but couldn't because he had no money. The way he went on, you'd think the only thing standing in his way was a cavern that should have been filled with gold. So now, as I stand here telling you this tale, I can see how it all fits. I'm certain, to Slinger, money equals power, and power is what he craves."

"That makes sense," Amanda said, nodding.

David rubbed his jaw again. "But a powerful man is a ruthless man. I need to be very careful when I put my plan in motion. There can't be any cracks or holes he can slither through and disappear, because that's what snakes do—they just worm their way into the shadows and vanish."

"You mustn't do anything to put yourself into harm's way," Amanda said fervently.

"I don't plan on it any more than you planned on losing your brother, or I planned on losing Gabe. But things happen."

Amanda's expression had grown rigid, like she already feared the worst.

"That sure came out wrong," he said, gazing intently at her. "You and I—we just came to realize we might have something good between us, didn't we?"

She sniffled and nodded.

"So, let's make sure we trap the rattler and put him where he belongs—in jail."

"That's where he belongs," Amanda said. "I can't stand Sheriff Slinger."

"Nor do I. Ada don't, neither. That makes three of us, and I'm sure there's a whole bunch more who wish they never laid eyes on him. So, here's what I'm fixing to do. I'm going to saddle up Kickabilly and head into town. You and Ada stay here and stay safe. You remember where I put the guns I hid?"

"Yes," she said. "I sure do."

"There are a few more guns in my office, in the gun case. They're all loaded—I hadn't hidden them yet. You and Ada take them and hide them wherever you can. Be real clever. Make sure the barn has a rifle, and the kitchen has one, too. Ada can handle a rifle okay if she has a mind to," David said. "And put the handgun in a place where you can get to it. I realize we haven't taken the time to teach you how to shoot, but the handgun is easy. All you got to do is hold it in front of your face and pull the trigger."

He lifted his arm, squinted, and squeezed a pretend gun trigger.

"Can you do that for me?" He regarded her with a steady gaze.

"Of course. Ada and I will get right to it."

"That's my girl," he said. "I'm going to go get Kickabilly saddled up so we can get on our way. I'm going to have a little chat with John Angus, and we're going to hatch a plan. We're going to catch that rattler."

For a few seconds, he didn't speak, just studied Amanda. Wasn't it a wonder that when this plan was put into motion and Slinger was put behind bars, he'd be able to come home to Amanda and maybe love her like she deserved to be loved?

The very thought lit a fire in his belly. And, by golly, he let that fire burn.

Chapter Thirty-Two

Kickabilly had a spring to his step as he picked his way along the trail heading into town, which suited David just fine. He wanted to get to town quicker than he would plodding along in a wagon with old Chester.

The air around him seemed muggy, and clouds gathered on the horizon like a thunderstorm might be on its way. He hoped he didn't get caught in a downpour again as he and Amanda had before—there was no time to lose when it came to coming up with a plan to stop Sheriff Slinger.

When he entered the town of Goldsprings, his buddy Arlo stood outside the general store. He waved David over like he intended on setting his jaw to wobbling—something David didn't want to do.

David slowed Kickabilly without stopping and said, "I've got some business to attend to, Arlo. Maybe we can catch up later." He tipped his hat, intending on continuing.

"What kind of business?" Arlo said, stepping from the wooden sidewalk to block Kickabilly's forward movement.

"The kind I can't do if you're in the way of my horse," David said, annoyance stirring the contents of his stomach into a froth.

"I ain't seen you much of late," Arlo pointed out.

"I ain't been around much to be seen," David said.

"So, let's catch up," Arlo said.

"Don't you have nothing better to do than flap your gums at me, Arlo?" David said.

"Actually, no. The wife's taken ill, and she's ordered me away from the house," he said, then spat a wad of chewing tobacco and saliva in the dirt near Kickabilly's hoof.

"Sorry to hear that. But if Estelle's well enough to kick you out of the house, sounds like she's well enough." David dropped the reins.

"Yep, I reckon so," Arlo said. "So, what's your business?"

David eyed him with suspicion. *He ain't in cahoots with Slinger, is he?* "My place got robbed the other day. Two of my horses are gone."

Arlo's face fell, appearing genuinely shocked. "I'm real sorry about that, David. Which horses?"

"Remember Bueno, the five-year-old I've been working with?"

"Sure do. He was a real fine horse, he was. So, he was stolen, huh?" Arlo spat out another juicy wad of tobacco.

"Yes," David said. "He and Calico are gone."

"That pretty little Appaloosa you had? The mare?"

"Yep," David said again.

"That's a crying shame. Did anything else get stolen?" Arlo said. The sincerity in his eyes told David he wasn't involved.

"My dog Blue. I had to put him down. Both his legs were broken, and there wasn't no way I could fix him. I buried him out back beneath the laurel tree, next to Gabe. I figure Blue's spirit is still watching over the cattle," David said as a lump of emotion clogged his throat.

"Oh, that's just awful, David! So, then, you're headed to the sheriff's, am I right?"

"That's right. I need to see if he's found anything with his investigation." David picked up the reins again, eager to get on his way.

"Mind if I tag along?" Arlo said.

Inwardly, David groaned. *How in tarnation am I going to get rid of Arlo?* "Slinger told me specifically not to tell no one about what happened. I've already told you too much," he lied. "But, since you're my friend, it made sense to tell you what's what."

Arlo seemed to puff up with pride. "Okay, I get it, I get it. But you'll tell me if the sheriff has any leads, right?"

"I'm not sure I can. Like I said, I already told you too much." David glanced at the dusty road ahead. Save for that thunderstorm they'd had that had caught him and Amanda unawares, they hadn't gotten too much rain of late. As a result, dust clouds billowed along the road, landing on the clothes, hair, and skin of everyone downtown.

He glanced at the hangdog expression on his friend's face. "Tell you what. What do you say if you and I get a drink at the saloon real soon? We can have a catch-up session then."

Arlo's face brightened. "I'd like that. This marriage business has gone and taken all of your time."

It has, indeed. In ways I'll never share. "I'll see you, then." With a cluck and a kick, David urged Kickabilly ahead.

Along the way to the sheriff's office, he concocted a cover story in case Slinger was around. *I'll just tell him I'm checking on the investigation, same as I said to Arlo.* That thought made him feel better about fibbing to one of his closest friends.

With the sheriff's office in his sights, he urged Kickabilly on. Another groan left his lungs when Jim Sawyer stepped out of the barbershop.

"Hey, David," he said with a wave. His newly cut short, wet hair clung to his scalp and his Stetson hung by his side in his hand.

"Jim," David said with a nod, hoping he could continue on without the chit-chat.

"Ain't seen you much of late," Jim said, stepping off the sidewalk, same as Arlo had, to block Kickabilly's way.

Here we go. David shook his head. "You should get to church more often, I guess."

"Reckon so. What have you been up to? How's married life?" Jim fit his Stetson on his head.

"Good. Look, I've got to head over to the sheriff's to make an inquiry. I got robbed a couple days ago. Two horses, Bueno and Calico," he said quickly, wanting to give as many details as he could to minimize further questions. "The sheriff's making some inquiries, but I'm kind of in a hurry, so..."

"Bueno and Calico? What a shame," Jim said.

"We can meet up for a drink sometime soon, you, me, and Arlo. What do you say?" David eyed the sheriff's office up the way. "And I can fill you in."

Angus dismounted his horse, having just arrived at the building from the opposite direction. When he spied David, he nodded.

"That sounds good. I've got to get your advice on some issues I've had with one of my horses," Jim said, stepping to the side of David's horse.

David reeled in his attention, turned to Jim, and said, "I'll have a listen, and then be happy to tell you what I think. There's the deputy sheriff now. I've got to head on over and see what he knows."

With a nod, he urged Kickabilly forward. A minute or so later, he dismounted in front of Deputy Sheriff Angus.

The deputy stood outside, draping his horse's reins over the wooden bar next to the sidewalk. "David," he said. "What can I do for you?"

"Slinger around?" David looked this way and that.

"Nope," Angus said, crossing to the front door. "He said he has business outside of town today."

"I'll bet he does," David said, following him inside. He closed the door behind him. "I've got some news to share with you," he said, digging into his pocket.

"What kind of news?" Angus settled into his desk chair in the corner.

"I found this letter this morning," David said, fishing free Gabe's letter. "It proves what I suspected. The sheriff is corrupt. He's in cahoots with a gang of bandits, sharing the profits." He handed the folded parchment to Angus.

The deputy blew his breath out. "I'm not saying I don't agree with you, but that's a mighty strong accusation." He crossed one leg, resting his ankle on his knee.

"Read it, Deputy," David said, gesturing toward the letter. "You can see for yourself."

Angus removed his hat, set it on top of the worn wooden desk, and smoothed out the parchment with his palms. Then, he began to read.

David pulled a wooden chair near the deputy's desk and sat, nervously rubbing his jaw and cheeks as he waited.

A loud *tick, tick, tick,* came from a clock on the wall. Outside, a couple of horses whinnied.

David studied the deputy intently, watching for signs of a reaction.

The deputy let out a couple of deep breaths as he read. When he'd apparently finished, he pinched the bridge of his nose. "This is pretty big, David."

"I know it is," David said, sitting up tall.

"And Henry Neil and Jim McCarthy are involved?"

David's head bobbed up and down. "That's what my brother said."

"Makes sense," Angus said, stroking the handlebars of his mustache. "Those two are in here all the time, chatting with Slinger. I wonder who else is involved?"

"Don't know," David said. "Do you see them around with anyone else?"

"I do, I do," the deputy said, lines creasing his face. "So, Gabe says he stored the stolen money in this here desk, am I right?"

"That's what he said," David said, sitting forward.

"I've gone through these drawers many times. I made sure they were cleaned out before I dropped my stuff in." Angus opened one of the sturdy drawers and looked inside.

"I'm sure you have, but Gabe weren't no fool. He wouldn't just leave the money inside a drawer for Slinger to find." David rose and stood beside the deputy's desk.

"Oh, like maybe there's a false-bottomed drawer in this desk?" Angus said excitedly.

David's eyebrows rose. "I didn't say that. Didn't know there was such a thing."

The deputy rapped his knuckles on the bottom of a drawer and said, "Nope, not this one."

"What are you looking for?" David asked, peering inside the drawer.

"I'll know when I find it, son," the deputy said, continuing to rap on the drawers. When he tapped his knuckles on the bottom right one, his eyes shone with excitement. He emptied the drawer of its contents, setting the telegrams and envelopes whose waxed seals had been broken on top of the desk. "This is the one. Listen..." He rapped on the floor of the drawer a few more times. "Hear that? Hear how it's kind of hollow sounding?"

"I guess so," David said, scrunching his eyebrows together.

"Do you have a knife? We need to slide a small blade into the side of this drawer." The deputy held out his palm.

"I've got one in my saddlebag. Be right back." David tromped outside, scratching his head. *A false-bottom drawer? What in the tarnation is that?*

When he returned, he removed his hunting knife from its sheath and handed it to the deputy.

Angus took it and carefully slid the tip of the knife between the edge of the apparent bottom of the drawer and the side. He wiggled the handle of the blade, but nothing happened. "Hmm," he grunted. He ran his fingertips along the edge of the wood, and his eyebrows rose. "Here we go. There's a notch in here." Once more, he fit the tip of the blade in the drawer where the notch was located.

Again, nothing happened.

"Maybe I got it wrong," the deputy said, his eyebrows stitched together. He rapped a few more times on the drawer bottom with his knuckle. "No, it sure sounds hollow to me."

"Let me try," said David.

"Suit yourself," the deputy said, handing over the knife. He and David switched positions.

David fit the blade into the notch, wiggled it, and tugged. He tugged again. And again.

The bottom popped open.

"Would you looky there? A magnet was holding it in place," David said, fingering a small, round metal piece. He lifted the false bottom out. "And, look!"

He stepped aside, revealing a cloth pouch similar to the one he and Amanda had found Gabe's letter inside.

"Oh, my," Deputy Angus said. "I think we found ourselves some evidence." He removed the pouch, untied the cord around the neck, and slid free a stack of cash along with a gold piece. When he held the pouch upside down, several more gold pieces fell into the desktop with soft thuds. The deputy whistled. He brought his fingertips to his mouth and stroked his mustache. "But if this is all the evidence we got, it can be his word against mine kind of situation."

David drummed his fingers on the wood. "Maybe we can set a trap of sorts. What if you were to say you wanted in on the deal? Tell him you heard about it, and you'll keep your trap shut if you can get a cut of the action." His heart thumped hard with excitement at the thought of putting the man responsible for his brother's death behind bars.

Angus snapped his fingers. "I like that! That's a good plan." He gathered all the money and inserted it back inside the pouch. "I think you should leave the rest of the particulars to me, David. I've got to think a spell before I put the plan into motion."

"I agree," David said. "Slinger's a wily one. He'll try to slither his way under the door if he thinks he's being played."

"But rest assured... we *will* bring him to justice. If he thinks he can get away with this kind of behavior under my watch, he's nothing but a fool." Angus nodded at David. "I'm sorry you had to go through this—the loss of your property, but especially the loss of your brother. Just know that I'll do everything within my power to put things to rights."

David reached out to shake Angus's hand. "Thank you kindly, Deputy." He turned around and strode from the office, encouraged that something might go right for a change.

Chapter Thirty-Three

Determined to confront the sheriff the same day David had brought him news of Slinger's corruption, John stayed downtown late into the evening. His wife, Sarah, probably had supper prepared, but she'd lived with him long enough to know sometimes his job kept him from regular hours with his family.

She and their two teenage sons would eat, and then she'd set aside a plate for him for when he returned home.

Shadows from the furniture stretched across the floor as the sun descended outside the window. John rose and lit the lantern on his desk before settling back into his seat. He fiddle-faddled with this and that, trying to stay busy. *Where is he? What's the hold-up that he has to be gone all day?* Finally, he sat at his desk, counting the money they'd found in Gabe's desk.

There was enough here to support several families for an entire year. He counted it a second time. When he was just about to count it again, he heard a commotion outside the door. Quickly, he thrust the gold, silver, and paper money back inside the pouch, shoved it in the drawer, and pretended to study one of the telegrams scattered across his desk.

The front door flew open, and the sheriff staggered in. "What in the blazes are you still doing here, John?" Slinger said in a too-loud voice.

"I had some work to attend to, is all," John said, setting aside the telegram.

"Did you now?" He crossed the room on unsteady legs, heading toward his desk. Placing his palms on the desktop as if to hold himself upright, he carefully made his way to his desk chair. He practically fell onto the chair, landing with a grunt.

"Been out drinking?" John said. "You look a bit bousy, like you've had your share of barbed-wire booze."

"What's it to you?" Slinger said in a belligerent tone of voice.

"Ain't nothing to me if you were on your own time, but you're still in uniform," John said.

Slinger flopped his hand around in front of his chest, and he made an unintelligible sound. "Which one of us is the sheriff, and which one of us is the deputy?"

John stayed quiet, picking up the telegram again and staring at it intently. "Did you get your business done today?"

"What?" Slinger slurred.

"Your business... you left this morning saying you had business outside of town. Did you get it done?" John pressed.

"Oh, I reckon I did, all right. Don't quite remember at the moment." Slinger propped his head on his palms.

John drummed his fingers on the desktop. "So... I found something that might be of interest to you today."

"And what might that be?" Slinger looked like he might drop his head any second now, landing with a thud on the oak surface.

John slid open the drawer, pulled free the pouch, and waved it in the air. "Did you lose something?"

Slinger sat upright, instantly sobered. "Where did you get that?"

"It doesn't matter where I got it. What matters is what I'm going to do next," John said coolly, dropping the velvet pouch on the wood with a heavy thud.

Slinger bolted to his feet and sped across the room, his hand reaching for the bag.

John seized it and swung it out of reach.

"That's mine. It belongs to me. Now, hand it over," Slinger demanded.

"Nope, not happening." His nose wrinkled at the stench of body odor and whiskey emanating from the sheriff.

Slinger fumbled with the gun in his holster, finally fishing it free.

While Slinger bungled about, John got to his feet, drew his gun, and held it steady, pointed at Slinger's head. "I'm not drunk, Mark. Like I said, you're bousy. I can lay you out in two seconds flat."

The sheriff reached up and scratched his head with the hand holding the gun. "I haven't had that much to drink."

"Keep telling yourself that." John cocked the trigger of his handgun. "I suspect you've got a belly full of bluestone. Now, here's what we're going to do."

"What?" Slinger said, weaving where he stood.

"I want in on the action," John said, tossing the velvet bag inside the drawer and slamming it shut. He kept the gun pointed at Slinger's head with his other hand. "I'll get a cut of this money, plus any more money coming in, and I'll stay quiet about whatever activities you've got going with McCarthy and Neil."

"They's friends, is all," Slinger said, looking like he might fall to the ground. He placed his palms on top of John's desk to hold himself upright. "You've got nothing on me."

"I've got more than you know," John bluffed.

The sheriff gave him a flinty-eyed glare. "Who put you up to this? Brown? It was Brown, wasn't it? That slimy little weasel is always sticking his nose where it don't belong."

"It wasn't Brown," John said.

"It sure was. Gabe had that pouch stored at his ranch somewhere, and it was full of gold."

"I don't know nothing about that," John said. "Brown didn't give me this. Gabe was too smart to store your stolen goods at his ranch. He stored it somewhere else, apparently. A friend of a friend gave this cash to me and said it's money stolen by you. I already have a telegraph ready to go down at the post office; I told a friend to send it if I don't show up there when I leave tonight. It's directed to the Skullwood Flats Marshal. It contains all the facts I've got... enough to put you behind bars for the rest of your life."

Slinger's eyes hardened as he stared at John. Finally, he said, "I've got to sit down and think on this for a few."

"You have about two minutes before I head down to the post office," John warned.

Slinger swayed from side to side. "I'll have to check with my partners."

"What, you ain't man enough to make the decision on your own?" John asked, taunting him.

"Of course, I'm man enough." Slinger staggered toward his desk chair and fell into it again. He dropped his gun on top of the desk. "I think you're bluffing."

"And I think you're an idiot if you think that," John said as he lowered his gun and put it back in his holster. "You don't know me very well. I was the sheriff in a town up north. Ever hear of Washoe Township?"

He puffed out his chest with pride. He'd been sheriff there for over seventeen years, and he'd served the people as best he could.

"I know you was," Slinger said, rocking as if in his own private boat. "I was the one who hired you, remember? I also know about the scandal you were involved in and why you came crawling to Goldsprings to be the deputy sheriff." A wicked leer crossed his face.

John's face grew warm. "I was cleared of all wrong-doing."

Last year, he'd been accused of "carrying on" with Lady Harriet Tilton, a socialite of ill repute. The one in the wrong was a rival of his, Franklin Beecher, the mayor, who had been involved with the woman. When John had had the mayor charged for impropriety, some of Beecher's cronies had started the rumors, intending to destroy John.

John had done nothing wrong, but for a time, his family had suffered the gossip and whispered lies that echoed through the town like a telegram message.

"Doesn't mean the people forgave you," Slinger said.

He was right. The stress on John's family became too tremendous, so John had sought employment elsewhere. He thought his fortune had changed when he was hired for this job. Now he suspected that Slinger had only hired him so he could keep the scandal as a weapon in his back pocket, should he ever need it—like now.

"Like I said, my name was cleared of all wrong-doing. And the marshal in Skullwood Flats is an old friend of mine. He knows I didn't do what I was accused of. He'll be more than happy to look into your corruption should the need arise."

Slinger huffed out a sigh. "Tell you what... we can give you ten percent of what's leftover. But my partners and I work hard to keep things on the down-low and keep things in motion. We can't have a loose cannon in our organization with a past such as yours."

"My past was exemplary. I want an equal share," John said, his expression stony.

"Fifteen percent," Slinger countered.

"I'm heading to the post office right now." John got to his feet and crossed to the front door. "But, before I do, you might want to hear about a shipment of gold I heard about. I'm sure you'll reconsider. It will make the gold in that pouch seem like nothing."

Slinger bolted to his feet and lurched toward the deputy. "All right, all right, all right. Equal shares." He thrust out his hand, his eyes glittering with greed.

John eyed the sheriff's hand for a second before shaking it. *The sheriff's a wily one. I'd better watch my back.* He took Slinger's hand, shook it, then stepped back.

"So, tell me about this gold," Slinger said, suddenly as sober as a church lady.

John, with his hand on the brass doorknob, said, "The Wells Fargo Stagecoach is on its way to a city I'm not at liberty to tell about. It's taking a different route. I heard it will be carrying the largest shipment of gold bars the country has ever seen. Imagine a chest filled with two-hundred-ounce bars." He grinned.

Slinger made his way back to his chair and sat down with a heavy thud. His brow furrowed. "Why haven't I heard of such a shipment? Me and the boys keep an ear to the ground."

"If you were Wells Fargo, would you want to announce you're carrying a load full of gold bars through the flatlands? No, sir, you would not. This shipment has been kept quiet— real quiet." John let go of the doorknob and let his hand fall to his side.

"Right, right," Slinger said, his expression that of a scheming man. "So, where will we find this stagecoach?"

"Do you think I'm stupid? If I tell you right now, you'll go on and tell your bandit friends. Then, you'll take the gold all for yourself." John leaned against the door.

Slinger rubbed his thumb back and forth across his lips. "So, what do you propose, then?"

"We're going to meet under the mesquite tree at the far end of town, at eleven o'clock tomorrow. Then, you and your boys and I will head out to a secret location."

Slinger rubbed his jaw and cheeks. "All right. We'll meet up tomorrow. I'll let my boys know. You sure you're not fooling with me?"

"Why would I do that when so much is at stake? I can't take down an entire stagecoach by myself. I need help." His gaze slid to his desk. *I sure can't leave him with the pouch David brought me or the one I found.* He crossed the room, opened the desk drawer, and removed the fabric bags.

"Where you going with that?" Slinger said, lurching to his feet.

"Don't worry, we'll split this soon enough," John said, holding out his palm to Slinger. "I'm keeping this as collateral, so you don't filch it."

He strode toward Slinger's desk and picked up the gun the sheriff had left there. *If he weren't so drunk, he'd already had this weapon drawn.* Pointing the revolver at Slinger, John said, "And if you try anything on me as I make my way outside, you're a dead man."

Slinger threw his hands into the air before slouching back in his chair. "I wondered if you had a backbone in you."

John kept a steady gaze on the sheriff as he backed his way out the door. Once outside, he made haste for his horse, pitched the money pouches in his saddlebag, and mounted Little Joe, his pinto. Then, he took off in the direction of David's house, intending to fill him in on the plan.

A full moon, round as a dinner plate, rose over the mountains as Little Joe loped across the landscape. John urged his horse onward, hoping to arrive at David's before the family tucked themselves into bed for the night.

Once they left the safety of the town, the coyotes could be heard singing their mournful tune. Little Joe's ears pricked, and he stayed watchful and alert.

John slowed his horse to a walk. Having spent time as a cattle wrangler in his early days, John knew the nighttime vigil all too well. He'd herd cattle from before the sun appeared on the horizon into the early evening when everyone gathered near a place plentiful with grass and water. While waiting for a supper of son-of-a-gun stew, basically "ever'thing but the hair, horns, and holler" of a cow, or chuckwagon chicken, bacon-wrapped in flour and fried in tallow, he'd take a nap, using his saddle as his pillow. After supper, when everyone bedded down for the night, he often had night watch duty. Singing songs and softly playing the harmonica kept the livestock calm. The last thing they needed was a stampede if the cattle or the horses spooked from the coyotes or a thunderstorm.

So, as John rode across the high desert toward the Brown's ranch, he sang. His voice emerged clear and strong as he belted out *Bury Me Not On The Lone Prairie* and *Green Grow the Lilacs.*

Little Joe seemed to calm, leaving John to keep an eye out for predators or Indians.

When they crossed the shallow creek, John knew they were almost at David's. Little Joe successfully forged the creek, picking his way past the trees until the home was in John's view. Soft golden light illuminated the windows, letting John know at least one of the occupants was awake.

He arrived at the house, dismounted Little Joe, and strode toward the front porch in the dark, only to be met with a rifle pointed at his head. "Easy. It's me, Deputy Angus," he said, lifting his palms in the air.

"Oh," David said, lowering his rifle. "This Slinger business has got me spooked. Can't be too careful."

"Understood," John said. "So, we've got ourselves a plan. Can you meet me out beneath the mesquite tree on the far side of town at half-past eleven? I've tricked Slinger into thinking that we've got a Wells Fargo shipment of gold coming through an undisclosed location, and I'm going to take him to rob the stagecoach. He's meeting me at eleven."

"How'd you manage that?" David said.

"The sheriff came into the office drunk like he'd been making a blue blotter out of himself. It wasn't hard to convince him when he heard the word 'gold,'" John said. "I'll get word to some more law officials to arrive, and you'll show them the letter your brother wrote you. When I hand over the stolen money to them, we'll have enough to take Slinger and his cronies in." He reached around to squeeze the back of his neck. "It's going to be a long night, but it'll be worth it to put Slinger behind bars."

"I appreciate it, Deputy, I really do," David said. "And you can bet I'll be there. I'll be able to finally rest easy once we've put my brother's killer behind bars."

Chapter Thirty-Four

Anxiety gnawed at David's insides as he milked the cows in the dim light of dawn. He'd rolled from his bed nearly two hours ago, before the sun set its mind to rise, but he simply couldn't sleep. He *had* to get up and get to the day and then head on into town to catch the rattlesnake—Sheriff Slinger.

Familiar smells of hay, fresh milk, and dairy cow wafted in the air, lending comfort to the moment. David loved being a rancher and tending to the needs of his livestock.

As he wrung the teats of Daisy, one of his milk cows, the sound of soft footsteps moving in his direction made him look over his shoulder. The footsteps were far too delicate to belong to the hired hand—they had to belong to Amanda.

Sure enough, she proceeded toward him, a lovely smile on her beautiful face.

"Good morning," she said in her lilting voice.

"Mornin'," he said. "Did you sleep well enough?" He'd been fixing to invite her into his bed but hadn't got the nerve up to ask her.

"Oh, I tossed and turned a bit. There's too much on my mind to get a good night's rest. How about you?"

"The same. I've been up a while," David said.

She stood before him, twisting her hands around and around.

"What's got you in a fret, Amanda?" Perched as he was on the milking stool, he leaned his forearms on his thighs and studied her face.

"Mind if I help you?" she said, her gaze fixed to the floor.

He paused. "Well..." He thought a minute about the right thing to say to not hurt her feelings. The urge to do things speedily today kept him moving through his chores at a rate that could break a man's neck.

"If you're thinking I'll slow you down, and you'll have to sit with me and offer instruction, that's not what I meant at all. I'm aiming to milk the cow next to you, all by my lonesome. If I don't get it right, I'll leave you to finish. But I've been practicing." The words tumbled from her mouth like they cascaded down a waterfall.

"You've been practicing? How?" David said, his eyebrows rising in surprise.

"Ada filled one of her thread gloves with vegetable scraps from the soup pan. She held the glove and had me practice the movement like this." Amanda worked her fingers as if she held a cow's teat. "And I managed to get the juice flowing through the threads, so I reckon I can take a try on a cow to help you get on your way."

"Well, aren't you a clever one?" David chuckled. "Never heard such a thing as practicing on a glove full of soup scraps." He rose and fetched another milking stool, as well as a bucket, and propped it next to Rose, who stood docilely chewing her cud. "You can get to milking Rose. I'll finish up with Daisy and get to work on Lilybell. Then, we'll be done, and I can get on my way." David grinned at Amanda. "Thank you kindly for helping."

"I want to be a good wife and helpmate. I'm happy to assist." Amanda plunked her behind on the stool.

The warmest feeling David had ever experienced filled his chest. "So, you remember what to do?"

"Sure do," Amanda said. "Put my fingers like so..." She demonstrated finger placement. "Then, play that cow's piano."

David let out a laugh. "That's right, you play that cow's piano." Turning toward Daisy, he placed his fingers on the cow's teats and set to milking.

Soon, the air was filled with the wet sounds of milk streaming into the metal buckets from Rose and Daisy's mammary glands. For a few comfortable minutes, the pair worked to empty the cows' udders before David rose, set his bucket in the aisle, and fetched another. He brought the new bucket, as well as his milking stool, to sit next to Lilybell. "You're doing a real fine job of it, Amanda."

"Thank you." Her pretty cheeks blushed a rosy hue.

They continued to milk the animals. The warmth in David's chest spread throughout his limbs. Working side by side with his wife felt as comfortable as swinging his leg over Kickabilly and heading off to check the fence line or herding cattle. There was just something about it that felt natural and proper. Too bad the moment of comfort had to come from a moment of tragedy—one that he would make right on this very day.

He finished up with Lilybell at about the same time Amanda finished milking Rose. "Thank you for helping out. You've done a wonder," he said, reaching out to squeeze her shoulder. He still felt awkward about touching her as much as he longed to do.

She reached up and lay her palm on his fingers, pressing down. "I told you—I want to be a good wife to you, so if I can help you out by milking a cow, I'm going to do it. Do you need anything else?"

"If you don't mind hauling the bucket of Rose's milk into the kitchen, I'll be right behind you with these two other buckets. You and Ada can set them up in the icebox." David cast a warm smile in her direction.

"That sounds fine," Amanda said with a nod. She hefted the bucket and proceeded, with David by her side hauling his load.

Once he'd finished with the milk, he set to feeding the pigs and the horses. Next, he spread hay for the cattle. After that, he saddled up Kickabilly and walked him over to the house.

Amanda stepped onto the front porch as he arrived.

"Where are you headed?" he said amicably.

"I've got to weed my garden. Are you fixing to get into town?" She clutched a pair of thread gloves, made from unbleached black yarn, no doubt to protect her hands from nasty weeds and the like.

"Yep. Send me some luck. We want to catch the sheriff and make him pay for his crimes." David stood awkwardly before her, hesitant. *Just kiss her, you fool.* "Well," he said.

She smiled. "Well...?"

He leaned forward, placed his hand on her shoulder, and kissed her softly on the lips. The contact felt warm and sweet, like cream and hot apple pie.

When he withdrew, she stood with shining eyes and lifted her fingertips to her mouth.

"I'll be back this afternoon," he said with a nod. Then, he spun on his boot and mounted Kickabilly. With a kick of his heels, he spurred his horse into action, cantering down the road.

A short time later, he slowed Kickabilly to a walk as they neared the town. He hoped he didn't run into Arlo or Jim wandering about. Today, he couldn't afford to stop for anyone—he had to meet the deputy at the appropriate time. He headed past all the shops and businesses in the downtown stretch of Goldsprings. Once he passed the downtown, he proceeded past the houses and aimed for the mesquite tree in the distance.

The lonely tree stood near a trickle of a creek that often dried up in the summer. As it was still spring, it continued to hold a bit of water. Townsfolk sometimes had picnics out here.

As he approached, David made a mental note to take Amanda up on her picnic idea someday.

Ahead, the deputy sat by himself on top of his horse, beneath the mesquite tree—no sign of Slinger and his gang, nor any law enforcement.

"Where's Slinger?" David said, his brows stitched together.

"I ain't seen hide nor hair of him this morning." Angus crossed one wrist over the over and rested them on the saddle horn. "I've got a bad feeling about this."

"So, what do you think happened?" David said, reining his horse to a stop.

"I think he got suspicious, is what I think. He could have been too drunk to remember, but I've shared a drink or two with the sheriff, and he can hold his drink like a reservoir holds water." He shifted side to side in his saddle. "I've asked the other law officials to scout around the outskirts of town to see if he's skulking about."

"Maybe he got the meeting places mixed up? Maybe he thinks you're going to meet him at the office?" David said, his heart beginning to race.

"I already thought of that and I've checked there. I've checked at Dirty Dick's, too. I sent a man to check in with one of the women Mark's been courting; I even sent a couple of men out to his house—so far, there have been no sightings of Sheriff Slinger. It's like he's a ghost in the wind." Angus wiped his hand in the air in front of his face.

"What about Neil and McCarthy? Seen them around town?" David said. He lifted his hat and rubbed his forehead before replacing the Stetson back on his head.

Kickabilly pranced on his hooves, as if feeding off of David's agitation.

"I found McCarthy staggering from the saloon, but no sign of his sidekick, Neil. When I asked him of the sheriff's whereabouts, he played stupid," Angus said.

"It probably weren't hard to do. I swear, that man is as dumb as a bucket of feed. He never seems to have a lick of sense about him," David said. "His mind's as simple as the day is long."

"You got that right," Angus said.

"So, what do we do next?" David said, his earlier anxiety creeping around his insides like a burglar threatening to steal any good sense he might have left.

"I don't rightly know," Angus said. "Do you have any ideas?"

A horrifying thought wormed its way into David's mind. *What if the sheriff headed out to the ranch? He could have watched me leave from that copse of trees out back and slithered out of the shadows when I took off.*

"Where are your men?"

He lifted the reins and Kickabilly continued to prance, pivoting in a tight circle instead of standing stock-still. "Easy," David soothed.

"They should return shortly," Angus said. "Like I said, they were headed to check at Mark's house. Why?"

"Did he mention anything about me when you confronted him last night?" David said.

"Not that I recall." The deputy squeezed the bridge of his nose. "Wait... that's incorrect. He said something about how it was you who set him up and, 'that slimy little weasel is always sticking his nose where his nose don't belong.'"

"Of course, he did. I'll bet he didn't like Gabe so much, and he sure doesn't like me. He's made his feelings clear this past two weeks—he gives me lip service when I come to him with a concern. At the same time, you can see in his eyes he's scheming and setting his sights on escaping the conversation. So, what I'm thinking is, I'll bet he didn't believe your story. He knew the bag of gold was out at my ranch. He's come out a few times to supposedly check on me, all the while asking to see the barn and talking about a pouch Gabe had, like I told you. So, I'll bet my bottom dollar he's at my house or headed there." He squeezed the back of his neck hard like he was fixing to pull it free from his shoulders. "I got to get back there. Find your men... find them and come on out to my place."

"Jumpin' Jehoshaphat! Why didn't I think of that? I'll bet you're right. Get on out there, and I'll get the others and be there shortly." Angus spurred his horse into action, heading out opposite David.

David dug his heels into Kickabilly and added a "heya!"

Kickabilly reared slightly, then took off at a mad gallop.

David kept his horse running through the plains and up into the foothills, heading for his home. All the while, he held a fervent prayer to God in his heart. *Keep my Amanda safe, Lord. Both her and Ada. Keep them safe and free from harm.*

Kickabilly's mouth foamed by the time they arrived at the ranch.

David reined him into a prancing walk as he cast his gaze around frantically, searching for signs of the sheriff. He found what he was looking for when he spied Slinger's horse tied beneath one of the mesquite trees. "So help me, God, if he's laid a hand on my girl..." he muttered, unable to finish the sentence. He leaped from his saddle and tied Kickabilly to a fencepost as he sprinted toward the house.

It was eerily quiet inside his home. There were no clatters of pans or dishes from the kitchen and no sign of Amanda or Ada anywhere.

Where in the blazes can they be? David raced up the stairs, only to be met with the same eerie silence.

He stormed back downstairs, checking his office, the front room, the dining room, everywhere he could think of. Unable to find either woman, he hurried outside, where he headed for the barn.

The sound of voices sent a chill up and down his spine.

The frantic cries of his wife and Ada, mixed with the sheriff's words, let David know Slinger had them both trapped in the barn.

Chapter Thirty-Five

David's lungs froze, unwilling to let any air in or out as he stood outside the barn, listening to the rants and ravings of Sheriff Slinger.

Nearby, his horse's body heaved as he worked to catch his breath from the fast-paced galloping he'd just accomplished to get David home in as short a time as possible.

"Let me go!" Amanda cried. "Let Ada and me go!"

"Not until that wretch of a man you married arrives," Slinger said.

"What did he do to you? Hasn't he suffered enough?" Amanda said in a desperate-sounding voice.

"Oh, he ain't going to suffer none. Not if he hands me what I came for," Slinger said. "His brother left me a mess of gold out here. Angus only showed me a little of what's out here." A beat of silence stretched into the air. "I hear you and Gabe was going to get hitched... that you was one of them mail-order brides." He let out a sinister-sounding laugh. "That sounds more like a prostitute, if you ask me. How much did Gabe pay you to come out here?"

David bristled where he stood. Amanda was anything but a prostitute—she was the most angelic creature he'd ever laid eyes on.

"Gabe didn't pay me a dime. He asked for my hand in marriage," Amanda shot back.

"And so, when he didn't turn up, you thought you'd snatch up his brother... you're a bit of a conniver, ain't you?" Slinger said.

Anger flared inside of David as he listened to the disrespectful manner in which Slinger spoke to Amanda. He finally got his legs to move and stealthily crept around the barn.

"I'm nothing of the sort. David's a good man. He asked me to marry him for having come so far with no family to my name," Amanda said.

"Well, isn't that a sad little story? Had I known you were up for grabs, I would have taken you for myself," Slinger said.

"I wouldn't marry you if you were the last man on earth."

Slinger laughed. "You're a feisty one, I'll grant you that. I love a feisty woman."

Amanda let out a yelp.

I'm going to tear that man's limbs from his body if he's touched her in any way. David kept up his steady tiptoeing around the corner, heading for the barn door.

"Why'd you do it, Sheriff? Why'd you kill David's brother?" Amanda asked.

"I had to, woman, not that it's any of your concern. Gol durn fool was getting in my business, pretending to be asleep in his office chair all while secretly plotting against me. A friend of his told me he kept records on me and my whereabouts, fixing to turn me in to the marshals. I had to put a bullet through his head to keep his tongue from wagging. Just like I'm fixing to do to you if you keep flapping your gums at me."

Amanda screamed. "No!"

A bullet exploded and tore through the wall of the barn, a few yards away from David.

He sprinted toward the doorway and bolted inside, half-expecting to see Amanda laid out dead on the ground.

"David!" she cried when he burst into the barn. She lay on the floor, her ankles and wrists bound with rope.

"There you are, you little weasel," Slinger said at the same time. A smoking revolver hung from his hand.

Ada lay slumped in the corner on a hay bale, tied similarly to Amanda, with a smear of dried blood spread across her cheek.

"What did you do to Ada?" David roared.

"I didn't do nothing to her except teach her not to backtalk me," Slinger said, looking mighty pleased with himself. "I knocked some sense into her with the butt of my revolver. She'll be fine."

"She'd better be, or I'll put a bullet through your head so fast you won't have time to blink," David said, realizing his rifle was still hanging on his saddle.

"Big talk coming from an unarmed man. Where's the gold?" Slinger demanded.

"I don't know what you're talking about." David scanned the barn for anything he could use as a weapon.

"I'll bet you do. I'll bet it was you who put Angus up into trying to trick me. He showed me a little bag of gold and said it was something Gabe had gathered. There's more where that came from. I know it. Angus showed me a fraction of what Gabe had. And I know for a fact the gold was stored out at your ranch. You set me up. And *you* stole some of *my* money." He waved the gun in the air.

"I told you before and I'm telling you again, I don't know anything about a bag of gold. You're dreaming, Slinger."

Slinger shot his gun again, sending a bullet through the roof this time.

He's lost his fool mind, David thought, as he jerked from the deafening noise.

Amanda looked frightened, all trussed and bound on the floor.

She has every right to be scared. David longed to comfort her, but he had to get her away from Slinger and his raving.

"Stop bluffing. I know the gold is out here! McCarthy knew it was out here. He stayed on Gabe's trail all the time, in the shadows in secret. He saw Gabe dismount from his horse out here and pull the bag of gold from his saddlebag!" Slinger yelled. "Where did you hide it? Tell me!"

And there's the proof I was after. When the sheriff was out here snooping around, all the time he was looking for that pouch of money. "I don't know what you're talking about!" David yelled back.

The sheriff lunged at David, grabbing him by his shirt. "I want my gold!" he bellowed, saliva spraying from his mouth and striking David's face.

David's brain raced, trying to come up with something, anything to say to Slinger to get him away from his property. *I've got to talk some sense into him. He's a lunatic!* When the sheriff released him, David wiped his face with his shirt-covered arm.

In the corner, Ada stirred, moaning.

"Ada!" Amanda cried.

David started to rush to Ada's side, but Slinger aimed his gun at him. David thrust his hands in the air.

"Don't move. You're going to show me where the gold is, or I'm killing each and every one of you." Slinger spoke in a low, deadly voice.

"Now, Sheriff, let's see to reason," David said, thinking fast. *I've got to calm down his fool mind.* "Why on earth would Gabe hide the gold out here?"

Ada shook her head and blinked. "Amanda! David! Are you all right?"

The sheriff swung his revolver in Ada's direction. "Shut yer mouth, woman, or I'll put a bullet through your head."

Ada clutched her hands beneath her chin and whimpered.

"Come on, now, Sheriff," David said, using the same tone he used for soothing horses. "Gabe weren't no saphead. Why would he bring the gold to our home? If he did, he knew he'd put Ada and me at risk, as well as Amanda, who he thought would become his wife."

Slinger narrowed his eyes at David as if considering his words. He reached up and scratched his chin with the hand holding the revolver.

"You're welcome to look around," David said. "Didn't I let you look around before? I opened my house to you and let you look everywhere, and you didn't find a thing. So, I sure don't know where else we can look, unless we set to digging holes in the yard. And wouldn't I have noticed if the dirt was out of sorts like someone had taken a shovel to it to bury gold? I'm out here every day, working from dawn until dusk, and I ain't seen no hole."

Where in the blazes are the deputy and his men? They should be out here by now. He strained to hear any sound of galloping hooves, but the only thing he heard was the pounding of his own heartbeat.

The sheriff continued to stare at David, his eyes a flinty gray. "Why should I believe you?"

"Why shouldn't you believe me? I don't want you on my property any more than you want to be out here. I'm sure you hoped to just conduct your business and be on your way. I want that, too. Why would I keep trying to reason with you and prevent you from finding this so-called gold that's supposedly out here?" David held his palms in front of him.

"Because you want my gold, that's why," Slinger bellowed.

"I don't need your money, Sheriff. You know that. I've got all the money I need. Why would I waste my time taking what's yours when I got plenty of my own?" David reasoned.

Slinger studied him through one squinty eye. "Maybe you have some of your gold stored out here?"

David laughed. "My daddy weren't no fool. He made Gabe and me store what's ours inside a safe deposit box in a bank far away from here. Our money's secured—it's secured from you, it's secured from me. I can't even get to it if I wanted to," he lied.

"Then your daddy *is* a fool. A man should be able to put his hands on what's his by rights," the sheriff said, stroking his jaw.

"Maybe so... but I'll tell you what. You want to look around here for gold, go ahead and look around. But let's untie the women-folk." He glanced at Amanda.

She bore a strange expression, like she was trying to tell him something.

He gave her a subtle shake of his head, indicating he couldn't read minds.

"What do you say, Sheriff? Can we let the women-folk go?"

"I don't trust that woman of yours as far as I can throw her. And Ada? She's old, but I'm sure she still has some gumption in her. The women remain as they is until we find the gold." He waved the gun in their direction.

David sighed. "Where would I store gold around here? You give me one good place to look, and you and I can go look."

The sheriff stood in place, eying David suspiciously.

"Go on, then," David said. "Let's you and me scare up some gold." He strode toward a wooden box where he kept horse blankets.

The sheriff whipped his gun in the air and pointed it at Amanda.

She let out a whimper.

"Don't you harm one hair on her head," David warned.

"Or, what? I'll do as I please, given I'm the one who's holding a weapon," Slinger said.

"I was only going to check the box for gold... doesn't that seem like a likely place to look?"

The sheriff redirected the revolver at David but sidled toward the box.

David put his hands up and inched in the same direction. When he stood in front of the wooden crate, he slowly lifted the lid. "Go ahead and look," he told Slinger.

Slinger continued to point his Smith and Wesson at David as he leaned over and rifled through the horse blankets with one hand. "Ain't nothing in here but wool."

"That's what I've been trying to tell you, Sheriff. I ain't got no gold out here. We can continue on looking for fool's gold, or you can let the women go and be on your way." David glanced at Amanda.

She inclined her head again, appearing to silently communicate something to him.

I wish I knew what you were trying to say. And where is the deputy? He should have arrived long ago. What in tarnation am I going to do to get rid of the sheriff? David shrugged.

Just as the sheriff was about to open his mouth and say more nonsense, Amanda blurted, "I know where the gold is!"

"Amanda! Stay out of this!" David said.

"But I'm telling the truth, David," she said, her eyes pleading with him. "I found more gold while you were out this morning. Untie me, and I can show you where it is."

Chapter Thirty-Six

One hour earlier...

Amanda stood on the front porch of the ranch, watching David disappear from sight atop Kickabilly. He was setting off to do something dangerous—confront and apprehend Sheriff Slinger. But she knew, having witnessed his steadfast behavior and determination, if anyone could get Slinger, it was David.

As she stood there, she wrung her hands, a nervous habit she'd developed since her ma and pa had died. She held her hands before her and stared. *David would tell me to do something useful rather than stand around and fret.* So, armed with new determination, she marched into the house, intending to clean it from top to bottom. She paused when she stood in the doorway of the unfurnished sitting room and sparsely furnished formal dining room.

I've never bothered to fix these rooms up. Shame on me. I have all the money I need, but I never took the time to accomplish the tasks I agreed to early on.

She ran back to her room and fetched her pen, ink, and a piece of paper. Then, she sat in the lone chair in the dining room and drew plans.

I think we need a fine table and chairs in here for when we have guests. We can have Arlo and Jim and their families over, to start. We'll add wallpaper to the room and a sideboard for all of Ada's fancy china that she keeps in the kitchen. Maybe we need new silverware.

As she sketched and made lists, she grew more and more excited. Once she'd finished, she scurried into the kitchen to show Ada.

Ada stood at the stove, stirring a delicious stew smelling of pork and vegetables.

"Ada, look! I've drawn up some plans for the formal dining room. What do you think?" She thrust her drawings and scribbles in Ada's direction.

Ada set her spoon to the side of the stove, wiped her hands off on her apron, and took the paper in her worn hands. As she scanned Amanda's notes, she nodded. "These look fine, Amanda. Real fine." Her eyes misted over. "David's mama would be so proud of you."

Amanda felt the heat rolling up her neck and face. "Thank you. I wish I could have met her. She did so many things to this place to make it look pretty."

"Oh, she loved this place. If she and the boys' father hadn't died, David and Gabe would have built their own homes and lived nearby. Then, we'd all gather here for holidays and such. But the good Lord had his own plans, I suppose." She wiped her eyes with the corner of her napkin. "Listen to me. I'm a sentimental old fool."

On impulse, Amanda reached out to hug Ada, something she'd never done.

Ada stiffened for a few seconds, then embraced Amanda back. When she released Amanda, a few tears slid down her face. "I'm so glad you're here, Amanda. I think you're well-suited to David. It's a shame Gabe died, it really is, but I know in my heart you and David were meant to be." After wiping her tears again, she stood up straight and handed the piece of paper back to Amanda. "I know a woodworker we can talk to, to get the table made. His name's Bo Carter. He lives in town. Next time we head in there, we can meet with him and give him your plans. He's easy to work with, and his craftsmanship is outstanding."

Amanda grinned, feeling the kind of warmth in her chest she hadn't felt for a long, long time. It felt like she was creating a real sense of family with Ada and David. "That sounds wonderful, Ada. Maybe we can surprise David."

"I don't know how surprised he'll be, given the wallpaper chore. You and I will have to tackle that. I helped David and Gabe's mother with some of the wallpaper, and it's not easy. But, with a little gumption on our side, we can get 'er done." Ada returned the smile.

"Do you think the hired hands will help?" Amanda asked.

"Oh, golly, no." Ada grimaced. "We don't want those men clomping around the house, getting underfoot. They're best suited to outdoor work." She glanced at her stove, alerted by the sound of bubbling, boiling liquid. "I'd best see to the stew. I have biscuits to make, a pie to bake..."

"And I'll help you as soon as I can," Amanda said. Glancing out the window, she added, "Look! There's someone on horseback heading for the ranch."

Ada turned her head and immediately paled. "Oh, my gracious! That's Slinger. I thought David headed into town to deal with him. This can't be good."

"We've got to hide!" Amanda cried, her eyes glued to the window. "Where can we go?"

"Let's head out the back door and scoot on out to the barn. There are more places to hide out there," Ada said. She moved the pot of stew from the burner and stoked the wood. "Let's hurry!"

Amanda raced for the door, flinging it open. The abundant flora from the back garden would shield them as they made their way to the barn. She hurried out the door, with Ada close on her heels.

The galloping hooves grew closer as the women made their way across the lush yard.

The galloping ceased, and Slinger said, "Whoa, whoa."

Sweat trickled down Amanda's face and neck as she moved as fast as she could toward the barn, their intended hiding place. They had to head out into the open to get to the barn. Looking every which way, she saw no sign of Slinger, save for his horse's tail swishing to and fro near the front of the house.

As they raced around the barn, Slinger's horse let out a loud whinny while Slinger pounded against the door. "Ada!" he bellowed. "Amanda! Open the door. I know you're in there."

As he kept up his caterwaul, Amanda quietly opened the barn door. "Get in here," she hissed to Ada. "Hurry!"

Once inside the large wooden building, she looked around for places to hide. "Where can we go?"

Poor Ada looked as white as flour. "Let's get in the tack room. He won't think to look in there."

"Good idea," Amanda said, hurrying to cross the barn floor.

Chester nickered from his stall as she passed it.

"I'm sorry, Chester," she said. "I can't give you treats right now. After the sheriff leaves, I'll be sure to get you some."

She stopped when she stood before the tack room door. Slinger continued to bellow from their front porch as she slid open the latch and made her way inside the small room. Ada quickly joined her.

Reins and harnesses hung from the wall, while saddles rested on stands with blankets and padding beneath each one. Huge horse blankets and coiled ropes hung from the opposite wall. A sizeable handcrafted sign at the back of the room said *The Brown Ranch.* But there was really no place to hide.

Amanda stood on her tiptoes, trying to get an equine coat from the hook.

"What are you doing?" Ada said.

"You make sure the door is good and tight. We'll huddle beneath the saddles and cover ourselves with the woolen coverings. Maybe we'll look like we belong here," Amanda said, having pulled the blanket free from its hook. She reached for the next one and made her way to the corner of the room.

Ada quietly closed the tack room door, plunging them into darkness. "Where are you headed?"

"In the back corner," Amanda whispered. "Use the side wall to feel your way back here. But let's keep our voices down."

Amanda's heartbeat hammered in her ears, and her mouth was as dry as a bone as she pulled the heavy wool around her body. Fear flooded her bloodstream.

Everything sounded too loud to her ears.

Ada's footsteps sounded like a team of Clydesdales as she crossed the room and her shin bumped into Amanda's leg. "There you are."

"Get down here with me," Amanda whispered. "Here..." She fumbled around to find the second covering and thrust it in Ada's general direction.

Together, the two women huddled beneath the smothering wool.

All Amanda could hear were the rapid pants of her and Ada's breathing as she clutched the wool over her head. "Let's remove the blankets unless we hear the sheriff in here. I can't breathe."

"Good plan," Ada whispered.

"What do you think he's doing? I don't hear him hollering anymore."

"I don't know. Probably helping himself to some stew," Ada said under her breath.

"Do you... do you think...?" Amanda couldn't finish the sentence.

"Let's not worry about David." Ada's fingers fumbled to find Amanda's hand. She clutched it in hers, lending strength to Amanda. "He's a resourceful, capable man."

Yes, but I'm sure Gabe was resourceful, too, and look what happened? Amanda rolled her lips between her teeth. *I don't know what I'll do if anything happens to David.* She squeezed her eyes shut, forcing back the tears that threatened to spill.

"It's in the Lord's hands," Ada continued quietly. "I don't think He would have brought you two together only to rip you apart from one another."

"I don't know," Amanda lamented.

"Well, I do, so *hush.*" Ada gripped Amanda's hands tightly with her own.

The two women sat in silence, waiting.

Amanda strained to hear something, anything, indicating Slinger's whereabouts. "I'm not moving until I hear Slinger's horse hooves moving away from here."

"I agree," said Ada.

The silence unnerved Amanda as she waited. She felt like she could hear the flies crawling on the wall and dust motes swirling in the air. Her own breath sounded like a windstorm in her ears.

But then, footsteps approached, and the barn door opened with a clatter.

"Oh, no!" Ada whispered.

"Pull the blanket over your head!" Amanda whispered back, ducking beneath her covering.

The footsteps came closer. "I should take you with me, you old horse," Slinger said, presumably to Chester. "I could sell you to some factory to make glue. You'd fetch me a good price." He paused a beat. "Did you see two women come in the barn? I know they're in here because they left the back door open. I've got me some good wits."

Ada let out a small whimper. She'd probably left the door open.

"Shhh," Amanda soothed.

"Now, where would two stupid women think they could hide?" Slow, plodding footsteps echoed through the barn. "Would they be hiding in your stall?" Wood rasped against wood as the sheriff no doubt opened Chester's stall. "Get on out of here," Slinger said, accompanied by the sound of a slap from his hand.

Chester let out a frightened whinny, and his loud steps clattered into the barn and out the door.

Oh, no. Slinger's set Chester free. Amanda's breath caught in her throat.

"Nope, they ain't in here," Slinger said. "How about in the feed bin?" A loud whack of wood against wood rang out. "Nope, they ain't in here," he repeated. "Where are you?" he said in a sing-song voice. "Come on out and show yourselves. I won't hurt you, I only want you to help me find the gold Gabe left here."

Gold? What gold? David said he gave the whole pouch to the deputy. Amanda pulled her knees tight against her body.

More clatters rang throughout the barn. The sheriff must have overturned bins, tipped over barrels, and tossed objects to the side. He began to curse, and nonsensical ravings poured from his mouth.

"I deserve the gold," he shouted. "It's all mine. I worked this town like a magic man to gain the power and status I deserve. It's mine, I tell you, all mine!'

Oh, Lord, he's lost his fool mind. Amanda's heartbeat thundered so loud she felt sure the sheriff would soon hear it. She fumbled through the coverings to find Ada's hand. Once she held it, she bore down on Ada's fingers.

"David Brown's going to pay. I killed his fool brother, and he's next. He can't stand in my way!" Slinger cried. "Now, where are you, Ada? And that sweet little thing, Amanda? Let's us have us some fun together, what do you say?"

Amanda wondered if she would crush Ada's bones. Her eyelids began to flutter and, unable to help herself, she felt light-headed. *We should have brought guns out here. Instead, we're weaponless against a madman.*

The slow-moving footsteps headed toward the tack room.

Amanda wondered if she might faint.

Ada's hand felt cool and clammy.

"Well, well, well," the sheriff said. "I didn't think to look in here." He rapped against the tack room door. "Hello? Anybody in there?" A chuckle left his throat. "First, I'll cut the old woman's throat and watch her bleed out. And then, I'll have my way with David Brown's wife. He won't be able to stomach her once I'm done using her for my own pleasure."

Yanking back her hand, Amanda pressed her fist into her mouth, stifling a sob. *Please, God, please don't let him lay a finger on me or touch Ada.*

The door flew open, banging against the wall.

Slinger laughed. "Look at those quivering lumps beneath those horse blankets. That couldn't be Ada and Amanda, could it? They thought they were so clever, trying to hide from me. You dumb women... You can't hide from me."

Amanda's limbs began to quiver and shake beneath the wool.

Footsteps approached, and the blanket was yanked from over her head.

"Well, well, well," Slinger repeated, leering at her. "It looks like this must be my lucky day."

Chapter Thirty-Seven

With a scream, Amanda lurched to her feet and shoved the sheriff backward.

"Why, you little..." he shouted as she wriggled around him and raced from the tack room.

Feed, barrels on their sides, and other debris littered the barn floor.

Amanda picked up a small, empty barrel, whirled around, and threw it at the sheriff as he lumbered toward her.

The barrel struck him in the chest. He stumbled and fell back with a loud "oof." Scrambling to his feet, he let out a roar as he powered in Amanda's direction.

Amanda seized Chester's harness, which had fallen to the floor, and whipped it at Slinger.

It caught him in the face, leaving red marks across his cheeks. Slinger cursed and grabbed the harness before it landed on the floor as Amanda scurried toward the door.

Slinger caught the back of her skirt, hauling her backward.

She slammed into his sweaty torso.

"Is this how you want to play, huh?" In swift order, he yanked her arms behind her back and tied them with the rope end of Chester's harness. Then, clutching the harness, he hauled her toward the tack room. "Get out here, you old woman," he shouted to Ada, who still huddled on the floor. With his free hand, he reached for a couple of ropes hanging on the wall.

"Please, don't hurt Amanda. Take me, instead," Ada cried, getting to her feet.

"Like I'd want your shriveled old body when I've got this sweet young thing right here," Slinger said. Still holding the rope connected to Amanda's arms, he used his other hand to grab Ada's upper arm. He yanked both women from the room. "Here's what we're going to do," he said, heading toward the hay bales at the back of the barn. "I'm going to secure the two of you, and you're going to tell me where the gold is."

"What makes you think there's any gold out here?" Amanda said.

"Because I'm not stupid, that's why."

"I knew you were a wretch from the minute I laid eyes on you," Ada said. "I took one look at you and knew you were bad to the bone. I warned Amanda to stay away from you. You're nothing but an evil, evil man."

"Well, aren't you something to have had thoughts like that," the sheriff said. He shoved Ada on top of one of the bales.

She landed with a cry. "You're going to pay for your sins, Slinger, I guarantee it."

"Quit whimpering," he said. "You're making me ill with all your talk." He pushed Amanda toward another hay bale.

Unable to stop her forward momentum with her hands tied behind her back, she fell hard to her knees on the wooden floor.

"That's exactly where I want you, woman... on your knees. But not yet."

He let out a horrible laugh that shook Amanda to her bones.

Before she could get up, he shoved her onto her belly and wrapped her ankles with one of the ropes. "Easiest calf I ever roped," he said, adding a chuckle. "You didn't even put up a fuss."

"That's because I'm not a cow," Amanda cried, wriggling against the dusty floor in her restraints.

"No, you ain't. You're a fine filly, you are, and I'm going to have some fun with you once I find the gold."

Amanda rolled to her side right as Ada lurched from the hay bale and kicked the sheriff in the leg.

He swore before whirling to face her. "I've had about enough of you, you old hag." He whipped his revolver out of his holster and backhanded Ada with the butt of the gun.

Amanda screamed as Ada fell on top of the hay. "What did you do to her?"

"Your eyes work as well as mine do," Slinger said, using the second rope to truss Ada's ankles and wrists. "What does it look like I did?"

"Did you kill her?" Amanda said.

"'Fraid not. The old biddy's still breathing." Slinger put his hands on his hips and scanned the room. "Now, where would Brown hide the gold? It ain't in all these feed bins."

Amanda's bones pressed against the unyielding floor. "We don't have any gold out here."

"You sure do. I told you before, I ain't stupid." His dark eyes continued to scan the barn.

The welcome sound of approaching footsteps caught her ears. *Oh, thank God! It must be David!*

The sheriff continued with his ravings as Amanda strained her ears to hear the gallops. *What if it's the sheriff's gang here to help him?* This thought paralyzed her. *Still... it might be David. And if it is, I have to prevent Slinger from hearing him. I have to keep him talking.*

"Let me go!" Amanda cried. "Let Ada and me go!"

"Not until that wretch of a man you married arrives," Slinger said.

"What did he do to you? Hasn't he suffered enough?" Amanda said, her voice laced with desperation.

"Oh, he ain't going to suffer none. Not if he hands me what I came for," Slinger said. "His brother left me a mess of gold out here. Angus only showed me a little of what's out here." He paused, leering at her. "I hear you and Gabe was going to get hitched... that you was one of them mail-order brides." Another one of his maniacal laughs left his throat. "That sounds more like a prostitute, if you ask me. How much did Gabe pay you to come out here?"

"Gabe didn't pay me a dime. He asked for my hand in marriage," Amanda said. Bile shot into the back of her throat.

"And so, when he didn't turn up, you thought you'd snatch up his brother... you're a bit of a conniver, ain't you?" Slinger said.

"I'm nothing of the sort. David's a good man. He asked me to marry him for having come so far with no family to my name," Amanda said.

"Well, isn't that a sad little story? Had I known you were up for grabs, I would have taken you for myself," Slinger said.

"I wouldn't marry you if you were the last man on earth."

Slinger laughed. "You're a feisty one, I'll grant you that. I love a feisty woman."

Slinger crouched and reached for her breast. Before he could touch her, she cried out and kicked at him with her trussed-up legs. Slinger only laughed.

"Why'd you do it, Sheriff? Why'd you kill David's brother?" Amanda asked.

"I had to, woman, not that it's any of your concern. Gol durn fool was getting in my business, pretending to be asleep in his office chair all while secretly plotting against me. A friend of his told me he kept records on me and my whereabouts, fixing to turn me into the marshal. I had to put a bullet through his head to keep his tongue from wagging. Just like I'm fixing to do to you if you keep flapping your gums at me." He lifted the gun clutched in his hand and pulled the trigger, aiming over her body.

Amanda screamed. "No!"

A bullet exploded through the wall.

David burst through the doorway, his eyes wide with fright. His shoulders fell away from his ears when he saw her.

"David!" she cried as relief washed through her.

"There you are, you little weasel," Slinger said, and he and David proceeded to argue about the gold.

As they verbally sparred, a plan popped into Amanda's mind—the gun she'd hidden lay at the top of the hay bales, the very hay bales next to her. She had to convince Slinger to let her go.

She tried to catch David's gaze as he spoke to the sheriff. Trying to reason with Slinger, he was using that voice he used when he gentled horses.

From the hay bale, Ada moaned as she awoke. "Amanda! David! Are you alright?"

The sheriff trained his gun at her. "Shut yer mouth, woman, or I'll put a bullet through your head."

David redirected the conversation, distracting the sheriff.

David, please look at me. Amanda tried with all her might to capture her husband's attention.

Finally, his gaze met hers for a few fleeting seconds. With her eyes, she pleaded with him. *Will you trust me?* His brow furrowed, and he turned away.

Amanda tried again to catch David's attention as he and the sheriff sidled toward a wooden box where he kept extra horse blankets.

As if sensing her silent communication, Slinger whipped his gun in her direction.

She let out a yelp as David said, "Don't you harm a hair on her head."

"Or what? I'll do as I please, given I'm the one who's holding a weapon," Slinger said.

"I was only going to check the box for gold... doesn't that seem like a likely place to look?" David said in that same soothing voice.

The sheriff trained the gun on David and sidled toward the box.

David lifted the lid of the blanket bin. "Go ahead and look," he said to Slinger.

Once more, he glanced at Amanda.

Her eyelids fluttered as she willed her thoughts to reach him. *I've got a plan. You've got to trust me.*

David shrugged, and she took the gesture as consent, blurting, "I know where the gold is!"

"Amanda! Stay out of this!" David said.

"But I'm telling the truth, David," she said, her eyes once more pleading with him. "I found more gold while you were out this morning. Untie me, and I can show you where it is."

Slinger paused in his search and looked at her, his eyes glittering with greed. "I knew you had it out here." His head pivoted toward David. "I knew you were lying."

"Amanda, don't. Slinger's a lunatic," David said. "Let me handle this."

She met his gaze with fierce regard. "I *know* where the gold is. I found it this morning. You've got to trust me."

Something in David's eyes softened, as if he finally trusted her plan. "Okay, Amanda. I believe you. Untie her," he said to Slinger.

Slinger's gaze shifted back and forth between Amanda and David as if he was considering his next move. "I'm tying you up, though," he said to David.

"Okay," David said, once more meeting Amanda's gaze.

She gave him a subtle nod.

Slinger untied her, and she scrambled to her feet. Then, he proceeded to tie David's arms and legs. Training his gun on Amanda, he said, "Show me where it is."

Amanda's limbs quaked as she said, "It's right on top of this hay bale. I hid it up here when I found it."

The sheriff waved the gun at her. "Well, go on, then. Get on up there and get me the gold."

Amanda began to climb the hay bales, hoping her shaking arms and legs would hold her steady. The stack of hay stood tall, and the higher she climbed, the more frightened she became. When she'd hidden the gun up here, she'd been scared out of her wits. Today, with a gun pointed at her head, her terror was unparalleled. Her thoughts became fuzzy as her fear increased. With shaking hands, she reached between the bales of hay. *Where is the gun? I thought I put it here.*

"What's taking you so long?" the sheriff bellowed from below.

"It's up here. I know it is. Give me a minute more, and I'll find it." She continued to shove her hands between the bales of hay, coming up with nothing.

"You've got a few more seconds before I shoot you all dead," Slinger said, letting loose a bullet into the hay.

It struck the bale with a dull thud and an explosion of straw.

Below, Ada cried out, and David yelled, "No!"

Amanda let out her own whimper of fright and climbed higher, continuing to shove her hands between the scratchy straw. *What if it shifted too far for my hands to reach?*

Finally, her hands closed around the metal. "I found it!"

"Get on down here and give it to me!" Slinger roared.

As she picked her way down the haystack, she wrapped her fingers around the gun handle and shielded it with her skirt. Climbing down the bales proved difficult with only one hand, so she moved slowly.

"Hurry up! Or I can just put a bullet through your back and get the gold when you fall to the ground," the sheriff said, taunting her.

She tried to hasten her movements. When she sensed she was low enough, she whirled and pulled the trigger several times, aiming wildly.

One of the bullets caught the sheriff in the shoulder and he fell back with a cry, dropping his gun.

Amanda leaped from the hay bales and rushed to David's side, kicking the sheriff's gun out of the way.

David's eyes shone with pride as he looked at her.

With fumbling hands, she untied the knots around David's wrists and ankles. Once he was freed, David shouted, "Look out!"

Amanda whirled.

The sheriff staggered to his feet. A stain of blood bloomed across his shoulder and chest as he lurched toward David.

David leaped out of his way, lunging for the sheriff's revolver. He picked it up and trained it on Slinger right as Deputy Angus and several other men raced through the door.

Epilogue

Pride surged through David at Amanda's bravery as she quickly untied the ropes binding him.

Right as the ropes fell from David's legs, the sheriff, with blood staining his shirt where Amanda had clipped him in the shoulder, lurched toward him. With seconds to spare before the man was on top of him, David snatched the sheriff's gun from the floor and aimed it at Slinger's heart.

Deputy Angus and a couple other men raced into the barn, guns at the ready. They trained their weapons on Slinger.

The two additional men wore silver badges on their chests, identifying them as U.S. marshals.

One of the marshals yanked Slinger's hands behind his back, while the other kept his gun on the sheriff.

"Mark Slinger, you're under arrest for armed robbery, conspiring against the citizens of Goldsprings, and murder," Angus stated.

"You ain't got nothing on me," the sheriff bellowed.

"We've got plenty on you," Angus said, affixing a belly chain around Slinger's waist and attaching the adjoining cuffs to his wrists. "One of your associates has already talked."

"Who was it? Who talked? I'm going to kill him!" Slinger said. "And I still say you got nothing on me! Them others—they was the ones always getting into trouble. I didn't have nothing to do with their activities."

"Tell that to a judge in a court of law," Angus stated calmly. "Take him away, boys. I'll join up with you in a moment."

The marshals nodded. One of them gave Slinger a shove, and the three men proceeded outside.

Amanda rushed to David's side. "Oh, David, you were so brave!"

David looked at her with loving regard. "I'd say you're the one who's brave," he said, wanting nothing more than to pull her close—just not in front of the deputy. "Let's get Ada out of these ropes. What do you say?"

"Oh, of course!" Amanda said, turning to untie Ada's restraints. "Are you okay, Ada? You took a nasty blow to the head."

Ada's face was slightly swollen, and purple and red bruises had formed where the sheriff had hit her with his gun. "I'll be all right," she said, palpating her cheek. "We'll dab some of that healing salve you made on my face, and I'll be fine by morning." Slowly, she pushed herself to stand. "My goodness gracious. I'm glad that foul wretch of a man was taken into custody. Thank you, Deputy."

Angus tipped his hat at Ada. "I'm happy to oblige. He was nothing but a poison seed in Goldsprings. We found several of the sheriff's gang headed out here, ready to attack your ranch at the sheriff's orders."

Amanda pressed her palm to her mouth and stifled a gasp.

"We caught them at the shallow creek. They had crates of guns and ammunition hidden out there in the woods. Paper money, too. They had a whole cache of goods. We've accosted them and they're heading to the same place as Slinger."

"Where's that?" Ada said.

"The state penitentiary," Angus told her. "I doubt they'll ever see the light of day again." He turned toward David. "Nice work, capturing Slinger."

"You can thank my wife," David said, beaming at Amanda. "The sheriff had her and Ada trussed up out here like cattle. But Amanda had the good sense to trick Slinger using his greed as bait. She told him she had found some more gold out here and hid it in the hay bales. He untied her and tied me up while she climbed all the way to the top to find a pistol she hid up there. I had the gals hide some of my guns around the property where they could find them, and I did the same. No sense being unprepared when a madman is on the loose."

"Well, that was real fine thinking, Mrs. Brown," Angus said, nodding at Amanda. "Real fine. What made you think he'd come out here, David?"

"Just a hunch. The man's obsessed with his gold, and he thought I had barrels of it stored out here. He's a greedy one, he is." David shook his head.

"Greed ain't going to do him a lick of good where he's headed. He'll probably be chained to a wall for the rest of his days," Angus said.

"That's where he belongs," Ada said.

"He does, indeed. Apparently, he and his gang have been wreaking havoc all over in these parts. They've been out to Skullwood Flats and into towns further west, robbing trains, stealing from banks, and such."

David whistled. "So, it was worse than we thought."

"Apparently so. Maybe the boredom of being a sheriff got to him. Our days can be long without a lot to do. Sometimes, we have to clean the streets and help a woman with a rat problem in her house. Other times, we have to get to politicking, reaching out to the community to keep our jobs. When there's danger afoot, we have to wrangle up a posse to take down a criminal, much like we did today." Angus folded his arms across his chest. "Sometimes we don't get along so well with other law enforcement, like the U.S. Marshal. One of the ones who came out today is a friend of mine, Caleb Curtis. If he and I weren't so friendly, they might not have been eager to help us. We got lucky. But regardless, there are a lot of reasons why the sheriff turned to criminal activity."

"Oh, I think the sheriff was born mean," David said, matching the deputy's folded-arm stance. He glanced at Amanda, and she nodded as if agreeing with him. "I sat near him many a time in the saloon. He was always bellyaching about some travesty or another... about how he came from a poor family, he didn't get to go to the school he wanted, he couldn't buy the farm he wanted, and so on. If you listened to him, you'd think that money was his only problem in life, like someone was always waving a bag of gold in his face, just out of reach."

"But, like you said, he was born a bad seed," Ada said. "He had to be plucked from the jar so all the other seeds wouldn't get tainted."

"There were certainly a few bad seeds that needed to be plucked." Angus glanced toward the door. "I'd best be getting on my way. The marshals and I have a long day ahead of us." Tipping his hat, he said, "David. Mrs. Brown. Ada. You all take care, you hear?"

"We will," David said.

"Oh! One more thing," the deputy said, looking over his shoulder at David.

"What's that?" David said.

"We got a good tip from a horse trader friend of mine that we found your horses, Bueno and Calico."

David brightened. "You found my horses?"

"Yep. They're up north in a holding pen, waiting for you to claim them," Angus said with a smile.

"Thank you much, Deputy. That's wonderful news!"

After the deputy had exited the barn, David said, "Let's head on in the house and get cleaned up, what do you say? Amanda can get you fixed up, Ada, and we can put this ordeal behind us."

When they stepped outside the barn, old Chester stood a few yards away, contentedly grazing in the grass surrounding the field.

By Chester's side was the mustang that David hadn't had the time to train yet.

"Well, isn't that something," David said, eying the two horses. "Amanda, go on in the barn and fetch me Chester's harness, will you please?"

"Sure," Amanda said, rushing toward the barn.

When she returned a few minutes later, she handed the harness to David.

"Thank you kindly." Holding the harness, David took an easy stride in the direction of the two horses.

He affixed the harness around Chester's massive head, deciding to turn him out in his round pen so David could set to righting the debris and feed-cluttered barn.

The mustang walked along behind, with his nose a few inches away from Chester's rump.

When David led Chester into the pen, the mustang walked in, too. "Would you look at that—you think Chester, a horse nearly twice your size, is part of your herd?" He chuckled, backing out of the pen and closing the gate behind him.

He strode toward Ada and Amanda, who stood watching him.

"So that mustang thinks he belongs with Chester, huh?" Ada said, her hands propped on her hips. "Isn't that a wonder?"

"Sure is. That fool mustang grazes outside the pastures and has shown no interest in the other horses, but, apparently, he took a shine to old Chester." David eyed the two horses as they stood companionably side by side. "What was Chester doing outside his stall? Usually, he prefers to remain in the barn by his lonesome."

"Sheriff Slinger turned him out," Amanda said. "Spooked him, and Chester escaped. I guess he didn't get far. I thought he'd take off, and you'd have lost another horse."

"Oh, my horses know where the feed comes from. They won't ever stray too far," David said. "Let's head on inside." He took Amanda's hand in his and led her toward the house.

Ada glanced at him, and a mysterious smile crossed her face.

"What are you grinning about?" David said.

"I'm glad to see you enjoying your wife, is all," Ada said.

"Huh," David said as heat flushed his neck and face. "Ain't it my right to enjoy her?"

"Yes, David, it's surely your right," Ada said, adding a chuckle as she entered the back of the house first.

David tugged on Amanda's hand, holding her back. Emotion seemed to get the best of him, and his throat choked up. "I'm right proud of you, Amanda."

"Thank you," she said, turning to face him. Her eyes shone as she regarded him. "I was in a fret when I watched you leave. I had a bad feeling about the day. But I figured you'd tell me the best thing to do was to find some hard work to do instead of worrying, so that's what I did."

David grinned. "I guess I got me a fine wife, didn't I? She might be a bit clumsy, but she's learning how to get her legs beneath her." He chuckled.

Amanda cast her gaze at the ground. "I reckon I am." She let out a big sigh. "When we saw the sheriff heading our way, I was so worried that something had happened to you. Ada told me you're a capable, resourceful man, so I clung to that notion the best I could. We ran out the back door and hid in the tack room, pulling horse blankets over our heads. But the sheriff... he found us out there. Oh, David, I've never been more scared in my life! Slinger, he was raving about the gold, threatening to have his way with me and that he'd make sure I was sullied and you wouldn't want me, and..." Tears spilled down her cheeks.

"Easy, girl," David soothed, drying her eyes with his thumbs. "You're alright. I'd have been heartsick had the sheriff harmed a hair on your head. But I wouldn't want you any less." He held her face in his palms and studied her. His throat choked up. "You did fine today—you and Ada. You kept your wits about you, even though you were scared. That's all a person can ask for, that even if scared, he acts."

"Thank you, David. You've already taught me that. I needn't stand around wringing my hands when there's a chore that needs to be done or something needs mending."

Amanda's eyes glistened. "I'm so glad you're okay," she said through her tears. "I love you with all my heart."

Before he had time to react or respond, Amanda lifted her face and pulled him down for a kiss.

David kissed her back with a fierceness he'd never before experienced. He poured every ounce of passion into loving her. And, from her yielding response, she did the same.

When they managed to untangle from one another, it took a few minutes to get his wits about him to figure out what to do or say next. "You're the best thing that ever happened to me, Amanda. I... I..." He swallowed back the lump in his throat. "I reckon I love you back with all my heart."

"Oh, David, do you mean that?" Amanda said, with her hands on his hips.

"I do, Amanda. I really do. And, um..." He glanced skyward, seeking courage.

"What is it?" Amanda asked gently.

For a few seconds, he couldn't speak. The words all tangled up in his throat. "What do you say to move into my... to *our* bedroom? I can think of nothing finer than to cozy up by your side every night I lay my head down to rest."

"Oh, David. I'd be right pleased to sleep by your side," Amanda said. She threw her arms around him, practically tackling him to the ground in her typical "gangly colt" fashion.

"Whoa, whoa, girl, you're about to knock me over," David said, then laughed. "Good thing I'm strong."

"Good thing," Amanda agreed, pulling him down for another kiss.

This time, the kiss was tender and sweet.

When they eased apart, David said, "You know, reading that letter—that letter from Gabe. That's what finally set me free. When he suggested I love you and care for you if something untoward were to happen to him, well..." He stopped speaking again as another wave of emotion strangled his ability to speak. "I guess that's what I did without knowing what he intended. I made the right choice."

"Yes, you did. You truly made the right choice." Amanda beamed at him.

"What do you say we head on into the house, wife?"

"I'd like that, husband," Amanda said.

The back door opened, and Ada trudged outside, bearing jars of lemonade. "Let's sit outside and celebrate. I've put the healing salve on my face, said a few prayers, and now..." Ada's gaze slid back and forth between them. "Now it looks like we can sit a spell and thank the good Lord that Slinger has been caught."

"Amen to that," David said, reaching for a jar.

"Amen to that," Amanda echoed, her hand brushing his as she reached for a beverage.

"Here's to family," David said, lifting his jar to touch Ada's and Amanda's. He reached for Amanda with his free hand, tugging her toward one of the stumps.

Ada followed.

They all settled in the yard. A few birds sang and tittered, hopping about in the bushes beneath a clear blue sky. A good amount of clean-up loomed ahead of them, as well as some healing. But as long as he had Amanda by his side, David knew everything would get handled. And he felt like the luckiest man in the whole wide world.

He had a wonderful wife in Amanda, and an excellent housekeeper and friend in Ada. And, when it came down to it, was there anything more precious than family?

Extended Epilogue

Amanda hummed as she bustled about the kitchen, trying out a new recipe, something called Gold Hill Rocks. "This sure is a lot of butter," she said to Ada, creaming a pound of the churned milk-fat with an ample amount of brown sugar.

"That's what gives them treats their flavor," Ada said, chopping two whole chickens into smaller pieces. The whack of her knife against the cutting board echoed rhythmically into the room.

"I think the flavor comes from all these other ingredients." Amanda stared down at the neat penmanship of Estelle, Arlo's wife, running her finger over the smudged, flour-dusted paper. "Let's see, there are six eggs, walnuts, raisins, five cups of flour, salt, and cinnamon. That will give us about thirteen dozen cookies."

"And David and those two ranch hands of his will have them all eaten in a day or two if we let them," Ada said with a sniff. "Still, it was mighty kind of Estelle to give you the recipe."

Amanda and Estelle had become fast friends. When Amanda and Ada went into town, they often stopped by Estelle's to share a cup of tea and a Johnnycake or a sweet, like Gold Hill Rocks, before heading back home. And Estelle, Arlo, and their two children often stopped by for a nice dinner, eaten in the newly decorated formal dining room that Amanda and Ada had completed. On her last visit into town, Amanda had begged Estelle for the Gold Hill Rocks recipe, wanting to delight David with the tasty treats.

Ada gave a final whack to the chicken with her cleaver and set the knife to the side. "Now, here's your chicken. What should I do next to prepare it?"

"Coat 'em up with flour, eggs, and apple cider. I'll make the marinade as soon as these cookies are in the oven," Amanda said as she carefully measured flour.

"Marinade on fried chicken... haven't we become fancy out here," Ada said with a smile.

"It's the marinade that gives it its special taste. David says he loves it," Amanda said, smiling at the thought of her husband. "Ma always said, 'It's the tart lemon taste of the marinade contrasted to the sweet batter that really sets the dish off.'"

"It surely does taste fine," Ada said, reaching for a bowl to make the batter.

Several months had gone by since that horrible ordeal with Slinger. Amanda and David had fallen into a comfortable, easy rhythm out on the ranch together. They shared an excellent, loving relationship now that David had found peace in his soul over his brother's final letter, Slinger had been apprehended, and they had survived the tribulation intact.

The gold and cash she and David had found in David and Gabe's hidey-hole had gone to improve the town. And last they'd heard, Slinger had received a life sentence and would never be seen or heard from again.

Angus had become Goldspring's sheriff, and one of David's friends, Jim Sawyer, had assumed the role of deputy sheriff.

Amanda dropped spoonfuls of cookie batter on the baking trays and slid the trays into the oven. As she closed the oven door, David entered the kitchen through the back door.

"How's my pretty wife?" he said, coming behind her to kiss her neck.

"I'm fine, sweetheart, but the afternoon meal isn't finished." She reached back to stroke his stubble-covered cheek, getting flour on him in the process.

"Who says I need a reason to come in the kitchen and see to your welfare?" David said, wrapping his arms around her midsection. "I also need to keep watch on 'Little Bit' here." He stroked Amanda's slight bulge—not long after she'd moved into their conjoined bedroom, she'd gotten with child.

She'd only recently told him, once she was sure.

Amanda practically purred at his affection. David often found excuses to come inside between chores to check on her. Or she'd head outside with a jar of lemonade and a Johnnycake, just to surprise him and be in his presence.

"Well, I say, keep your visit short. You're in my way when you tromp around my kitchen while we're preparing a meal," Ada said with a sniff.

David laughed. "Okay, okay, I got my moment of loving... I'll head back outside."

"We'll call you when it's ready," Ada said.

David kissed Amanda's neck again and exited the kitchen.

***

After consuming their midday meal, everyone at the table seemed sated.

David leaned back in his chair and patted his belly. "That was one tasty meal," he said, gazing adoringly at his wife. "I sure got lucky when I married you."

Amanda blushed, staring at the table.

Michael and Billy grunted their agreement, pushing away from the table to head back outside.

And Amanda and Ada stood to begin cleaning the dishes.

David caught Amanda's hand as she swished past him. "What do you say we take a ride?"

"Today?" Amanda said.

"Yes, today. Why would I ask you if you wanted to head out on the plains next week?" David said with a cheeky grin.

"Mind if I help Ada with the kitchen first?" Amanda said.

"Oh, you two go on and leave me to my lonesome," Ada urged with a wave of her hand. "I'll be fine."

"Are you sure?" Amanda said.

"I'm as sure as the day is sunny. Go on, then," Ada said, shooing her and David with her hands.

"Which horses shall we take?" Amanda said, turning to her husband. "Bueno and Kickabilly?"

"Oh, we'll hitch up old Chester. No sense putting you and Little Bit in harm's way by letting you ride side-saddle. I'd rather you were sitting next to me with Chester's faithful, plodding gait," David said, rising from his seat. "Come outside in a few minutes, and we'll be ready to go."

"All right. I'll help Ada in here and then head on out."

David nodded, picked up his hat on the counter where he'd deposited it, and placed it on his head.

Fifteen minutes later, after stacking all the dishes and retrieving a couple buckets of water from the well, Amanda made her way outside.

Chester stood patiently in the yard, hitched to the wagon.

The mustang, which David had named Pareja, Spanish for "partner," stood by his side.

Pareja and Chester were inseparable. They slept side by side in adjacent stalls and were turned out every day in their own section of pasture. Pareja didn't get on too well with the rest of the herd, but he loved Chester like they were best friends.

When David and Amanda practiced riding, her on Kickabilly, and David on Pareja, the mustang would start whinnying for Chester the second they began to head back to the ranch. Only the whinnying had been more of a frantic scream. And when Chester was hitched to the wagon, Pareja trotted along beside him, never straying from his buddy's side whether they trekked across the plains or tied Chester up in town.

As she sat next to David, she took his hand in hers.

His head pivoted, and he smiled at her. "I meant it at the supper table, Amanda—I sure got lucky when I married you. It took me a while to realize it, but it's true."

She gave his callused hand a squeeze. "I'd say we both got lucky. The curse of my bad luck has gone and left me."

"It surely has."

"So, are we heading where I think we're heading once this ride is through?" Amanda asked as she stroked her belly. She found it a comfort to caress the life she and David had created. She couldn't wait to hold their baby and teach him or her the ways of the world.

"If where you're thinking is Gabe's grave, then I reckon you'd be right," David said as Chester picked his way across the shallow creek. "We haven't paid our respects for a while, so I figured today would be as good a day as any. But first, I thought we'd take a drive to that wildflower field you like."

Amanda nodded, scanning their whereabouts. When she spied the field, she urged David to stop.

Once Chester came to a halt, she started to climb from the buckboard, but David blurted, "Hold up there, Missy. Don't you be climbing from the wagon without assistance."

Amanda smiled as she waited for David to round the wagon and help her from her seat. She'd grown more sure-footed in the past few months, what with all the hard work she performed around the ranch, but David had become protective ever since she told him a week or so ago that she was with child.

He stayed by her side as she strode toward the field. Amanda picked a handful of flowers, then bundled them into her hands. "Cut me a measure of that Crossvine, will you please?"

David obliged her, slicing with his hunting knife through a length of the sturdy vine growing amid the wildflowers. "Here you go," he said, handing her the cutting.

She wound it around the wildflowers and managed to tie a knot of sorts into the vine.

"Ready?" David said.

She nodded and he guided her back to the wagon, where he helped her up.

As they meandered back toward the ranch, David grew silent, eying the land with pensive regard. "I always love being outside. I get my peace from being alone with my animals, appreciating the world around me."

"I know you do," Amanda said, as a stab of sadness threatened her good mood. She'd been so blissful lately, but maybe she'd missed interpreting some of David's moods.

"But I've learned in these last few months that I'd rather enjoy my quiet time with you than without you." He gave her a side-eyed glance. "You and I can ride together in companionable silence, only it's filled with so much love I can barely breathe at times."

"Oh, David." Amanda's heart soared, and tears pricked the back of her eyes. "That's the kindest thing I think you've ever said to me."

"It's in my heart, girl," David said.

When they pulled up to the laurel tree, Amanda waited for him to help her from her seat. Clutching the wildflowers, she made her way to the gravesite, where both Blue and Gabe were buried. Crouching, she placed them next to the grave and removed the dead flowers she'd left behind on their last visit.

David stood by her side, his eyes moist as he stared at his brother's grave. "Well, Gabe... I'm sorry we ain't been out to see you much lately. Been busy, is all. But I want to thank you again for the sacrifices you made on our behalf. I already told you the sheriff will never see the light of day again. And I've been fixing to tell you the good news—Amanda is pregnant with our child. We're planning on having a whole mess of children. I wish you was around to know them. But then, if you was around, I'd be getting to know you and Amanda's kids." He winced. "Anyway, I hope you're happy for Amanda and me. I hope you wish us well from wherever it is you've landed. And again... thank you." His last words emerged as a strangled sob.

A wind kicked up, stirring the tendrils around Amanda's face. "I think he hears you, David. I think this wind is his answer."

David nodded as he gathered himself together, wiping his eyes with his thumb and forefinger, and said, "Well, I reckon that's enough for today." He paused, turning to her. "Thank you, Amanda, for being patient with me while I sorted out my heart."

Amanda bit her lip as she gazed at her husband. She'd never been happier in all her life.

That night, before she turned into bed by David's side, she sat in the room adjacent to their bedroom, which had become her study. Penning the letter by the light of a kerosene lantern, she wrote,

My dear Julia,

How rich and wonderful my life has become. I'm so in love with David. And guess what? We're now with child. It's going to be the first of many children.

I've turned into a good horseback rider, but David won't let me ride by myself as long as I'm pregnant. He's such a loving and patient man.

Today I made a new recipe called Gold Hill Rocks. The name isn't accurate because they're anything but rocks—they're buttery cookies full of things like nuts and raisins. And we fixed my ma's fried chicken recipe, which David loves.

My garden continues to grow a bountiful crop and has kept us in good stead all season. The winter vegetables I just planted will see us through the long months of snow and cold.

I hope you'll come and visit us in the fall when the leaves are turning, like you planned. I'll be huge with child by then, but I could use the company.

I hope your life with Marshall is the same as mine, filled with love and all you ever hoped for. I didn't think I could ever have this much happiness. I guess that's what comes from hard work and persistence—that's what David says, and I think it's true.

I'll write again soon, I promise.

Your loving friend,

Amanda.

Then, she turned off the lamp and exited the room, carefully making her way to be by her husband's side.

THE END

Also by Lydia Olson

Thank you for reading " **An Unforgettable Love by a Twist of Fate**"!

I hope you enjoyed it! If you did, here are some of my other books!

Some of my Best-Selling Books

#1 The Sheriff's Compassionate Bride

#2 A Western Flame to Redeem their Past

#3 Healing the Bride's Broken Heart

#4 A Second Chance for a Redeeming Love

#5 A Sheriff's Haven for the Rebellious Bride

Also, if you liked this book, you can also check out **my full Amazon Book Catalogue at:**
https://go.lydiaolson.com/bc-authorpage

Thank you for allowing me to keep doing what I love! ❤

Made in the USA
Las Vegas, NV
27 September 2021